BETRAYED

Murder in the Bahamas

A Suspense Novel By Robert Terwilliger

SPRING TIDE PUBLISHING
Palm Beach Shores, FL

Mystery and Crime
Sub genre suspense

Copyright © 2005 by Robert Terwilliger

Published by Spring Tide Publishing, Palm Beach Shores, FL

First Edition

The characters and events in this book are fictitious.
Any similarity to real persons, living or dead
is coincidental and not intended by the author.

Library of Congress Cataloging-in-Publication Data

Terwilliger, Robert
BETRAYED! MURDER IN THE BAHAMAS: a novel by Robert Terwilliger—
1st ed.

1. Drug smugglers and boat thieves – Fiction
2.The Bahamas – Fiction 3. Palm Beach, Florida – Fiction
4.Walkers Cay, The Bahamas – Fiction 5. Freeport and Lucaya, Grand Bahama Island – Fiction 6. Eye Spy store in Ft. Lauderdale – Fiction
7. Mores Island – Fiction 8. McLeans Town – Fiction 9. Jail at Freeport – Fiction
10. The prison ward at The Rand Memorial Hospital – Fiction
11. The hospital ward at Freeport Jail –Fiction 12. Rosa's Bar and Grill – Fiction
13. Lucayan Marina – Fiction 14. Bob Marley Square – Fiction 15. Bell Channel Marina – Fiction 16. Channel Apartments – Fiction 17. Atlantic Beach Resort – Fiction

Printed in the United States of America

ACKNOWLEDGEMENTS

Numerous people assisted in making this story possible. I'd like to thank all the officers of the Royal Bahamas Police Force who worked so diligently to locate the engines from my 27' Edgewater powerboat and arrest the men who stole it. Assistant Police Superintendent Basil Rahming, Detectives Johnson and Campbell, Corporal Seymore, and Private Cash worked tirelessly to find my engines and the criminals.

Lieutenant Lee Palfray with the Florida Fish and Wildlife Conservation Commission, Division of Law Enforcement was a priceless resource regarding the drug smugglers and dealers and their modus operandi. Lieutenant Mark Pignato of the West Palm Beach Fire and Rescue helped me with the medical procedures and terms regarding the treatment of a trauma patient and the trauma center at St. Mary's Hospital. Roland "Red" Davies, retired U.S. Coast Guard, shared numerous drinks and stories regarding his experiences based on thirty years of service protecting and guarding the Southeast Florida coast.

Ann Scurry, who's editing, sentence structure, and grammar were invaluable in making the novel readable and easier to understand. A special thanks to Kate von Seeburg who diligently did the final copyedit and fixed more errors than I thought a writer could make in lifetime. Michele DeFilippo who did a superb job on the cover and the interior design.

Lorelei Pignato and Neil Evans, who listened patiently day after day as I was developing the early chapters. Also, they gave me valuable support when we were searching for the Edgewater in the Bahamas.

Thomas Lockhart, dock master at Lucayan Village Marina. Our good friends at Walkers Cay, Clark and Connie Balsinger and mate Jason Brown who shared their extensive knowledge of The Bahamas and made writing this novel a joy. A special thanks to Joe Zado and the entire staff at Walkers Cay.

My son, Robert lived with us for a year and took great care of our boats and fishing equipment.

And last but most important, my wife and life partner Melody, who read and edited the novel numerous times. She tolerated my grumpy moods when I suffered writer's block and celebrated when I got it right.

Between 1690 and 1720, The Bahamas was a pirate's paradise. The seven hundred islands and cays allowed pirate ships to hide from and attack French and Spanish ships returning from the New World laden with gold, silver, and spices. After the galleons were relieved of their precious cargo, the islands' many limestone caverns provided the pirates with convenient caches for their treasure, some of which may still be there today.

Charles Town, later named Nassau, quickly became headquarters to many of the most infamous pirates who roamed the Caribbean. The Charles Town port was surrounded with shoals and shallow water channels, making it well-suited for the shallow draft vessels favored by pirates but not for the large, deep draft British man-of-war ships. In addition, Charles Town offered abundant natural resources: food, water and timber.

In 1703, the British left The Bahamas unprotected because of numerous attacks staged by the Spanish and the French fleets on the islands. As a consequence, it quickly grew into islands full of the most notorious pirates of the age. Blackbeard, Charles Vane, Jack Rackham, Samuel Bellamy and others had free reign to repair and refit their ships and spend their loot in Charles Town, the capital of The Bahamas. They quickly became the law and authority because no one was able to stop them. Their pirate's gold and booty formed the basis of a thriving community that attracted rogues, merchants and wild women from far and wide.

One of the most notorious pirates during this era was Charles Vane. He initially served under Captain Henry Jennings, who pirated the ships and crews working to recover the sunken Spanish Treasure Fleet of 1715. Vane first sailed for himself in 1718, when he went to the West Indies.

Later that year, Vane rejected Bahamian governor Rogers' offer of pardon by burning a captured French ship in order to escape two British warships that were pursuing him. Soon after, Governor Rogers sent a former pirate, Captain Benjamin Hornigold, to track down Vane, but again, he was able to evade capture by escaping to the Carolinas.

He captured several ships outside of Charlestown, South Carolina, but he soon had a falling out with his crew when he refused to pursue what they thought were worthy ships to plunder. His assistant, Yeats decided to be his own captain and left in the middle of the night with some of the treasure and slaves from a recently captured brig.

Vane and his remaining crew fled the Carolinas in early September 1718 when the governor of South Carolina dispatched Colonel William Rhett with armed sloops to catch him. Unfortunately, Rhett followed misinformation that Vane was heading south, when Vane actually went north. He joined Blackbeard at Ocracoke Island, North Carolina in early October and participated in a weeklong party with other pirates before Vane continued to New York.

By late November, Vane had fallen on hard times and decided to head back to the Caribbean. He went to an area south of Cuba between Jamaica and the Yucatan, and for a few weeks had moderate success plundering various vessels.

In February 1719, while en route to the Windward Passage, Vane's two sloops were wrecked on an uninhabited island in the Bay of Honduras during a hurricane. Most of the crew drowned, but Vane and one other crewmember managed to survive, eating turtle and fish.

An old friend Captain Holford discovered Vane but didn't trust the stranded pirate enough to invite him aboard. They were soon rescued by another vessel, but Vane was taken into custody after the captain discovered his true identity. On March 22, 1720, Vane was swiftly tried and hung in Port Royal, Jamaica, at Gallows Point. His body was hung in chains at Gun Cay.

John Rackham arrived in The Bahamas around 1718. His nickname was Calico Jack because he wore gentlemen's clothing made of calico, a special cloth from Calcutta, India. He began his pirate career as a quartermaster on Charles Vane's ship. When Vane decided to split his crew between two ships, Rackham was chosen as captain of the second ship. After a quarrel over liquor, Vane and Rackham went their separate ways.

Soon after, the governor of Jamaica sent vessels to capture Rackham and his men but Calico Jack and his crew jumped overboard and escaped in two small boats. They sailed to

Charles Town and in May of 1719, Governor Rogers pardoned them. Many of the crewmembers wandered off to work on trading ships while others became privateers.

While in Charles Town, Calico Jack met and fell in love with Anne Bonny. Anne already had a husband, James Bonny, a retired pirate who wasn't interested in losing Anne to Calico Jack. James threatened to report them to the governor for punishment but Calico Jack and Anne fled the island.

In August 1719, the two lovers stole a ship named *William* and they returned to their pirating ways after being law-abiding citizens for only a short time. After giving birth to their baby, Anne accompanied Calico Jack, dressed as a man. The odd couple spent over a year attacking small vessels around the West Indies. After capturing a Dutch ship, they took on a sailor who Calico Jack thought was spending too much time around Anne. The crewmember turned out to be a woman named Mary Read. Upon discovering her identity, Rackham realized the benefit of her friendship to the pair.

Anne Cormac Bonny was born around 1697 in Cork County Ireland. Her father, a successful lawyer, had an affair with Peg Brennan, one of his house servants, and decided to run away with her and their love child. They moved to Charlestown, South Carolina where Anne grew up and eventually met James Bonny, a part-time pirate. James convinced Anne to marry him in an attempt to steal her father's plantation. Anne's father discovered their plot, disowned her, and gave the couple twenty-four hours to leave town. They left South Carolina for The Bahamas where Anne met Calico Jack and set out on a crime spree that would make her one of the greatest of lady pirates.

Mary Read, Anne Bonny and Calico Jack ran out of luck in October 1720, after Governor Rogers found out about their return to piracy. A government sloop caught up with them at the west end of Jamaica while the crew was drunk and unable to fight.

The entire crew was arrested and taken to Jamaica to be tried for piracy. The proceedings caused quite a stir because of the two female pirates, but the women escaped the noose because they were both pregnant (with Calico Jack's children). The remaining crew was hung on November 27, 1720. Calico Jack's body was gibbeted and hung as a deterrent on Deadman's Cay near Port Royal, Jamaica.

Blackbeard's true name differs between official records, personal accounts, and fictionalized history. Edward Teach or Thatch or Drummond was born in either Bristol or London, England around 1680. Like many other young men of his time, he probably served aboard a British privateer in the West Indies during the War of the Spanish Succession and chose piracy over unemployment at war's end.

Very little is known about the most famous and notorious pirate. It seems that Blackbeard rarely passed up an opportunity to build his reputation and persona as a devilish fiend, but first hand reports seem to suggest that his reputation was more of a carefully crafted tool of the trade. Most accounts suggest that he was generally kind to those who were cooperative with him but intolerant of those who were not.

He arrived in Charles Town, The Bahamas in 1716 as an understudy of Benjamin Hornigold, and after a few months of successful apprenticeship acquired his own ship, the former French slaver *Concord*. It was renamed—*Queen Anne's Revenge* and fitted with some 40 guns.

In 1717, reports began circulating about the new governor, Woodes Rogers, and his crusade against pirates. Blackbeard chose to head north, and in January 1718, settled in the village of Bath Town, North Carolina. Not only was the town a good place to settle in and sell his plunder, but also he was able to buy a pardon and protection from Governor Eden, who welcomed the economic boost the pirates brought to the area.

Blackbeard continued his pirating ways, and soon commanded four ships and more than 300 men. In May of 1718, he captured a pilot boat and several ships off the port of Charlestown, South Carolina, set up a blockade and held important citizens for ransom.

After the loss of the *Queen Anne's Revenge* on a sandbar and one other ship in a failed rescue attempt, Blackbeard returned to Bath Town, sold his loot, the two remaining ships and bought a house. He spent the summer of 1718 trying out the lifestyle of a regular citizen but managed to irritate his neighbors when he held a weeklong party with many of his pirate friends at Ocracoke Island in October.

In November 1718, Virginia Governor Spottswood sent Lieutenant Maynard with two sloops to capture or kill Blackbeard. During the pursuit, Blackbeard's sloop *Adventure* was grounded, but thinking he had the advantage in numbers, he ordered his crew to board Maynard's ships. It was a trick: Maynard's troops were hiding and a fierce fight ensued. Maynard shot Blackbeard in the shoulder, and another officer slit his throat and then decapitated him.

When his body was inspected, it had more than 25 wounds, including 5 from gunshots. His severed head was put on the bowsprit of Maynard's ship, which sailed back to Williamsburg with the remnants of the crew in custody. Thirteen of them were hung in March 1719.

M ost of the pirates who came to Charles Town, The Bahamas during the Golden Age of the pirates were caught and hung by the British navy but many of their descendents remained in The Bahamas. Records indicate that Blackbeard had fourteen wives and fathered forty children. He claimed his prowess was from the conch he ate while living in The Bahamas.

Some people claim the ghosts of Calico Jack, Anne Bonny, Mary Read, Blackbeard and Charles Vane still roam the streets of Nassau. However unlikely that may be, many of their descendents, who have become twenty-first century pirates, do roam the Caribbean today smuggling drugs, killing unsuspecting captains and their guests aboard luxury motor yachts and eluding satellite blockades, surveillance balloons and the U.S. Coast Guard.

And just like their forefathers, when they get caught, some go to prison and some are hung from the gallows until they are dead.

> *"You can run...but there's no where to hide in The Bahamas."*
>
> *Viper Bob Edwards*

VIPER BOB

chapter 1

1961
PORT-AU-PRINCE, HAITI

Consuelo Rodriguez was born on May 3rd, 1961, in Port-au-Prince, Haiti. Her family, like eighty percent of the population, lived in abject poverty. Since the 1950s, Haiti has been the poorest country in the Western Hemisphere. Two-thirds of all Haitians depend on agriculture to make a living, which consist mainly of small-scale subsistence farming.

François "Poppa Doc" Duvalier became president of Haiti in 1957, and was a ruthless dictator until his death. When he died on April 21, 1971, Jean-Claude Duvalier, Poppa Doc's 19-year-old son, became Haiti's second president for life. Both Duvaliers maintained power by relying on their feared secret police, the Touton Macoutes (pronounced to-to ma-kute), whose techniques included rape, torture, murder and voodoo.

Like most girls in Haiti, Consuelo never went to school. As a child, her prize possession was a Raggedy Ann doll her father found in a trash bin near the docks in Port-au-Prince.

When Consuelo was nine years old, the Touton Macoutes killed three members of her family. Her father, fearing the Touton Macoutes had marked the entire family for political re-education, which meant execution, fled the capitol. They moved to Cap Dame-Marie, a remote fishing village located on the peninsula one hundred and fifteen miles southwest of Port-au-Prince.

Her father was not a smart man but he was right about one thing. The Ton-tons Macoutes would not follow them to that part of Haiti. A seven thousand foot mountain separated Cap Dame-Marie from the rest of the country. There was a single, rugged road over the mountain and no airstrips in the region, so the few people who came to the small village usually did so by boat.

Cap Dame-Marie is at the western tip of the island where Haiti is separated from Cuba and Jamaica by a large body of water known as the Windward Passage. From top to bottom the Windward Passage is two hundred miles long, and at the narrowest point, Haiti is a mere forty-five miles from Cuba.

As the cool waters of the Atlantic travel north approaching the Windward Passage, the first land they touch is just west of Cap Dame-Marie. Here, an unseen plateau extends into the passage. As the water approaches the Windward Passage it travels across a seabed that is eight thousand feet deep. When it reaches the plateau at Cap Dame-Marie, millions of gallons of water must either go around, or up and over the six thousand foot high plateau.

The top of the plateau is relatively flat and extends southwest for sixty-five miles, nearly half way to Jamaica. It's fourteen miles wide and in the middle is a small, solitary, uninhabited island that is one and a half miles wide.

As water is forced over and around the plateau, it stirs up the seabed, bringing plankton and small baitfish into the shallower waters. Predator fish, including blue-fin tuna, wahoo, dolphin, marlin and sailfish follow the baitfish, making Cap Dame-Marie a fishing paradise.

Consuelo's father made a decent living as a fisherman until more bad luck struck the beleaguered family. When Consuelo was fourteen, her father drowned in a fishing accident and from that point, her life went from bad to worse.

Consuelo quickly learned the only asset she possessed was her body. She became a prostitute and would do anything, with anyone who wanted her, accepting money, fresh fish, even fruit and vegetables for her services. Unfortunately, she was too young to know how to protect herself and soon she was pregnant with her first of three children.

Five years later her third son, Chino, was born. By then Consuelo looked like a woman in her forties. Most of her teeth were gone and the remaining ones were rotting like bananas in the hot Caribbean sun.

In 1991, Consuelo's luck changed when a fishing boat from Port-au-Prince spent three months working around Cap Dame-Marie. The man who owned the boat met Consuelo at Le Grande Prix, a local waterfront bar. Soon he started visiting her every weekend. His wife died the previous year and his sister kept his two young children while he was away fishing. He became fond of Consuelo and when it was time to return home he asked her to move to Port-Au-Prince and live with him. Consuelo, who was thirty years old, gladly moved with her three sons back to the capitol of Haiti, where life improved.

The three Rodriguez boys knew they didn't share the same father. Their mother told them, "I don't know who your daddies is, and I don't really care."

Life in Port-au-Prince was as different from Cap Dame-Marie as Consuelo's three sons were from each other. Henri, who was fifteen, preferred the simple life in the small village where he was the man of the family. Thirteen-year-old Peter was uncomfortable with his new home and didn't like his stepfather or his new brother and sister. Chino, who was eleven, found his new life exciting. There were endless opportunities in the capital to make money and have fun, something he couldn't do in Cap Dame-Marie.

In 1992, Chino joined a local gang that sold small quantities of drugs on the streets of Port-au-Prince. He got along well with the other gang members and at an early age exhibited organizational skills. Over the next four years, the gang graduated from selling drugs, to smuggling them between Haiti, Jamaica and The Bahamas.

Chino enjoyed the thrill of running a boat at full speed across the water at night. He was a good driver and his young eyes could spot land or rocks sticking out of the water. So, when the gang started smuggling drugs out of Jamaica, Chino was picked to drive the boat. Once a month he and his mechanic went to Jamaica to pickup marijuana.

The two hundred sixty-four mile route to Jamaica began at a warehouse in Port-au-Prince Harbour and ended at a rural, deserted beach east of Kingston and had three legs. The first leg was one hundred ten miles due west from Port-au-Prince through Canal du Sud, to a point just north of Cap Dame-Marie. Then it turned southwest and went one hundred sixteen miles to the corner of Jamaica. The final leg was a short, nine and a half miles along the Jamaican coast to a small cove thirty-five miles east of Kingston. The entire trip took six hours and thirty-five minutes, at an average speed of forty miles per hour and required one hundred sixty-five gallons of fuel.

Once a month a second team would take the marijuana from Jamaica and cocaine the gang got from Columbia, South America, to Sandy Point, in The Bahamas. The route to Sandy Point was more complicated and much more dangerous than the run to Jamaica. The U.S. Drug Enforcement Agency and The Bahama Drug Enforcement Unit were always on the lookout for drug smugglers entering The Bahamas from Haiti.

The Bahamas route was four hundred and forty-three miles, and had five legs. The two man team would leave Port-au-Prince in their drug laden boat and travel north one hundred miles to Le Mole, Haiti. Le Mole is a small town on the northwest corner of the island. When they reached Le Mole, the mechanic would check the engines to make sure they were ready for the nighttime trip. If they had a mechanical failure after the smugglers left Haitian waters, either the U.S. or Bahamian drug enforcement agencies would most likely find and arrest them. Before leaving, the two men would put a one hundred-fifty gallon fuel bladder onboard and fill it and the boat's fuel tank.

The first leg was one hundred forty-nine miles and went northwest past Great Inagua Island and continued north to Mira Por. Mira Por is a shallow, dangerous outcropping of coral that is twelve miles west of Acklin Island, well inside Bahamian waters.

The second leg continued northwest in open water, to a white buoy at Nuevitas Rock that marked the entrance to another shallow water bank.

The third leg stretched twenty miles across the bank and exited between Hog Cay and White Cay, south of Georgetown in The Exumas.

The next one hundred miles was in deep, open water until it reaches the Middle Ground Bank. Like most of the shallow banks in The Bahamas, this one was strewn with coral heads, shoals and sand bars. The only mark for entering the Middle Ground Bank was a GPS waypoint. Upon reaching the waypoint, the route went northwest on a heading of 326 degrees, past Finley Cay to a pair of flashing beacons at Six Shilling Cay that announced the entrance to Northeast Providence Channel.

The final leg was fifty miles to the west side of Great Abaco Island. At the flashing white beacon at Sandy Point, it rounded the southern tip of the island and went eight miles up the coastline to a small cove called Bamboo Point.

During the February 1996 trip to Sandy Point, an engine overheated, reducing the boat's speed to twenty-two knots. The strain was too much and within an hour the other engine overheated. The boat drifted for two hours before the Royal Bahamas Defence Force found the boat and the trail of drugs that had been dumped overboard. The boat was only sixty-five miles north of Haiti, off the coast of Great Inagua. The two young Haitians were arrested and later convicted of smuggling drugs into The Bahamas. They were sentenced to fifteen years in prison.

Chino, who craved more action, wanted to take over The Bahamas route and in March 1996, Chino and Patrick, his mechanic, started making two runs a month. They went to Jamaica when the moon was full because they weren't concerned about being caught. Two weeks later they went to The Bahamas when the night sky was dark with a new moon.

Every time Chino made the trip to Sandy Point, a fifty-foot fishing trawler named *Bank Walker* was anchored in the cove at Bamboo Point awaiting Chino's arrival. Chino would maneuver his boat next to *Bank Walker* and tie up to the white

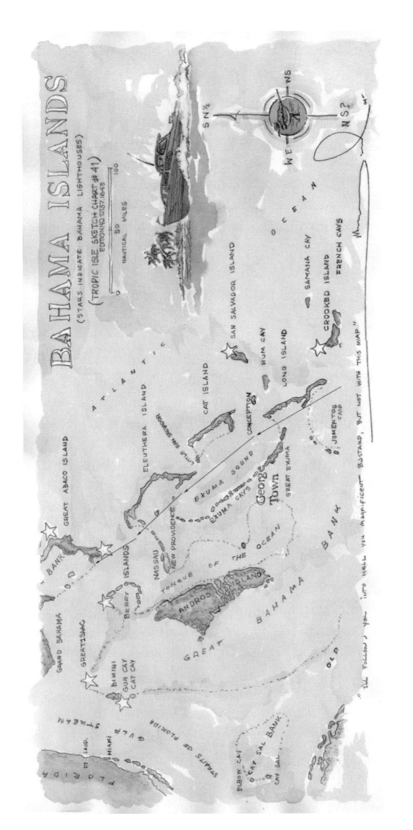

trawler. A big man, named Manny, would lower a cable from an electric winch and they would begin unloading the bails of marijuana and boxes of cocaine. When the drugs were removed, a gas line was passed to Patrick and he replaced the fuel they used to make the eleven hour trip.

Chino's native language was French, but he had an ear for languages. Over the next two years he taught himself English and soon he sounded just like a Bahamian. On one trip he asked Manny, "Why you name your boat *Bank Walker*? I heard a lot of boat names but I never heard of *Bank Walker*."

Manny laughed and said, "While you be takin' on gas, I'll tell ya."

When they were finished unloading the drugs, Manny invited Chino aboard and handed him a cold beer and told Chino his favorite story, one he heard from a famous movie star who came to Sandy Point many years ago to bonefish. Manny began:

One day the manager of a bank came home with a bottle of champagne and twenty-five roses. It was his twenty-fifth wedding anniversary. He called to his wife, announcing his arrival. But he couldn't find her. He looked all over the house and when he got to the kitchen he found a note taped to the refrigerator door that said—

> *Dear Herbert, You're a wonderful man and you've been a good provider for the past twenty-five years. But, I have fallen in love and have run off with a bank walker.*

> Muriel

> *PS, Please don't come looking for me.*

Herbert was heartbroken. He couldn't believe his wife left him for another man. So, he drank the bottle of champagne and didn't stop drinking for the next six months. He lost his job at the bank and they foreclosed on his house. But, he continued drinking. One afternoon he was sitting in a tavern in Mississippi telling his tale of woe to a totally uninterested bartender. When he was finished, he said to the bartender, "You know what? I worked in the banking business for twenty years. I know what a bank teller is. I know what a bank manager is. But I've never heard of a bank walker."

A woman sitting across the bar said, "I know what a bank walker is." Herbert rushed over to find out more about the man who stole his bride of twenty-five years. "Oh, pray tell," he asked, "what's a bank walker?"

She said, "Here in Mississippi it gets real hot in the summer months. So in the late afternoon the young boys and girls like to run down to the riverbank, strip off their clothes and jump into the cool water. Most of the boys are shy. After they strip, they cover their private parts with their hands and jump in the water as fast as they can. But the well-endowed boys like to strut down to the water's edge, walking slowly, so everyone can see their manhood. Those boys are called bank walkers."

Manny laughed so hard at his own joke, he choked on his beer. Once he recovered he said, "I is a bank walker. I gots the equipment to satisfy my women."

He started laughing again as he reached for two more beers.

In 1998, Chino turned eighteen. Since joining the gang he had saved almost a thousand dollars. The money was part of his plan to escape Haiti for a better life in The Bahamas. On his next trip to Sandy Point, he took all his cash plus an extra driver. He was going to join Manny on *Bank Walker* and stay in The Bahamas.

Manny agreed to help him, but warned him, "I'm glad to help you, Bro. Just don't mention my name if you gets caught." So, in June of 1998, after they unloaded the drugs, Manny took Chino with him to Nassau, the capitol of The Bahamas. Manny introduced him to Edward "Blackbeard" Knowles, a friend who operated a drug gang and the next day Chino was selling drugs to American and European tourists who came to Nassau to vacation and party.

Chino joined a three-man team selling drugs. The team was comprised of the salesman, the banker and the runner. Most drug dealers use this approach because it provides maximum protection from the police as well as other gangs who try to rob the team of their drugs or money. The team works like this:

The salesman would approach a prospective buyer called The Client. He would start a conversation with the client that quickly led to drugs, and he would ask, "You want a little candy to help you party?"

If the client said yes, the salesman asked him what kind of candy he liked. Next, the salesman told the client the price. If the client agreed, the salesman would tell the client he didn't have the candy on him but a second person would deliver the candy.

The salesman would walk over to the banker, who would be sitting at a table, and tell him the price, quantity and product. The runner would go to a nearby secure location, such as a local business, where the drugs were kept. He would get the product and bring it back to the site.

When everything was ready, the salesman would tell the client to walk over and pay the banker. As soon as the banker received the money, the runner would give him the product.

While the drug team worked, a security person acted as a lookout. His job was to alert the team if a police officer was approaching and to guard the location where the drug inventory was kept. Depending on the location and the number of teams working an area, there were between one and four security people. When a police officer was spotted the security person signaled the other guards and the banker.

The banker always kept a close eye on the security person, who stayed in a highly visible location. Within seconds after the alert was given, the team would disperse. They waited for a call or signal from the security person telling them it was safe to go back to work.

Chino quickly distinguished himself as an excellent salesman and as he worked, he was always looking over his shoulder. Not only was he concerned about getting caught selling drugs, but he didn't have any Bahamian citizenship papers and he was afraid that if he got arrested he would be deported to Haiti.

chapter 2

Six months after leaving Haiti, Chino and his team were working an outside bar in Nassau. As he was waiting for a client, a young Bahamian boat boy sat down and ordered a beer. They looked so much alike Chino thought, *This guy could be my twin brother*. Almost immediately, Chino's evil mind began to hatch a plan.

The boat boy introduced himself as Ernie and Chino said, "No way, Mon, my name's Bernie." Instead of telling his unsuspecting double he sold drugs, he told him, "I scored some great dope earlier today. Hey Bro, tonight I'm goin' to a new club in Nassau where the women are totally hot. You wanna join me? We can pick up a couple of babes, do some dope and party all night."

Ernie couldn't believe his good luck. "Sure, Mon," he said, "I got nothin' more important to do."

Chino said, "I got some wheels. How's about I pick you up about nine. We can get somethin' to eat and then head out to the club." Chino suggested both men wear jeans and a white T-shirt, to further suggest they were brothers.

Chino had a very different evening planned for Ernie. He went back to his apartment and filled a small baggie with high-grade cocaine, rolled four joints of White Widow marijuana and called a friend.

"I met a girl from New York today and I want to borrow your boat. She wants to make love on a boat underneath the stars," he told his friend.

Chino left his apartment at eight o'clock, stopped at his buddy's house to get the boat keys, and then drove to an old two-story apartment building in Potters Cay, a slum area in Nassau, where Ernie rented a room. Chino suggested they smoke a joint before leaving. Ernie quickly agreed, saying, "Yea, Mon, the dope make the food taste better."

Ernie had never smoked White Widow before and he wasn't used to such powerful marijuana. He was stoned in a matter of minutes. They got in Chino's car and Ernie relaxed in the front seat. He dreamed about what a great time he was going to have tonight and how lucky he was to have met his new friend.

Chino ordered two Whopper meals. Then he pulled into a remote parking space to smoke another joint and eat the meal. The tinted windows in Chino's dark blue Ford Escort didn't allow anyone to see the two men as they puffed on another White Widow joint—as if anyone cared.

After Ernie finished his meal he said, "I could use one more."

Chino said, "Yea, me too, Bro. But, first, let's try a little coke." He told Ernie to open the glove compartment and pull out the small baggie.

Chino expertly arranged the cocaine on a small piece of glass, cut it into four lines and handed it to Ernie and said, "Here Bro, try some of this." Ernie snorted two lines of the high-grade cocaine. Chino didn't need to pretend to snort the other two lines; Ernie was slumped in the seat, in his own private dream world.

As soon as Ernie was wasted, Chino started the car and drove to the Nassau Club where his friend kept a 38-foot Hatteras sport fisherman. He drove down an alley on the west side of the marina and parked. Chino reached in the back seat and got a bag that had a black leather jacket, a baseball cap, and a black wig inside. He slipped the wig on Ernie's head, and adjusted it. Then he put the baseball cap on Ernie to keep the wig in place.

Chino got out of the car and walked around to the passenger side. He helped Ernie out of the car and told him they were going to meet two babes who were staying on a boat. Ernie laughed and mumbled, "Yea, two babes on a boat, let's go." Chino put the black jacket on Ernie and zipped it up, completing the female disguise.

It was a short walk to the slip where the Hatteras was docked, but Ernie had a difficult time walking. He stumbled a number of times but Chino had his arm firmly around his shoulder and steadied him as they entered the marina. A security guard looked at them and Chino said, "*Sea Yea Later.*" That was the name of his friend's boat and pointed to it. The guard nodded as they walked like a pair of lovers down the dock to the boat.

Once they reached the boat Chino guided Ernie out onto the slip and sat him down. Then he stepped on the boat, which was almost level with the dock. Chino eased Ernie onboard and held him while he unlocked the salon door. Once inside, Chino sat Ernie on a tan leather couch, pulled the bag of cocaine out of the jacket pocket, and had Ernie snort two more lines of the highly potent drug.

Chino went up on the flybridge* and started the engines. The twin Detroit Diesels roared into life. While they were warming up, he untied the dock lines and left them on the dock. Chino was an expert at navigating in the dark from his drug smuggling days. Within fifteen minutes *Sea Yea Later* was headed out Nassau Harbour and into Northeast Providence Channel. Ten miles later Chino eased back on the throttles and the Hatteras slowed down until it was resting peacefully in nearly six thousand feet of water.

Chino left the engines running and went down below to the cockpit. He opened a locker door and pulled out an anchor with one hundred feet of line the owner used as an emergency anchor. He walked into the main salon and shook Ernie who was lying on the couch. He was completely wasted and could only mumble a few words before going back to dream land.

Chino sat Ernie up on the couch, removed the baseball cap, wig and jacket. He emptied Ernie's pockets and put his wallet and room key on the carpeted floor. Chino lifted him off the couch. Ernie's legs buckled like rubber sticks under the dead weight of his body. He had almost no control of his arms and legs and continued to mumble indiscernible sounds. Chino dragged him out the salon door, onto the cockpit and laid him face up on the deck. Then he wrapped the anchor line around his legs, tying it tightly, until he was sure the rope wouldn't come undone any time soon.

---

* A glossary of nautical terms begins on pg. 349.

Chino lifted Ernie off the deck onto the gunwale and rolled him overboard, quickly throwing the 40-pound anchor after him. Ernie never knew what happened to him. There was so much high-grade cocaine in his body he may have died that fateful night of drowning or cardiac arrest from the drugs. But no one would ever know what or who killed him.

With a 40-pound anchor attached to his legs, Ernie's rate of descent was about 600 feet a minute. When his body reached 200 feet his internal organs, like his lungs and bladder, were crushed from the pressure. It took Ernie's body nine minutes and twenty-four seconds to reach the ocean floor, five thousand six hundred-fifty feet below Chino and *Sea Yea Later*. Soon, the rapidly decomposing body would become food for the bottom feeders that roamed the deep, cold waters of Northeast Providence Channel.

Shortly after Ernie's body reached the seabed, Chino was approaching the entrance to Nassau Harbour. He maneuvered the Hatteras into its slip at Nassau Club, replaced the dock lines, and made sure the boat was properly secured to the dock. Finally, he straightened up the salon and put all of Ernie's belongings in the black jacket.

Then he sat quietly on the flybridge and waited for the security guard to make his rounds of the marina. Fifteen minutes later, the guard slowly got up, leisurely walked to the opposite end of the marina and out the east dock. He began checking the yachts and fishing boats that were resting quietly in the calm marina waters.

When the guard was at the opposite end of the dock, Chino got off *Sea Yea Later* and walked toward the stairs leading up one floor to the main entrance of the marina. He knew the gate he used to enter the marina was locked at ten, and the only way out was through the front entrance.

Chino was wearing the black leather jacket and baseball cap. In the event anyone saw him leaving the marina, they would have a hard time identifying him. But he really wasn't worried. No one was going to miss Ernie, because Chino Rodriguez was now Ernie Deal.

Chino went to Ernie's room at midnight. He put all Ernie's personal belongings in a heavy-duty garbage bag and took them to his car. He left the room key on a small table in the center of the room and left the door unlocked.

Two days later Ernie "Chino" Deal, moved to Grand Bahama Island and began working for Big Dawg, the leader of a local drug gang operating out of an area in Freeport known as the Ghetto.

VIPER BOB

chapter 3
SATURDAY
APRIL 8, 2000
FREEPORT, GRAND BAHAMA ISLAND

Chino was a natural born salesman and his team consistently sold more drugs than the other four. They normally worked a large casino near downtown Freeport and three nearby hotel pool bars. The casino provided a constant flow of tourists who came with cash in hand, ready to gamble, party and get high.

Chino liked his job and he liked the money; what he didn't like was his boss. After working for Big Dawg for almost two years, he still didn't know Big Dawg's real name. However, no one else did either. But, Big Dawg certainly fit him to a T. He stood six feet, six inches tall and weighed close to three hundred pounds. He had a loud bark, a very nasty bite and he threw temper tantrums over anything that displeased him. He routinely humiliated the men who worked for him by picking a fight and beating them up in front of their wife or girlfriend.

Chino's team made a lot of money for Big Dawg so he usually left them alone. Chino didn't fear the leader of the gang but he didn't respect him either. However, growing up in Haiti he learned a version of the Golden Rule at a very young age: He who has the gold makes the rules. Big Dawg made all the rules.

Chino was growing more and more frustrated with Big Dawg and his bully tactics. In Haiti, he had learned all aspects of the drug smuggling business and in Nassau and Freeport he had mastered the retail business. Chino truly understood the drug industry and, after some serious reflection, came to the conclusion that he could run the gang better than Big Dawg.

Without saying a word to anyone, Chino began to develop a plan he called "The Big Dawg Retirement Plan."

As he developed the plan, there were two major obstacles in order to take over and run the business. Chino needed Big Dawg's operating cash and drug inventory and the location of both was a well-kept secret. *They has to be somewhere in Freeport. He probably keeps his cash in a safe deposit box at one of the banks on East Mall Drive. But I don't got a clue where he keeps the drugs. The only way I'm gonna find out is to follow him.*

Following Big Dawg would be difficult, but more importantly, it would be dangerous. Twice in the past two years, Chino and Big Dawg got into a fistfight and both times he paid dearly. The first time Chino was lucky and he only suffered a broken rib. The second beating put him in Rand Memorial Hospital for two days. Chino was no match for Big Dawg and he knew it. *If Big Dawg catches me followin' him he'll kill me. All I can do is continue workin' and wait for an opportunity.*

Chino's team started work every morning at eleven and they quit when the tourists went back to their hotel rooms between three and four. Around nine, the tourists and the drug dealers reappeared for an evening of fun and entertainment.

One evening, Chino was relaxing at his apartment watching the six o'clock news on a Ft. Lauderdale station when he heard the anchorman say, "And now a Channel 11 exclusive update."

The update was about a California murder case where a husband was accused of killing his wife and dumping her body in the San Francisco Bay. The reporter said, "The Modesto police attached a tracking device to Peter Scott's truck. They knew exactly where he went at all times, without using a surveillance team to follow him."

Chino was instantly excited. He thought, *That's it—I'll use a tracking device to find out where Big Dawg keeps his cash and drugs.* In the follow-up segment, a reporter from Channel 11 News was at a store in the Ft. Lauderdale area that sold tracking equipment. The manager of EYE SPY explained how the tracking device worked.

"The Modesto police probably used a device manufactured by GPS-Web™. It's the only tracking system that doesn't require a skyward pointing antenna," the manager explained.

The reporter asked, "How difficult is it to install?" The manager replied, "The portable GPS-Stealth™ Antenna is a covert, real-time, under vehicle tracking system that is magnetically attached. In less than thirty seconds, anyone can install one underneath the hood or the underside of a vehicle."

"That's amazing," the reporter replied. "How can the signal be sent from underneath the car?"

The manager continued, "The GPS-Stealth™ Antenna doesn't require direct line of sight or conspicuous *edge-of-vehicle* mounting in order to communicate with the GPS satellites.

It utilizes an adaptive learning algorithm that allows the GPS antenna to be hidden up to twenty-eight inches underneath the vehicle while achieving over ninety percent of the efficiency of a traditional roof mounted GPS antenna. The system operates day and night in all weather conditions."

"How is the unit powered?" the reporter asked. "The unit can operate for forty-eight hours of actual driving time before recharging. When the vehicle isn't moving the unit goes into sleep mode. Extra rechargeable battery packs can be purchased and used for quick field swaps. The GPS-Web™ is designed to handle constant long term tracking, not just occasional location requests," he said.

The female reporter looked at the manager who resembled John Travolta, and asked, "How much does the GPS-Web™ unit cost?"

"The tracking is done using our secure Internet website which provides unlimited use for forty-four dollars per month. The purchase price for the GPS-Web™ system is about two thousand eight hundred dollars. There are no contracts to sign, no activation fees and our customers only pay for the months they access our website. There are no cell phone accounts, cell activation and no roaming charges incurred when tracking cross-country."

The reporter looked at the manager, giving him her best smile and said, "That's sounds exciting," as if she was going to purchase a unit before returning to the TV station.

The next afternoon Chino called EYE SPY and spoke with the manager. "Hey Mon, are you the guy I seen on Channel 11 News last night?"

The John Travolta look-alike replied, "Yes sir, that was me."

"Hey Mon, I gotta ask you a question," Chino said. "I can put the GPS thing on the underside of a car and track it on your website. Is that right?"

"That's correct," the manager replied.

"Do it work outside of the U.S?"

"Yes sir, it works anywhere on the planet."

"Has you got one in stock?"

"No sir, but I can have a unit here in three to four business days."

"Cool. I wants me one."

"Wise choice and how would you like to pay for it?" the manager asked.

"I can FedEx a money order tomorrow. What's your address?" Chino asked.

Chino and the manager traded information and made arrangements for Chino to pick up the unit the following week.

The next morning Chino went to his bank and removed three thousand dollars from his safe deposit box. He went to the customer service counter and bought a cashiers check for two thousand-nine hundred ninety-six dollars and eighty-one cents. The Federal Express office was across the street from his bank, and in less than ten minutes his check was on its way. Inside the envelope he attached a note to the check. "This is for the GPS unit. I will call you in four days. Signed, Ernie Deal."

Four days later Chino called EYE SPY and the manager confirmed the unit had arrived.

"I personally checked it to make sure everything is operating properly," he said. "I installed the battery and you have an extra battery pack. Both are rechargeable. You're ready to go, sir."

"Thanks," Chino replied, "I'll pick it up Monday morning."That afternoon Chino drove to the Freeport International Airport and purchased a round trip ticket to Ft. Lauderdale. He would leave the following Monday morning on Continental Connection flight 9195 departing Freeport at 7:35 a.m. and return on flight 9300 at 5:34 p.m. The ticket agent reminded him to be at the airport at 6 a.m. to allow time to clear U.S. Customs before boarding the plane.

The following Monday, Chino flew to Ft. Lauderdale, picked up the unit, and spent three hours practicing how to gather information using the website. He wanted to be absolutely certain he could determine the exact locations Big Dawg visited. He couldn't afford an error of one hundred feet.

The next morning he got up early and installed the unit's software on his computer. He wanted to practice using the system before installing it on Big Dawg's truck. He decided to put the antenna on a friend's taxi and tracked him for a week, until he was absolutely confident he could use the system to track Big Dawg's every move.

A week later he was ready to put the antenna on Big Dawg's truck and learn where he kept the cash and drugs. That night, he drove to Big Dawg's house, attached the antenna to the underside of his black Dodge pickup truck and went to work.

While Chino worked selling marijuana and cocaine to the tourists, the unit silently tracked Big Dawg's every move. Chino gathered the information off the website and downloaded it to his computer every night before he went to bed. After tracking him for two weeks he was sure he knew where he kept the drugs.

Big Dawg went to three places every day: the Jungle Room Bar, a warehouse in the commercial area off Explorer Way and he visited his mother. Chino was sure he kept the drugs at the warehouse. But he wasn't sure about the cash.

Does he keep the cash at the warehouse, too? I can't believe he's dumb enough to put all his eggs in one basket. But Big Dawg never went to any of the local banks, so where else can the cash be?

He continued tracking him for another week but there were no new clues to help him discover the location of the cash. Chino was almost convinced Big Dawg kept the cash at the warehouse then one day it hit him like a ton of bricks. *That bastard isn't visitin' his mother every day. He keeps his cash in her house. That explained why his mother had two dogs. Those German shepherds aren't pets; they be guardin' Big Dawg's cash.*

The more Chino thought about it, the more convinced he was. It was simple, yet a stroke of genius. Keeping cash in a safe deposit box was definitely safe. But banks had security cameras and every time you entered or exited the bank they took pictures of you, whereas visiting your elderly mother everyday would be something the cops or a rival gang wouldn't think twice about.

The cash was the final missing piece of the plan. Without it, Chino couldn't bankroll the operation and the Haitian suppliers didn't offer a credit program—even to former gang members.

Finally, all the pieces had fallen into place but Chino still had a lot of work to do before the Big Dawg Retirement Plan was complete.

VIPER BOB

chapter 4

SUNDAY
MAY 7, 2000
FREEPORT, GRAND BAHAMA

How am I going to kill Big Dawg? How am I going to get into his mother's house? Is the money in a safe? If so, is it a key or combination safe? Where am I going to store the drugs? Do I need someone to help me? If so, who can I trust?

Chino made a list of things he had to do and arranged them in chronological order. As he worked through the list he realized he needed one person to help him kill Big Dawg and carry out the rest of the plan. There was only one person in the world he literally trusted with his life and that was Emanuel "Manny" Pender. Manny helped him get into The Bahamas and he was well aware of the dog eat dog mentality of the drug business.

More importantly, Manny could be trusted.

Chino spent a week working out the final details and reviewing his plan. He couldn't afford to make a single mistake.

His life literally depended on doing everything right and never once did he think about abandoning the plan.

When he was ready he called Manny and said, "I gots something real important to talk over with you. Let's meet at the Lighthouse Restaurant near Pender Point." Manny agreed and suggested they meet Sunday afternoon around four o'clock.

Pender Point is a slum area just west of Freeport Harbour. When you enter the town a sign says, Welcome to Pender Point—Home of the Beautiful People. However, Pender Point and its residents are anything but. The people are dirt poor, and live in old, dilapidated shacks. Their homes rumble and rattle every time a strong Atlantic wind blows out of the southwest, pounding their tin roofs and whipping through the mostly glassless windows.

At the west end of town the shell rock that runs through Pender Point dead ends. A single story, rectangular shaped building sits on the south side of the road and is the local hang out. A wooden sign four feet wide and three feet tall reads:

Bien Venidos
Lighthouse Restaurant
Abieto 11 AM–1 AM Dom-San
Welcome Open 11AM–1 AM Sunday–Saturday

Chino arrived first, at 3:30; Manny arrived a half hour later. Manny sat down and Chino ordered the Lighthouse special. They drank their beer and ordered another round as they talked about old times. Chino vividly remembered when he smuggled drugs from Haiti into The Bahamas but his best memories were of leaving Haiti and they both laughed about some of the stupid things they had done in the past. It had only been two years since Chino left Haiti but, he commented, "It seems like a lifetime ago," and in many ways it was.

Chino wasn't sure if Manny had ever killed anyone but Chino knew, under the right circumstances, he was capable. Both men had witnessed violence and a few executions by the drug lords. In this business, there was no shortage of men who wanted to share in the abundant number of women who were attracted to, and became addicted to drugs, not to mention the lucrative profits to be made.

Finally, Chino got around to the reason for the meeting. He explained his three-part Big Dawg Retirement Plan, when it would happen, and what he needed Manny to do. "I'll pay you fifty thousand dollars but I can't give it to you all at once. I can give you ten thousand dollars a month for five months," Chino explained.

Manny liked Chino. He thought, *He's a smart dude, but killin' Big Dawg be gutsy and, if it don't work, we both be dead men.* The two friends sat at the table in the back of the bar and talked for another half hour.

"If I do this, I'm riskin' my life," Manny said, "and honestly Mon, I be worth more than fifty grand."

"How about I double it to one hundred grand?" "Done," Manny replied. They shook hands and ordered another round of drinks.

Manny's primary job would be to lure Big Dawg to a remote location where Chino would kill him. Over the past five years, Manny met Big Dawg numerous times in the remote canals off the Grand Lucayan Waterway, where he delivered stolen engines to the gang leader.

The Grand Lucayan Waterway is a seven and a half mile canal that bisects Grand Bahama at a point four and a half miles east of Lucaya. Over thirty canals branch off the waterway.

The plan was for Manny to call Big Dawg and tell him he might have two nearly-new Yamaha outboard engines, and would Big Dawg be interested in buying them? Yamahas were easy to sell and it would be unusual for Big Dawg to say no.

"This Friday is a new moon," Chino said, "which means it be pitch black, the perfect time to steal a boat."

"So, this weekend it is," Manny agreed.

The timing of the plan was tight and critical. They needed Big Dawg to agree to pick up the engines Saturday night. Manny would call him on Wednesday and offer him the deal. If he didn't agree to Saturday, the plan would be postponed.

Chino tried to stay busy, but the next three days moved in slow motion. Every afternoon Chino went back to his apartment, logged onto the website, and checked Big Dawg's movements for the past twenty-four hours. Each day, Big Dawg pretty much followed the same routine, which made Chino more confident he was right. *He don't suspect nothin'. That be good.*

Wednesday afternoon, Manny called Big Dawg and told him about a possible deal for two Yamaha engines this weekend.

"Yea, we gots a new moon," Big Dawg replied. "Good time to steal a boat and I needs a couple of engines. OK. How much?"

"The usual, three thousand each."

"OK," came Big Dawg's reply.

"I'll call Saturday and let you know if I gots the engines."

Manny suggested they meet at The Wreck, a deserted area on one of the canals off the Grand Lucayan Waterway.

The Wreck was the site where a Volkswagen Beetle had been pushed into the canal a number of years ago, with two of Big Dawg's rivals in the front seat. It was a good location because there was a paved road within one hundred feet of the seawall and the water was deep enough for Manny's trawler. Also, for sentimental reasons, Big Dawg liked to go there. After a hardy laugh he agreed.

As soon as Manny got off the phone with Big Dawg, he called Chino and told him everything was set for Saturday night. Everything was set for what would be a very busy and dangerous weekend.

Saturday morning Manny called Big Dawg and told him, "The engines be on the way to Freeport. Meet me about 11 o'clock tonight at The Wreck."

Chino and Manny drove out to The Wreck one last time and went over the plan. It was simple, but both men wanted to make sure everything was ready. They couldn't afford a single mistake.

One potential problem was the local residents. There had been numerous complaints to the police about suspicious activities happening in the undeveloped areas near their homes. The sound of a gunshot might cause one of them to call the police so Chino decided to kill Big Dawg with a heavy lead pipe.

In order to make everything look believable, Manny arranged to borrow a pair of Yamaha engines from a friend. At 3:30, Manny left Arawak Marina where he kept *Bank Walker*, and went to a dock near his friend's house. They loaded the engines onto his stern deck and he returned to Arawak Marina. He stayed at the marina and kept himself busy for the rest of the afternoon and evening.

At 9 o'clock, Chino drove to the marina and parked near Manny's boat. Manny started the diesel engines. Chino jumped onboard, untied *Bank Walker* and they went out the channel. Forty-five minutes later they turned east off the Grand Lucayan Waterway and went down one of the canals. Three minutes later they came to the end of the canal. They were at The Wreck.

Manny eased the 50-foot trawler next to the seawall, exactly where they had agreed. Chino threw the forward anchor ashore and tightened the anchor line until the boat was resting against the seawall. Meanwhile Manny went to the stern and threw a second anchor ashore and secured the stern line. He put out a pair of large fenders to keep the boat from rubbing against the concrete seawall and shut off the engines.

Bank Walker was now resting peacefully in the small cove. The only noise was the crickets and the muffled sound of the five-kilowatt generator that provided electricity to power the appliances, electric winch and the lights onboard the trawler.

VIPER BOB

chapter 5

SATURDAY
MAY 13, 2000
FREEPORT, GRAND BAHAMAS

M anny and Chino were ready and there was nothing else to do. Now came the hard part: All they could do was wait for Big Dawg to arrive.

They were confident the plan would work, but they were tense. After all, they were getting ready to murder someone they knew, in cold blood.

At 10 o'clock, Chino got off the boat and took his place behind a large pine tree. If Big Dawg decided to come early he needed to be ready. The big pine tree was fifteen feet from the seawall, enabling Chino to reach the boat in four steps. He searched the ground between the tree and the boat. It was soft, white sand covered with chocolate-colored pine needles and leaves from the surrounding trees. Chino removed a few twigs and leaves. He didn't want to make any noise and lose the element of surprise when he attacked Big Dawg but the area needed to look natural.

At 10:30 a truck approached the area. The headlights shone through the dark night, bouncing off trees and shrubs, like a roving spotlight, and stopped one hundred feet from the trawler.

In an instant the area was transformed from darkness to daylight. Big Dawg had turned on a set of one million candle spotlights mounted on the cab of his truck. The vacant field was instantly lit up like Yankee Stadium during a night game. Manny was looking directly at Big Dawg's truck, jerked around to save his night vision, but it was too late. The high intensity lights temporarily blinded him.

Big Dawg sat in the truck for a couple seconds before he turned off the lights, plunging the area back into total darkness. He got out of the truck and walked toward the trawler. A single light bulb on the aft section guided him to the boat.

"Jesus Christ, Big Dawg, nothin' like announcin' where we are."

"Yea, I be talkin' on the phone," he replied. "Hey, them engines lookin' pretty good."

"I'm glad you can see 'em, cause I can't see a fuckin' thing."

When the powerful lights snapped on Chino was standing behind the large pine tree, which blocked the bright lights, helping preserve his night vision. He immediately closed both eyes and didn't open them until the lights were off.

As Chino stood behind the tree, waiting for Big Dawg to reach the trawler, a drop of sweat rolled down his forehead to the end of his nose. It hung there for a second before it dropped to the ground. It was the middle of May and the combination of the warm air, humidity and his nervousness made Chino sweat. His black shirt was soaked with perspiration.

Big Dawg continued walking to the boat, sidestepping numerous prickly bushes as he went and moving him closer and closer to Chino. When he reached the boat, Chino stepped from behind the pine tree. He was holding a ten-pound lead pipe in front of him with both hands. As he took the first step he started to raise the pipe, by the second step the pipe was over his head. On the third step his hands were behind him touching the back of his head. On the fourth step he aimed at Big Dawg's head and swung the heavy lead pipe as hard as he could.

The pipe began moving forward, its progress was slow because of its weight. Big Dawg never saw a thing. It was pitch black, but he must have sensed something. A second before the pipe crashed down on his head, he stepped to the left, causing the pipe to miss its mark and crash into his right shoulder. All three men heard the bone crack. Manny was sitting on the gunwale still blinded from the spotlights. Chino was taken completely off guard as Big Dawg spun around and attacked instead of falling down.

A normal man would have collapsed to the ground. But Big Dawg wasn't a normal man. He doubled up his enormous left fist and threw a roundhouse punch at whoever was behind him. He had no idea who it was, but he was going to kill him. His fist missed the target, but his momentum carried him toward the figure lurking in the dark behind him.

Chino's hands were stinging from the powerful blow he had delivered to Big Dawg's shoulder. As he started to raise the pipe a second time, Big Dawg's body smashed into him, driving him backwards. Chino grabbed a large branch from the pine tree with his right hand, which stopped his backward fall. But in the process he had to drop the lead pipe.

Big Dawg lost his balance after hitting Chino and fell to the ground. He instinctively held out his hands to break his fall. His right arm hit the ground first. Pain coursed though his body from the pressure placed on the broken shoulder. He stumbled forward like a raging bull, screaming and searching for the object of his anger.

Chino righted himself as Big Dawg adjusted his stance and charged. He hit Chino in the center of his chest, driving him into the big pine tree with his massive left shoulder.

The pine tree acted like a backstop, driving the wind out of Chino's lungs. He was gasping for air, trying to counteract Big Dawg's attack, but he was losing the struggle. Even with his right shoulder broken, Big Dawg was more powerful than Chino.

Big Dawg still had no idea who his attacker was but there would be plenty of time to discover that after he broke the bastard's neck. His eyes were bulging in their sockets, red with anger. In a perverse way he was starting to enjoy himself. He was winning the fight, as he always did.

Big Dawg could hear his attacker. Guided by heavy wheezing, he threw a punch, hitting Chino in the face. First, came the sound of his nose being crushed; then came a howl of pain. Big Dawg reached out with his left hand and wrapped it around his attacker's neck, like a king cobra snake and began squeezing the life out of his victim.

Soon the attacker was making gurgling sounds and Big Dawg knew within seconds this idiot would be dead. A morbid smile crept across his hot, sweaty face. His body reacted to the pleasure he was experiencing. Big Dawg knew he had won the fight!

Chino was struggling for air, but he couldn't force any down his throat. Big Dawg's massive death grip was choking the life out of him. Chino's legs buckled and he dropped to his knees. Big Dawg shifted his position and started pushing down on his neck and squeezing harder.

It would take Manny a couple minutes before he got his night vision back. Until then, he couldn't help Chino. He knew if Big Dawg killed Chino, he was next!

Chino was about to lose consciousness. His brain was screaming, *where the hell is Manny? I can't believe he ain't here helpin' me.*

He stopped struggling. His body was leaning forward as Big Dawg continued to apply pressure. As he started to give up the fight, his hands fell to the ground in front of him. When his right hand hit the ground, it touched something. The object was round and cold; Chino realized it was the lead pipe.

He wrapped both hands around the heavy pipe and, with every ounce of strength he possessed, Chino brought the pipe straight up between Big Dawg's legs. Big Dawg grunted, but nothing happened. The iron grip continued to crush Chino's throat, suffocating him.

That's when Chino knew he was about to die. He didn't have enough strength to swing the pipe again. He let it drop to the ground and with it fell any hope he had to survive.

Suddenly a blast of cold air rushed down his throat and Chino took a deep breath. As air started to flow into his lungs, he started gagging and choking on the cool, sweet oxygen. Big Dawg's three hundred pound body came crashing down on Chino and rolled to one side. Big Dawg started screaming and coughing, as he landed on his right shoulder.

At first Chino didn't know what happened. Then he realized the lead pipe must have connected and caused serious damage. He found the pipe, picked it up, and began hitting Big Dawg. He heard Big Dawg's skull crack and blood splattered all over his shirt and jeans. He kept hitting Big Dawg until his head was a bloody pulp. Finally, Chino collapsed on the ground, completely exhausted.

As he lay on the ground covered with blood, he heard Manny making his way through the bushes to where the two men lay. One dead, the other just returned from the dead. Chino looked up and smiled at his partner in crime. Manny shined a flashlight on both men.

"You're a fuckin' mess, Mon."

Chino laughed, exhausted from the fight. He was exuberant, having won another battle in his life's journey, beginning in the arms of his prostitute mother to becoming the leader of a multi-million dollar drug gang. Manny smiled at his friend and said, "You ain't big but you're one, bad motherfucker."

VIPER BOB

chapter 6

Manny and Chino dragged Big Dawg's body to the seawall next to *Bank Walker*. Manny got a tarpaulin off the boat and they wrapped the body in it and tied it with rope. It was after 11 o'clock and they still had a lot of work to do before the job was complete.

Big Dawg had ten keys on a heavy-duty metal ring that was attached to a chain and hooked on his belt. *In two years I've never seen Big Dawg remove that key chain from his belt,* Chino thought, *I'm sure that be where he keeps the keys to the double locks on the warehouse door, and that explains why he be so paranoid about that key chain.*

Big Dawg was larger than Manny, and it took both men to lift the body and dump it on the stern deck. Chino removed the key ring from Big Dawg's belt and emptied all his pockets. He put the key ring in his pocket. He put a wallet, penknife, a roll of bills and some coins in a Tupperware bowl. Then he placed the blue lid on the bowl and sealed it. Chino took the bowl into the pilothouse and put it on the floor in a corner. The key ring was a critical part of tonight's plan and he was going to keep it with him at all times. He thought, *How ironic, just a few minutes ago it was Big Dawg who was paranoid about this key ring. Now it's my turn.*

Manny started the twin diesel engines while Chino jumped ashore and pulled the anchors out of the ground, coiled the anchor lines and put them on the boat. Manny moved the boat away from the seawall and waited for Chino.

Chino took a pair of surgical gloves from his back pocket and put them on as he walked toward Big Dawg's Dodge Ram 3500 truck. He removed everything from the truck including the GPS antenna, the license plate and the registration that was taped to the passenger side of the front windshield. He put everything in a black heavy-duty plastic trash bag. He put the bag on the front seat and used a twist lock to seal the bag so nothing would accidentally fall out. He started the truck and drove it through the bushes toward the seawall.

He stopped about fifteen feet from the seawall and put the truck in park. He opened all the windows, got out of the truck, taking the trash bag with him. He walked over to the big pine tree, the same one he hid behind, and snapped off a strong branch. He walked back to the truck and rammed the foot brake as hard as he could. Then he put the truck in drive and jammed the branch between the seat and the gas pedal. The truck engine revved up, Chino released the brake and quickly stepped away as the truck lurched forward into the canal.

The engine continued to run as the wheels churned in the water, trying in vain to push the truck forward. Slowly, the truck filled up with water. Soon, the engine was silent and the wheels stopped spinning. Slowly, water filled the cab and when it reached the windows it began pouring in. The front of the truck pointed toward the bottom of the canal and it quickly disappeared, sinking fifteen feet to the bottom.

Manny brought *Bank Walker* close enough to the seawall so Chino could throw the plastic garbage bag aboard and jump onto the stern deck. Manny went out the canal and back to the Grand Lucayan Waterway. Once they were in the waterway, Manny went south three miles until he reached the narrow channel that led to the Atlantic Ocean. While Manny took the boat south into deep water, Chino tied a rope around Big Dawg's ankles and attached two heavy concrete blocks to the rope.

Twenty-one miles due south of the Grand Lucayan Waterway is an area known as Tuna Canyon, where fishermen troll for blue fin tuna and dolphin. The water is over three thousand feet deep and the canyon is ten miles long and one and a half miles wide. Chino selected this as Big Dawg's retirement home. At 2:15 they reached Tuna Canyon. Chino and Manny picked up the body, wrapped tightly with half inch dock line, weighted with concrete blocks, and tossed Big Dawg overboard to his retirement home. Chino threw his wallet and penknife overboard, too. The only things he kept were the key ring and the roll of money.

As Big Dawg headed to his retirement home, Manny and Chino drank a Kalik. Then they went back to Freeport where there was still more work to be done.

They docked the trawler at 5 a.m. and drove to a local restaurant near the marina that catered to fisherman. They were drinking coffee and enjoying a Bahamian breakfast of boiled fish and dirty rice by 5:30. Soon, they would begin phase two of Chino's plan.

Matilda Cockburn, Big Dawg's mother, rarely left her house. However, every Sunday morning she went to Zion Baptist Church and listened to Reverend R.D. Goodfellow preach the word of the Lord. She wouldn't miss church for any reason, even if she were sick.

Every Sunday morning at 8:30, Matilda went out her front door and let the two German shepherds out, into the fenced yard. Then, she walked two blocks to her church on Columbus Drive.

Today she wore a bright red dress, a birthday present from her son, Lucifer. Her white hat with lace was a Christmas present from him, as were the matching red purse and high heel shoes. She looked nice and she was so proud of her son for taking such good care of his Momma. Most of the other women in her neighborhood rarely saw their sons. She knew how much that broke their hearts, but her boy was different. Lucifer "Big Dawg" Cockburn was a good boy, in her eyes.

Fifteen minutes after Matilda left her house, Chino walked around to her back yard and tossed two raw steaks over the fence to the German shepherds who were jumping and barking. As the dogs devoured the sixteen-ounce steaks Chino returned to his car.

It'll take about fifteen minutes for them two dogs to fall asleep, he thought. Chino had ground up a couple of five-milligram sleeping pills and rubbed the prescription drug all over the steaks. He used just enough to put the dogs to sleep. He didn't want to kill them—that would raise too much attention.

By 9:15 both dogs were lying by the side of Matilda's house sleeping like babies. Chino and Manny opened the gate, walked up to the front door, inserted a key from Big Dawg's key ring and let themselves into the house. It took fifteen minutes to find the wall safe with the combination lock. Chino looked at Manny and said, "See. I was right."

One of Chino's customers was in the construction business. He traded the man some cocaine for a small amount of plastique, a putty-like explosive, and a remote detonator. Chino wadded the plastique around the combination lock and stuck the electronic detonator into the wad.

He covered the wall safe with two mattresses from the twin beds in the room. He took one of the bed frames and jammed it against the mattresses to keep them in place.

Manny went into the living room and turned the TV on and the volume up. He covered his ears with his hands and waited for the plastique to explode. Chino came into the living room and crouched behind a wall, next to Manny. He pushed the button on the remote control and the detonator did its job.

When it exploded, the blast threw the mattresses and bed frame away from the wall, and left the mattresses smoldering. The explosion was loud, but not enough to draw any attention from the neighbors. The house was set back off the road and Sunday morning the neighbors were either sleeping off the booze and drugs they had consumed Saturday night or they were at church.

Manny brought a black trash bag into the bedroom and Chino started filling it with cash. There was much more cash than either of them imagined. When the safe was empty they walked out the front door, through the gate and back to their car.

They drove to Big Dawg's warehouse and took the trash bag full of cash inside. Chino counted the money and was shocked at his good fortune. There were sixty bundles of cash in the trash bag and each bundle held ten thousand dollars in one hundred dollar bills. Manny looked at all the money and said to Chino, "I don't think you be needin' to pay me on the installment plan."

Chino smiled, picked up ten bundles and handed them to Manny and said, "When I was a kid growing up in Haiti, every year we went to Carnival in Port-au-Prince. There was this huge merry-go-round. Every time I rode the merry-go-round, I always sat on a big white horse and I'd try to grab this shiny, brass ring, but it was always out of my reach."

"Today," he said. "I got me that brass ring."

VIPER BOB

chapter 7

MONDAY
MAY 14, 2000
FREEPORT, GRAND BAHAMA ISLAND

The next day Chino announced Big Dawg had retired and he was taking over the gang and both businesses. Initially, there had been some problems, but Chino proved he was up to the task of running a multi-million dollar drug operation. Whenever someone asked him where Big Dawg was, Chino replied, "Oh, he retired."

He took the half a million dollars in cash and put one hundred thousand dollars in five safe deposit boxes at five different banks. With the cash spread out, he would never have to go to the same bank more than two times in a single month. Also, no one could kill him and get the cash.

He moved the drugs to Manny's boat Sunday morning after they left the warehouse. He didn't know if the police or any rivals knew about the warehouse and he certainly didn't want to be associated with anything Big Dawg owned. On

Monday he moved the drugs into two different warehouses in another part of Freeport.

Matilda Cockburn went to the police station numerous times. No one seemed to care about Lucifer's disappearance. There was no body and Matilda didn't mention the safe in her back bedroom that had been blown open.

Everyone who worked for Big Dawg was glad he was gone. Chino wasn't a bully and the gang quickly agreed it had taken some BIG balls to get rid of Big Dawg. That alone caused them to respect Chino.

Chino kept a very low profile, not changing his lifestyle one bit. He continued to drive his three year old white Honda, live in the same apartment, and wear the same type of clothes. The only thing that changed was he no longer worked in the team selling drugs. He was too busy running the businesses.

Other than the people directly involved in the drug and boat theft business, no one knew Chino was the new leader, and he intended to keep it that way.

Both of Chino's businesses stayed busy ten months out of the year. The Bahamas has two distinct tourist seasons. The winter season is from November to April, when Americans and Europeans flee the Snow Belt and cold weather for the warm environs of The Bahamas. The summer season is from May to September, it starts and ends when the kids are out of school.

Millions of tourists come to The Bahamas each year. Most vacationers fly to The Bahamas and stay at luxury hotels and resorts. Some arrive on mammoth cruise ships and spend their days shopping at straw markets and duty-free stores. Almost daily, boaters venture across the deep waters of the Gulfstream, in boats of all sizes and descriptions.

Well-known boat manufacturers like Edgewater, Sea Ray, Contender and Bertram sponsor weeklong rendezvous where like-minded boat owners gather to sunbathe, fish and have fun. They come to places like Walkers Cay, Green Turtle Cay, and Harbour Island. The most popular locations are in the Abaco Islands, which lie less than one hundred miles due east of the Florida coast, making all of them easy to get to in less than a day.

Like the drug market, tourists were the primary target for Chino's other illegal business. His gang steals hundreds of boats worth an estimated twenty to thirty million dollars each year. Chino sells the stolen boats to three different markets. The largest market is the drug smugglers' from Haiti. The second market is to re-power small commercial or private boats and the third is reselling the entire boat and motor.

Drug Smuggling Market—Drug smugglers represented about seventy percent of Chino's business. They use the boat or just the engines to bring their illegal products into The Bahamas and then on to the U.S.

Normally the smugglers use a boat for one or two drug deliveries, then sink the boat so it will never be found. If they were to use the same boat repeatedly, it would be much easier for the drug police to spot them.

Certain types of boats are better than others for hauling drugs. When Chino's gang stole one of these boats it would be taken directly to Eleuthera, an island fifty miles east of Nassau on the Atlantic side of The Bahamas. The island is seventy miles long, very narrow and the leeward side borders the Great Bahama Bank, which extends all the way back to Nassau.

The southern half of Eleuthera is sparsely populated, with small towns and settlements scattered along the leeward side of the island. Davis Harbour is the last town on the southern tip of Eleuthera and is three hundred twenty-three miles from Le Mole, Haiti. Most boats can't travel that far on a single tank of fuel. So, Chino kept a supply of fuel along with one hundred and fifty gallon bladders at a marina near Davis Harbour. The driver would stop and fill up the boat and the bladder with enough gasoline to make the trip to Haiti.

Within twenty-four hours after one of these boats was stolen, it would be at the smugglers' warehouse in Le Mole, Haiti. The boat would be hauled out of the water, put on a trailer and moved into the warehouse. In the rear of the warehouse was a forty by sixty foot room with a door. Boats were brought here after they had been pressure washed. The boat was painted a new color and twenty-four hours later, it was back in the water ready to take a load of drugs back to The Bahamas.

R e-Power Market—If a boat owner wanted to purchase an engine on the black market to re-power a boat he would deal with one of Chino's middlemen. Chino sold a nearly new engine for about one-fourth the price of a new one. A new Yamaha 225 horsepower engine cost about eighteen thousand dollars and Chino sold a nearly new one for about five thousand dollars. A buyer would tell the middleman what kind of engine he wanted and agree on the price. The buyer wouldn't even have to put up a good faith deposit.

Chino would contact a small group of commercial fishermen and tell them he had a contract for an engine or a pair of engines, the manufacturer and the horsepower. When someone found a boat with the proper engines, he would call

Chino. The first to call would get the contract and have a certain amount of time to deliver the boat to Chino.

As soon as the boat was stolen, Chino would tell them where to take it and he would have a tow truck waiting for them. A mechanic would remove the engines and take them to a warehouse where he would file or alter the serial numbers. Meanwhile, the fishermen who stole the boat would tow the engineless boat a couple of miles into the Atlantic Ocean and sink it.

Then the buyer would be contacted and a meeting would be set up to inspect, take possession, pay for the engines and arrange to transport them. The entire process would take a couple of days to a couple of weeks.

Resale Boat Market—Throughout The Bahamas and the east coast of the United States, there are hundreds of marinas and boat dealers. Most of them are dealers for one or more boat and engine manufacturers while others are completely independent. All of them are in the highly competitive, low-margin business of buying, selling and trading boats. A handful of these marinas and manufacturers deal in stolen, and legal, boats.

When Chino's gang stole a boat that was in exceptionally good condition, usually less than six months old, he would put these boats in a warehouse in the Freeport area. The boats would be kept for three or four months during which time the owner filed an insurance claim. The claim would usually be settled within ninety days, as long as a police report had been filed and the owner was not suspected of disposing of the boat himself.

When Chino had three or four of these boats he would contact a couple of these unscrupulous dealers and describe what type of boats he had. A representative would fly to Freeport, inspect the boats and negotiate a price for the entire lot.

These dealers and manufacturers have devised various ways to get titles for stolen boats, allowing them to sell stolen boats on the open market. Only a small percentage of these boats are ever recovered by law enforcement agencies. But, when they are discovered the boat is confiscated and the unsuspecting owner loses the boat and his money.

Boat theft is a profitable business and Chino made a lot of money for three reasons. First, only a handful of law enforcement officers are assigned to investigate these criminal activities. Second, a majority of the boaters visiting The Bahamas don't realize how vulnerable foreign registered boats are. Third, most boaters leave The Bahamas soon after their boat is stolen, return home and file an insurance claim.

Most boaters come to The Bahamas, dock their boat in a marina and stay at a local hotel or resort. Each year, more than three hundred boaters dock their boat and retire to their hotel room to eat, drink and party the night away. The next morning they return to the marina, expecting to take their boat out and enjoy a day on the water. Instead they discover their boat was stolen while they were having fun. The police are immediately called and, after a brief discussion, the officer files a stolen boat report. After that, very little, if anything, happens.

Within a few hours after their boat was stolen, the engines were removed and the hull was sunk in a couple thousand feet of water. It usually drifted aimlessly north along the ocean floor, carried off by the Gulfstream or local currents, never to be seen again.

Chino's gang targeted new or nearly new powerboats with expensive outboard engines. The typical single-engine boat would be worth thirty thousand to fifty thousand dollars. Twin-engine boats are worth fifty thousand to one hundred fifty thousand dollars. Because the value of almost every boat his gang stole was in excess of twenty-five thousand dollars, they were handled as grand larceny cases.

Within the Royal Bahamas Police Force is a group of detectives who work in the Central Investigation Department. CID as it is known, is responsible for investigating all major crimes committed inside The Bahamas, including boat thefts. Unfortunately, they have a very low success rate at recovering stolen boats or catching the thieves. Gangs like Chino's are well-financed, experienced and can afford excellent legal representation. However, the single biggest obstacle is time: By the time an owner has notified The Bahamian police their boat has been stolen, the engines have been removed and the boat is lying in a couple thousand feet of water.

In addition, most boaters can't stay around to follow up with CID or launch a search to recover their stolen boat. For these reasons, CID focuses on other crimes that are solvable. It's no surprise Chino's gang successfully stole a couple hundred boats every year.

Occasionally, a boat was stolen simply because the situation was right. There were no identified buyers for the engines nor was it a good boat for hauling drugs but the opportunity was too good to pass up.

These thefts tend to be the exception rather than the rule. Without a buyer, the boat or the engines must be kept in storage until a buyer is found, making it easier for the criminals to get caught with the stolen property.

These crimes of opportunity usually occur because an inside person working or living at a marina needs fast cash. He or she was privy to personal information about the boat and the crew, like when they plan to return to the U.S. Also, the insider knew one of the commercial fishermen who stole boats for Chino.

VIPER BOB

chapter 8

THURSDAY
OCTOBER 9, 2003
WALKERS CAY, ABACOS
NORTHERN BAHAMAS

Randy Morales was looking for some fast cash. *Shit, how did I get in this mess?* It was after 5 o'clock Thursday evening and Randy repeated to himself for the hundredth time, *I'm broke, dead fuckin' broke.*

Teddy Brown, Randy's boss and captain of *Sea Wolf*, a 38-foot Bertram sport fisherman, had been gone for eight weeks. Randy only worked three charters during that time and he was broke. Thank God he lived on the *Sea Wolf*, but he still had to eat. Two weeks ago he ate the last bit of food Teddy left onboard. *No food, no booze, and no fuckin' money. If it wasn't for Nicole, I would have starved to death by now.*

Tonight, there was going to be a big birthday party at the hotel for Tony Neubolt, the dock master for Walkers Cay Marina. *Tony be a popular guy and lots of people be comin' to the party*, Randy thought. *I'll load up on free food and booze—and sneak as much as I can back to the boat.*

Until the party started, Randy decided to go to Grand Cay, a neighboring island three miles east of Walkers, and see Nicole, his on again, off again girlfriend. Nicole worked as a barmaid at Rosa's Bar and Grill and tonight she didn't start until 10 o'clock. Randy thought, *I'll lay up with her for a couple of hours.* Nicole was twenty-two years old, extremely attractive and just thinking about her young, hard body got him excited.

Randy hitched a ride to Grand Cay with three locals who worked on Walkers and lived on Grand. They were coming back later for Tony's birthday party, so Randy asked if he could ride with them. Colin, the driver, said, "Sure, Mon. No problem."

Ten minutes later they arrived at the dock behind Rosa's Bar. "We be goin back at nine, so be here or we leave without ya," Colin said.

Randy went straight to Nicole's apartment but she wasn't there. Then he walked to Rosa's to look for her. Rosa's Bar and Grill was one of two bars on the island, and the favorite hangout for locals as well as fishermen visiting the area. Rosa's was a wild place and there was a party going on every night.

Nicole wasn't at Rosa's, but Randy saw two commercial fishermen he'd met a few weeks ago. They were his age and they were sitting at a table near the big screen TV drinking beer. Their fishing boat had been working in the area for the past couple of weeks and he remembered they were from Mores Island, which was about one hundred miles from Grand Cay.

"Hey Dude," Randy said as he joined the two men. Spider and Speedo looked up and said, "What's happenin', Bro? Want a beer?"

Randy nodded his head and said, "Yea, I'm dyin' of thirst."

While Speedo went to get three beers, Spider asked Randy, "How you doin', Mon?"

"Not good. My boss is still in Ft. Lauderdale, and I ain't made no money in a month. Charters are real slow this time of year."

Speedo returned with three bottles of Kalik.

Randy took a long sip of his beer and asked Spider, "You got any ideas how I can make some fast cash?"

"Yea Mon, I might know a way." The three men finished their beer and Speedo bought another round.

"What you got in mind?"

"We be goin' home tomorrow, and if you knows of a boat with good engines we can heist, we can take them to Freeport and sell 'em."

Randy thought for a minute, *My Melody had been at Walkers for the past two months and they have a 27-foot Edgewater center console powerboat.*

"Yea, there's a boat in Walkers with two Yamaha engines, but they be leaving in the morning."

Randy told Spider about *My Melody*. Spider said, "That sounds good, Mon. Let's take a ride and scope it out."

They got three beers, left Rosa's and took their 17-foot skiff to Walkers.

The sun was setting as the three men entered the small channel leading into Walkers Cay Marina. Resting in the calm water at the end of the center dock was *My Melody*. Tied up on the port side of the big yacht was a shiny 27-foot powerboat. The forty slip marina was only one-third full and there weren't any boats docked next to *My Melody*. Spider looked at Randy and said, "Mon, this look good. What kind of security does the marina got?"

Randy smiled at Spider and replied, "Absolutely none."

"How many people be on the boat?" Speedo asked Randy.

"Three people—the owner, his wife, and son," he said. "I talk to the son every day and he told me they be leavin' for the U.S. tomorrow morning."

"What time they go to bed?"

"Early Mon, maybe ten or eleven o'clock."

"Yea Mon, you gonna make some fast money tonight," Speedo predicted.

VIPER BOB

chapter 9

Theophilus Spider Dean turned twenty-one, three months ago, on July 16th. He and his best friend Speedo had been working as commercial fishermen for six years. For the past three years they worked on *Lady Gertrude*, a 55-foot fishing trawler. *Lady Gertrude* had been fishing the area around Walkers and Grand Cay for three weeks and the fishing had been good. The holds on the boat were bulging with conch, lobster and fish. Early Friday morning, the boat was going to make the one hundred and ten mile trip south to Marsh Harbour, where they would sell the catch to a local fish house.

Spider and Speedo worked all day Thursday, diving for conch and lobster. They returned to *Lady Gertrude* around three and helped the rest of the crew clean their catch and wash down the boat. Once all the chores were done, Spider and Speedo took their skiff to Grand Cay to have a couple of beers and dinner at Rosa's Bar and Grill.

Rosa's Bar was one of their favorite places to hang out. The food was good, prices were cheap, and the people were a lot of fun. The owner of Rosa's was a large burley man who was the dominant person on Grand Cay. He was built like a fireplug. Roosevelt was six feet tall, weighted three hundred and ten pounds, his skin was black as coal and his hands were the size of baseball gloves. In addition to the bar and grill, he owned the local seafood business and the grocery store. He was a quiet man but he was someone you didn't want to mess with. Whenever someone got on his wrong side, there was hell to pay.

Rosa's Bar and Grill was divided into two rooms, with the bar area twice as large as the restaurant. The bar was thirty feet wide and one hundred feet long with a pool table at one end, an oversize video jukebox and large screen TV at the other end. A three sided bar stood in the middle of the room, with six bar stools on each of the three sides. Half a dozen tables and chairs were in front of the 50" Sony large screen TV. That was where Spider and Speedo were sitting when Randy joined them.

The TV was always on at Rosa's. Sometimes the volume was high, sometimes it was low, and once in a while it was off. Tonight it was off and the two men were talking about a girl Spider met last week when he went to the Jungle Room Bar, in downtown Freeport, to meet with Chino.

Spider and Speedo had stolen a boat for Chino four weeks ago from the marina near Treasure Cay when the *Lady Gertrude* had been fishing near there. Over the past six years, the two men had stolen forty-nine boats, primarily for the engines. They work as commercial fishermen in the daytime and at night stole boats for Big Dawg and now Chino.

Stealing boats in The Bahamas was easy, and Spider and Speedo were good at it. There were numerous marinas in the Abaco Islands where boaters come to vacation and fish. The marinas have little or no security and the police consider boat theft a low priority.

When Big Dawg operated the gang, the fishermen had to steal the boat and remove the engines themselves, sink the hull and then bring the engines to Freeport. The large 200- and 250-horsepower engines weighed about six hundred pounds, so Spider and Speedo needed help to remove them. Many of the fishermen, including Spider and Speedo, entered into an arrangement with Manny Pender to help remove and transport the engines to Freeport.

Manny would meet the fishermen with his boat, *Bank Walker*, which had a powerful electric winch and help them remove the engines. While Manny took the engines to Freeport, the fishermen towed the stolen boat into deep water and sunk it. Manny's arrangement with the fishermen was he got one third of the money Big Dawg paid for each engine.

Spider and Speedo usually took a boat they stole to a place they called Hole in the Wall, where they would remove the engines and anything else of value. Hole in the Wall was located on the northeast side of Mores Island, where Spider and Speedo lived.

To get to Hole in the Wall from Walkers Cay they went southeast past Great Sale Cay, then south toward the lower tip of Little Abaco Island. From there they went due east between Cave Cay and Cashs Cays, navigating in three to five feet of water. Once they were past Cave Cay they went southeast for thirty-six miles in water that was fifteen to twenty feet deep until they reached the northeast corner of Mores Island.

Then they went down a narrow, deep water channel, turned right into a small cut, then turned right again, into a dead end channel. This was Hole in the Wall. The entire area was overgrown with mangroves, making it the perfect place to hide a boat.

In addition, it was only seventeen miles from Manny's house at Sandy Point. Spider and Speedo usually called him when they got to Hole in the Wall and by the time Manny arrived, Spider was ready to remove the engines.

Spider was an expert at removing the big outboard engines. It took him about thirty minutes to unhook the fuel, hydraulic and electrical systems. Then they were ready to unbolt the engines and remove them.

As soon as Manny arrived they would tow the boat, using their skiff, out to the deep water channel and tie it to *Bank Walker*. Spider would remove the cowling from each engine and hook the cable from the winch on *Bank Walker* into the lifting eye and hoist the engine off the boat. Speedo would join Manny on *Bank Walker* and place seat cushions from the stolen boat on the deck. Manny would expertly raise each engine off the boat and onto *Bank Walker*. As he lowered each engine onto the deck Speedo would position it so it rested comfortably on one of the seat cushions. It took about ten minutes to remove each engine.

When they were finished, Spider and Speedo were usually tired and hungry and Manny would take them to Sandy Point for breakfast and some sleep.

They would anchor *Bank Walker* in front of a secluded house that sat back off the beach, where Manny lived by himself. Then they took their skiff to the town dock to Paul and Mary's guesthouse where they would have a breakfast of boiled fish and grits. Spider's aunt and uncle owned the restaurant and while they ate breakfast they talked to Paul and Mary.

After breakfast Manny usually walked back to his house, while Spider and Speedo went down a waterfront road to Effie Thompson's house. Spider knew Effie most of his life and she had been his woman for the past five years. She and Spider had a son who was almost three years old.

Spider and Speedo had a routine they did every time they went to Effie's house. They would flop into the two chairs in the small combination living-dining room and Spider would tell Effie, "Gets us some smoke, Baby."

"Sure," she would say, and disappear into the bedroom. A minute later she would reappear with a large Ziploc bag of marijuana and a pack of cigarette rolling paper.

She would sit on the floor beside Spider, roll three joints, light the first one, take a deep drag and hand it to Spider. The threesome would sit in the small room, smoke all three joints, laughing and reminiscing about all the good times they've had together.

Soon Spider and Effie would go into the bedroom and get into the twin bed, where they spent many days and nights smoking dope and making love. Meanwhile, Speedo would stretch out on the couch and doze off, sleeping peacefully.

One afternoon Spider woke up and stumbled into the living room where Speedo was still sleeping. He shook him a couple of times but he didn't budge. Spider walked over to the refrigerator and got two ice-cold beers and opened them. He walked back to the couch and laughingly said, "Hey Bro, want some cold beer?" He poured beer on Speedo's face, immediately waking him out of a deep sleep.

"Come on Bro, we got to get back to *Lady Gertrude*," Spider said. "Ellison's gonna be pissed, we been gone all day." Speedo grunted and grabbed the bottle of Kalik from Spider before he could pour more beer on him.

They went back to Paul and Mary's for a late lunch, and then walked down the dock to their skiff, fueled it up and went back to *Lady Gertrude*.

When Chino took over the gang he made a number of changes that everyone agreed were improvements. He took responsibility for removing the engines. Now all Spider and Speedo had to do was take a stolen boat directly to Freeport. Chino's mechanic used a wrecker truck to remove the engines and took them to a warehouse.

Before Chino allowed a fisherman to steal boats for him, he made them attend a class on boat theft. He was both a leader and a shrewd businessman. He believed that if he taught the Bahamian fishermen the best techniques for stealing boats and what to do if they got caught, he would make more money and it would help keep him and his people out of jail.

Manny Pender, who became one of Chino's most trusted allies after Big Dawg retired, taught the class. Spider and Speedo were in the first group to take the class, even though they had stolen numerous boats with Manny's help.

Manny was an excellent teacher, in part, because he had years of experience at stealing boats and smuggling drugs. Pender University—or PU as he laughingly called it—taught the local fishermen every aspect of boat theft. Manny was proud of the fact that very few of his students had ever been arrested. Manny was in his mid-thirties, and had been stealing boats and running drugs most of his life. He had been arrested twice, but never convicted.

Chino, through his lawyer, provided bail money for anyone arrested for dealing drugs or stealing boats for him. His lawyer, David Thomas, was one of the best in The Bahamas. He defended some of the worst criminals in Freeport, and his record was nearly perfect. The bail money and legal expenses were handled as a loan from Chino and were repaid from future criminal activities.

Spider and Speedo mastered every technique in Manny's course. They could sneak into a marina undetected, cut the dock lines, and tow a boat out of the marina in less than three minutes. They learned the best time to steal a boat was between three and four in the morning when the boaters were asleep and the security guards were fighting to stay awake. The best weather for stealing a boat was when it rained because few security guards would go out in the rain and make their rounds. One of the most important things Manny stressed was to steal foreign registered boats. If they stole a Bahamian's boat, the police were far more motivated to find the thief. Any Bahamian who could afford a new boat worth fifty thousand to one hundred fifty thousand dollars was wealthy, by Bahamian standards. That meant he had other wealthy friends who could pressure the police to find the criminals.

Also, Manny taught the fishermen an easy, foolproof way to start a Yamaha engine. Speedo was particularly interested in this part of the class because it was much quicker than hotwiring the sophisticated systems.

Manny's technique was for the fishermen to steal a Yamaha starter switch with the keys and use it to start the motors of a boat they planned to steal. Using this technique it took about sixty seconds to remove the four screws securing the starter switch plate. Then they would unplug the seven-pin connector, plug-in their starter switch plate and start the engines.

Yamaha made seventy-five different keys for their ignition switches. Speedo had collected ten keys and three complete ignition starter switch plates over the past six years.

"Believe it or not," he would say to Spider, "some of them dumb ass owners actually left their keys in the ignition."

He had starter switches for single engine, twin engine and triple engine boats. If one of his keys didn't work it took Speedo about sixty seconds to replace the boat's starter switch with one of his. He often joked about how easy it was to start the engines saying, "Why do Yamaha bother to give the boat owner a key, why not just use an on/off switch?"

The majority of the boats they stole, Chino only wanted the outboard engines. After the engines were removed Spider and Speedo would tow many of the stolen boats to Hole in the Wall and strip the electronics and T-Top. They had a Cuban-American contact in Miami who sold the electronics to fishermen in the south Florida area and split the profits with them.

VIPER BOB

chapter 10

Great Abaco Island is seventy miles long, narrow at the top and bottom and wide in the middle. Marsh Harbour, the largest city, is in the middle of the island on the eastern shore where more than six thousand people make their home. The Great Abaco highway was originally built as a logging road in 1957 and connects Marsh Harbour to the southern tip of the island.

Traveling south, out of Marsh Harbour, The Great Abaco highway passes through The Bahamas National Trust sanctuary. This is a preserve for the endangered Bahamian parrot, but numerous other birds live in the sanctuary. Twenty miles south of Marsh Harbour, the highway passes the little village of Cherokee Sound, which has about one hundred fifty residents, all of them friendly. Continuing south, the highway goes to Sandy Point and terminates ten miles further south near Annotation Point. Here a lonely lighthouse, which is mainly seen by boaters, marks the southern tip of The Great Abaco Island. This is the same lighthouse Chino looked for when he was running drugs from Haiti to Sandy Point.

The fifty-mile drive from Sandy Point to Marsh Harbour takes an hour and thirty minutes, if you have a sturdy vehicle. At forty miles an hour, the trip is like riding the world's longest roller coaster. Trucks twist and swerve, as they defy gravity, trying to stay on the uneven road. Heads and spines are brutally punished as passengers bounce like a ping-pong ball between the roof and seat, as tires dive into and out of the numerous potholes.

Sandy Point is just one of the many remote areas in The Abacos. The people who live here are as sturdy and rugged as the mangroves that surround their town and overran the island thousands of years ago. They live a simple lifestyle and prefer being left alone. The few strangers who come here are mostly fishermen looking to battle bonefish that thrive in the flats, surrounded by the thousands of mangrove trees.

In The Abacos there are hundreds of remote waterways and channels covered with mangroves. Anyone can hide anything here. Due to its remote location there are few, if any, witnesses, making it the perfect place to carry out illegal activities. The combination of these factors has made this part of The Bahamas a haven for drug smugglers and other criminals.

One of the first things a stranger visiting Sandy Point might notice was there are no signs of any industry. Yet ninety percent of the two hundred-fifty people who live there own new or nearly new pick up trucks. Even Auntie Maude, the local bread lady, has a maroon one-year-old Ford F-100 truck.

This is where Theophilus "Spider" Dean was born and grew up with other young men who had little or no education and spent most of their youth in and around the water. Most of them were excellent swimmers. Spider could free dive to fifty feet and was able to stay underwater for more than three minutes. As he grew older he realized there were only a few ways he could make a living if he stayed at Sandy Point. He could fish, steal, or smuggle drugs. He and Speedo decided to do all three.

On Spider's fifteenth birthday, he and Speedo decided to become fishermen. They needed a small boat, something about 17-feet long with a motor, so they could earn money diving for lobster and conch. However, there was one small problem. They only had two hundred and thirty-one dollars between them, and that wasn't enough money to buy a boat. So, they decided to borrow a friend's boat, go to Lucaya and steal one.

Lucaya is a resort town, on Grand Bahama Island, seventy-six miles from Sandy Point. Saturday morning, three days after Spider's birthday, he and Speedo left Sandy Point at sunrise and four hours later arrived at Lucaya. Their boat used twenty gallons of gas to make the trip. Since they planned to return with two boats, they brought three plastic cans capable of holding thirty gallons of gas.

They docked at Lucayan Marina and bought fuel from Alonzo Hudson, the dock master. As they filled the main gas tank and three spare cans they told Alonzo they were from Mores Island and were visiting relatives who lived in Freeport.

They had never seen a marina and resort like Lucayan Marina. They asked Alonzo numerous questions and he told them the history of the complex.

"Who owns the marina?" Spider asked.

"Two retired European businessmen purchased the marina a couple of years ago. They tore down the old marina and built an ultra-modern facility, complete with marina, pool, outdoor bar and grill and waterfront condominiums. The complex is five miles from downtown Freeport and just a short ride by water to the ever-popular Lucaya Marketplace," Alonzo explained.

Spider and Speedo decided to take their boat to Lucaya Marketplace and have lunch before they set out to find a boat to steal. Spider drove their boat across Bell Harbour, they tied up next to the fuel dock and walked to Dry Throat Tavern, a popular restaurant where they ate fish and chips.

East of the marina are a group of exclusive waterfront developments build in the 1980s. The homes are built on a series of interconnected canals and from the air it looks like a giant spider's web. Two deep-water channels provide boaters easy access to Lucayan Marina and the Atlantic Ocean.

Most of the canal-front homes had docks with boats ranging from 15-foot flat boats, to expensive sport fisherman. Spider and Speedo spent four hours looking for a 15-foot to 17-foot Boston Whaler but they didn't find any boats that could be easily stolen. Finally, they decided to look in another waterfront development.

They went out Bell Channel and east four miles to the entrance of the Grand Lucayan Waterway. It took two more hours before they found what they were looking for. There was a new 17-foot Boston Whaler on a canal just south of the Casuarinas Bridge, the main bridge connecting the east and west sides of Grand Bahama Island. The boat was docked behind a large house set back about one hundred feet from the canal. The ground between the house and the dock was level, making it difficult for anyone in the house to see the dock or the small boat.

It was almost six, so they decided to go back to the market-place and replace the gas they used during the day. Afterward, they would hang out there until it was time to steal the boat. The marketplace, with its eighty waterfront shops, craft stalls, bars and restaurants was the perfect place to kill time. At the heart of the marketplace was Bob Marley Square, where live bands played and single girls danced and partied all night. Also, there were numerous places for them to relax and take a nap.

At 2:30 in the morning they left the marketplace and went back to the Grand Lucayan Waterway, easily finding the house where the Whaler was docked. The full moon shone brightly, lighting the island and the canal with a pasty white glow.

Spider got into the Whaler, untied the dock lines, and they towed it until they were outside the channel. Then they stopped, hotwired the motor, topped off the gas tanks in both boats and began the four hour trip back to Sandy Point.

The eastern horizon was turning from a gun metal gray to light blue as the boys saw the outline of Sandy Point, still ten miles away. Thirty minutes later they arrived at a secluded area known as Bamboo Point. The boys were exhausted from the long night and the boat ride. However, they were eager to start working on *their* new boat.

They pulled the Whaler out of the water, onto the sandy beach and began painting the hull and motor. By 2 o'clock, both boats were anchored in front of the cocoanut palms that cover the bleached white beach at Sandy Point.

The boys were excited and proud of themselves. In their world, this was a rite of passage. Now they could earn money, fishing. This meant they were men making their own way in the world.

Anyone who noticed the newest black-hulled addition to the small fleet of fishing boats at Sandy Point knew better than to ask the boys where they got it. Boats mysteriously appeared in this part of The Bahamas all the time.

VIPER BOB

chapter 11

THURSDAY
OCTOBER 9, 2003
GRAND CAY, ABACOS
NORTHERN BAHAMAS

It had been six years since Spider and Speedo stole the Boston Whaler in Lucaya. Now, as they prepared to steal their fiftieth boat, neither man was concerned about getting caught. Why should they? They were good at what they did.

They had earned almost one hundred sixty thousand dollars in the past six years stealing boats. It didn't matter to them that tonight they would steal a boat worth one hundred and twenty thousand dollars so they could make four thousand dollars.

As they left the small marina at Walkers Cay and went back to Grand Cay, Spider drove the skiff and Speedo and Randy sat in the bow.

"I'm gettin' thirsty. Let's go to Rosa's and have us another beer and somethin' to eat," Speedo suggested. "Good idea,

Bro," Spider replied, as he pushed the throttle all the way forward, causing the skiff to race ahead, skipping across the water as they headed for Rosa's.

They arrived a few minutes later and sat at a small table in front of the video jukebox. They ordered three seafood platters and washed down the fried grouper and snapper with cold Kalik beers. After dinner they ordered three more beers and watched TV, as they passed the evening away.

Spider had given Randy one hundred-fifty dollars against the four hundred and fifty dollars he would receive from the sale of the engines. When Chino paid them, Spider would give Randy the other three hundred dollars.

But, first they had to steal the boat. If everything went right, Randy would fly to Freeport tomorrow and collect the rest of his money. The one hundred and fifty dollars Spider gave him would pay for the round trip ticket to Freeport, a few beers and he would still have some money left over. Once he got his hands on the other three hundred dollars he figured he was good until his boss returned in a couple of weeks.

At 8 o'clock, people started leaving Grand Cay for the birthday party at Walkers. Randy hitched a ride with Colin, while Spider and Speedo waited on Grand. The plan was for Randy to stay at Walkers and watch the marina and the people on *My Melody*. He would act as the lookout until it was time to steal the boat.

The hotel at Walkers Cay sits on the highest point of the one-mile long island. The bar where the birthday party was being held was located in a promenade connecting the hotel lobby to the restaurant and gift shop. One side of the bar opened out onto the patio and a fresh water pool. A stone walkway led from the bar down to the marina and went past three cabanas perched on the south side of the island. They faced Tea Table Cay, an uninhabited string of flat rocks one mile south of Walkers. Just before the walkway reached the marina it went past a tiny chapel where Jebodia Rolle performed weddings and occasionally preached on Sunday to the twenty or so locals who worked and lived on the island.

When Jebodia wasn't preaching, he operated a charter fishing business that catered to the numerous sportsmen who came to Walkers. Jebodia had been a guide for over fifteen years. During that time he'd taken many famous, and not so famous, people fishing. Some of them caught record-size bonefish on the flats, where the feisty fish hide among the mangroves.

Beyond the chapel, the walkway dropped sharply and passed a long, narrow two-story building. On the first floor was Jebodia's charter fishing office, a small one-room liquor store and the Treasure Chest, the only grocery store on the island. The second floor of the building had two apartments the Symington family used when they were at Walkers. Roger Symington bought Walkers Cay in 1968 from Rosa Espinosa, a Bahamian woman who had owned the island for three years.

The Espinosas were a prominent and wealthy family from Nassau where Rosa's father made millions in the construction business. She had a vision to develop Walkers into a major, high-end resort but after three years, became bored and disillusioned in the project. In 1968, she sold the island to Roger Symington, a successful businessman from New York.

Roger was already a local landowner, having bought Big Grand Cay in 1964. He was fascinated with the local fish population, including the many species of sharks that thrived in the area. From the palatial home he built on Big Grand,

Roger launched numerous oceanographic studies of the sharks that lived below in the string of beautiful and unique coral reefs that protected the windward side of the islands.

Roger purchased Walkers because, like Rosa, he believed the island could be developed into a resort. As a successful and wealthy businessman, he could easily afford to develop the island into any kind of resort he wanted. His vision was to keep the island rustic and cater to sportsmen like himself. Over the years, many of Roger's friends visited the island to dive and fish. The island quickly developed a reputation for fun and good fishing and few people who went there were disappointed.

Over the years some very famous people visited the island including a U.S. president. Richard Nixon was one of Roger's most influential friends and on several occasions, vacationed at Roger's large house on Big Grand Cay. The large white building was situated on the highest point of the island, facing south, overlooking The Little Bahama Banks. After President Nixon's first visit to the island the locals started calling Roger's house on the hill the White House.

Spider and Speedo sat on the dock in front of Rosa's looking at the White House. At 11 o'clock they finished their tenth beer of the night. They left the dock and walked down a narrow street to check out the Cool Spot Disco, the other bar on the island. They decided to have some fun drinking and dancing with the local girls while they waited. Their plan was to steal the boat around 3 a.m., so they had four more hours to kill.

While they were waiting, Speedo called Chino and told him they were planning on picking up a couple of almost new Yamaha engines.

Chino said, "I'm not in Freeport and I ain't gonna be back 'til Monday. Manny's at Sandy Point, so do what you gotta do, but be careful."

That gave Speedo an idea so he said to Spider, "Hey Bro, let's take the boat to Hole in the Wall. We can pick up some extra cash by strippin' the electronics and T-Top and sell them in Miami. Manny can meet us with *Bank Walker* and then we can go to Effie's."

Spider replied, "Yea Bro, and we can party. Just like ole times."

Every hour Randy left the birthday party and took as much food and beer as he could hide under his jacket. He went down the walkway past the apartments and onto the center dock. Whenever someone asked where he was going, he said, "We got a bad pump on *Sea Wolf*, I gotta check it every couple of hours. I'll be right back." Each time he went to *Sea Wolf*, he put the food and drinks in the refrigerator and checked on *My Melody*, which sat ten slips down the dock.

There were only two boats between *Sea Wolf* and *My Melody*. Each time Randy walked down the dock, he stopped at both boats to see if anyone was awake or onboard. One of the boats, *Fun 'n Sun Too*, was a charter fishing boat. The owners, Mark and Lynn, and first mate, Johnnie, who lived onboard, were up the hill attending the birthday party.

Randy stopped thirty feet from *My Melody*. A light was flickering in the main salon, but the curtains were closed. He couldn't see inside the yacht but he quickly recognized it as light from a TV.

Inside the yacht, Melody Edwards was relaxed on the white custom-made leather couch watching a movie while

Randy sat outside on a picnic table for a couple of minutes watching the boat. He didn't see anyone moving inside the boat, so he left and went back to the party.

At three, when the party broke up, Randy went back to *Sea Wolf* and continued to watch *My Melody*. The curtains were still drawn and the light was still flickering. He figured someone forgot to turn off the TV.

Spider and Speedo waited at the Cool Spot Disco until a group of locals returned from Tony's party.

Speedo asked one of the men, "Hey Dude, was you at the party?"

"Yea, Mon, it was great."

"How come you back here?" Speedo asked.

"Cause the party be over, now we gots to buy our beer."

Speedo was relaxed as he finished his last beer of the evening. He was confident this would be another successful job.

VIPER BOB

chapter 12

THURSDAY
OCTOBER 9, 2003
GRAND CAY, ABACOS
NORTHERN BAHAMAS

Alphonso "Speedo" Albury was born on Man-O-War, a small island six miles, as the crow flies, east of Marsh Harbour, The Abacos. Speedo and his family moved from Man-O-War to Sandy Point when he was eight years old. There are hundreds of Albury's through the Abaco islands and they are the dominant family on Man-O-War. Speedo's father got into a vicious fight with Silas Albury, head of the clan, and almost killed him.

As a result they were no longer welcome on Man-O-War and Speedo's father moved the family to Sandy Point. Very few Albury's lived there and the ones who did, like many of the residents, had criminal pasts or something to hide.

Spider and Speedo were the same age and quickly became best friends. As Speedo grew up, there were two things he excelled at: diving and repairing motors. He learned how to hotwire any engine and when the two boys got into the boat stealing business, he learned everything he could about Yamaha, the most popular outboard engines in The Bahamas.

In January of 2000, Spider and Speedo were offered a job on a fishing boat owned by Ellison Braithwaite from Mores Island. Ellison was a fair man and they enjoyed working for him. During the three years they had worked for him he never said anything when they disappeared and were gone all night stealing a boat. He pretended he didn't know what they did on the all night expeditions but he was nobody's fool.

Lady Gertrude was a 55-foot wooden hull fishing boat built in Nassau in 1939. She was a sturdy vessel with three large holds below deck to store lobster, conch and fish. The crew was usually made up of nine men, including Ellison Braithwaite. Four teams of two men worked from small flats boats. Each team owned their boat and Ellison provided the fuel. He and Speedo, both excellent mechanics, repaired the motors and just about anything else that broke on the boats.

Ellison bought *Lady Gertrude* with money he and his wife saved over the eighteen years they had been married. When Ellison bought the boat, the first thing he did was change the name from *Invincible* to *Lady Gertrude*. His wife was a good woman and they enjoyed a good life together. Their six children were hard workers and the fishing business had been good to them. Gertrude and Ellison lived the kind of life they dreamed of as kids.

Each year Ellison took his family on *Lady Gertrude* and went thirty miles to the east end of Grand Bahama Island, where they spent the holidays with Gertrude's relatives. They would spend a week anchored in McLeans Town Harbour where they lived on the boat. Each day they visited family and friends and each night the clan gathered at a different relative's house for dinner and a joyous evening of singing and talking. Around 9 o'clock, the men would leave the house and go to one of the waterfront bars.

The Water's Edge, where most of the local fishermen gathered each evening, was Ellison's favorite bar. The older men talked about the weather and fishing. The younger men talked about trucks, wrestling and girls, but, not necessarily, in that order. During the holiday season most of the fishing boats were in port and many of Ellison's friends went to the Water's Edge for the evening ritual.

Ellison enjoyed having a few beers but he was a deeply religious man and he never got drunk or stayed out late at night. There was no shortage of things he and Gertrude needed to buy for the fishing business or their six children.

On December 26, 2000, Ellison went to the Water's Edge and met Spider and Speedo. He immediately liked them and since he was short a couple of fishermen, he offered them jobs on *Lady Gertrude*.

Spider and Speedo worked well together, taking turns diving and operating the boat. Spider was a good diver, but, not as good as Speedo, who could harvest more conchs and lobsters than any member of the crew. He and Spider worked hard and they made good money.

Their workday began after a breakfast of boiled fish and rice on the stern deck of *Lady Gertrude*, where the crew slept in hammocks. They left the mother ship by 8 a.m. and dove until late in the afternoon. When their boat was full, they went back to *Lady Gertrude* where Ellison was waiting to help them unload their catch.

They usually stopped diving between three and four and went back to *Lady Gertrude* to help clean the day's catch. During the day, Ellison cleaned the catch but he couldn't keep pace with the four work crews. Once the catch was cleaned, the lobsters went into the forward hold, conch went into the middle hold, and snapper and grouper went into the stern hold. The ice machine operated around the clock, making five hundred pounds of ice a day, which was continually dumped on the catch to keep it fresh.

Between the cash Spider and Speedo earned working on *Lady Gertrude* and the money they made stealing boats, each man earned about eighty thousand dollars a year. The Bahamas has no personal or income taxes, so they made an excellent living and there was almost nothing they couldn't afford.

When Spider and Speedo joined the crew, Ellison's oldest daughter, Inez, was seventeen years old. Speedo always had an eye for Inez and in January of 2001, on her eighteenth birthday, Speedo and the tall slender girl started dating.

Three months later Inez was pregnant and she and Speedo were both excited about having a baby. They decided to get married and asked Ellison to perform the wedding ceremony, which he agreed to do.

Speedo made good money and the couple could easily afford a house of their own but because Speedo was gone most of the time, they decided to live with her parents.

When Inez was ready to have their baby, her mother, who was one of the island midwives, would help with the birth and care of the infant. Ellison and Gertrude were excited about becoming grandparents and they made sure Inez took good care of herself.

VIPER BOB

chapter 13

FRIDAY 3:00 A.M.
OCTOBER 10, 2003
WALKERS CAY, ABACOS
NORTHERN BAHAMAS

It was 3 a.m. and time for Spider and Speedo to go to work. They left the Cool Spot Disco and walked back to their flats boat that was tied up at Rosa's. As they walked down the road, two locals—obviously very drunk and having a good time—in a golf cart almost ran them over. There were almost no cars or trucks on Grand Cay because the roads were too narrow for a car and gasoline was three dollars and sixty cents a gallon. Every household owned at least one golf cart, and most of them had numerous dents and scratches.

Spider and Speedo got into their boat and went north to Funny Cut, a narrow, twisting channel, fifteen feet wide, with jagged coral rocks as vicious as shark's teeth, that guards the channel. Once they were through the channel, they went up the leeward side of Grand Cay until they reached the end of the island.

Spider expertly guided the boat through one of three small cuts, then opened up the throttle and raced in a straight line for two miles toward Walkers.

Five minutes later, Spider throttled back to idle speed as they approached Walkers and looked for any people left over from the party. Sixty-watt light bulbs glowed in front of a few slips casting an eerie shadow up and down the dock.

They turned into the channel and glided quietly toward *Sea Wolf* where Randy was sitting on the gunwale waiting for them. As Spider eased the flats boat into the slip beside *Sea Wolf*, Randy grabbed the bowline and tied it to a cleat. Speedo, who was sitting in the bow, whispered to Randy, "How everythin' look?"

"It's quiet as a corpse. Everybody's gone or sleepin'."

"OK, then we be ready to do it. There's been one change in the plan. Our man in Freeport won't be back 'til Monday."

Randy was annoyed and lost his temper saying, "Shit Mon."

Speedo cut him off before he could say another word. "Shut the fuck up, Mon."

Randy realized he was talking too loud and nodded he understood, "OK, what am I suppose to do?"

"Come to Freeport on Monday," Speedo said. "We gonna deliver the engines Monday and get paid."

"OK, I'll be in Freeport Monday mornin'. Where can I meet you guys?"

"Come to the Jungle Room. We be there."

Randy replied, "OK."

"Now, let's get us a boat," Speedo ordered.

Randy got off *Sea Wolf* and walked down the dock, acting as the lookout. If he saw anyone, he would signal his new partners by asking, "Hey, Mon, what's happening?"

Randy was extremely nervous as he kept watch and was relieved no one came down to the dock. Spider quietly guided their boat to the end of the dock and eased it next to *My Melody* so Speedo could climb aboard the 27-foot Edgewater. The engines were raised out of the water, which would make towing the boat tricky. If the engines were in the water, they would act as a rudder but out of the water, the boat would weave back and forth. This meant they had to be extra careful not to make any noise.

Speedo took a sharp knife from his pocket and cut the stern lines that secured the rear of the boat to the yacht. Then he went to the bow and undid the bowline and pushed the boat away from the yacht. Once it was a few feet from the yacht, Speedo threw Spider a line and they quietly left the marina. It took them less than three minutes to steal the boat.

As soon as they were outside the marina, Speedo lowered both engines and Spider increased their speed. As they moved away from the marina, Speedo opened his canvas tool bag and took out a Phillips head screwdriver and removed the four screws holding the starter plate to the center console. Then, he took an identical starter plate from his canvas bag with two keys. He separated the seven-prong plug connecting the starter switch to the Yamaha engines, plugged his starter plate into the plug and started the engines.

Spider heard the engines start and slowed down to release tension on the towline so Speedo could untie it. When it was free, they took the boats behind Tea Table Cay, stopped, and put ten gallons of gas in the Edgewater's fuel tank. Fifteen minutes after stealing the boat, they were racing southwest toward Grand Bahama Island, forty-six miles away.

They didn't have enough gas to make the trip all the way to Mores Island. They decided Speedo would wait north of Freeport Harbour while Spider went to a marina and got more gasoline.

At 6:15, they arrived at a group of small, barren rock islands where Speedo could easily hide the Edgewater. It was too dark to navigate the channel into Freeport Harbour so they relaxed and waited.

Sunrise was at 7:17. But fifteen minutes before the sun started its daily trek across the sky, there was enough light for Spider to leave. He took the skiff down a narrow channel that went through Hawksbill Creek to Freeport Harbour. He pulled up to the dock just as an attendant was unlocking the fuel pumps. He filled up two ten-gallon gas cans and returned to Speedo.

While Spider went to get gas, Speedo called Manny Pender.

"Hey, Bro, what's up?"

"Just getting started, my man. How you hangin'?"

"Spoke with the boss last night and he said you was at home. We headin' your way. We got somethin' for you to take back to Freeport."

Manny understood. "OK, Bro, when you gonna be here?"

"We be at Hole in the Wall by eleven."

"OK, Bro, see you there."

As soon as the Edgewater was gassed up, they went to Dover Sound, the northern entrance to the Grand Lucayan Waterway. Thirty minutes later, they exited the waterway and went southeast toward Mores Island. The two boats went in a straight line for sixty-five miles to Mores Island and Hole in the Wall.

Hole in the Wall was seventeen miles from Manny's house. Manny looked out his front door at the large blue and green Bahamian flag attached to one of the antennas on *Bank Walker*. He saw there was a mild wind blowing out of the southwest this morning. *Bank Walker* was a heavy wooden boat that could go between ten and twelve knots depending on which direction the wind and the current were going. He figured with a southwest wind it would take him about ninety minutes to reach Hole in the Wall, so he decided to leave at 9:30.

Spider and Speedo made good time and reached Hole in the Wall before 11 o'clock. They drove the Edgewater into a cluster of mangroves and used rope from the Edgewater's anchor locker to tie the boat to a large mangrove tree.

Then they went to work.

While Speedo removed the cables and hoses attached to the engines, Spider removed the fishing equipment. There were six rods and reels in the holders on both sides of the boat. He pried the lock on the center console door with a large screwdriver. Inside he found a deep drop fishing rig and a downrigger they could sell along with the electronics to their Cuban contact in Miami. The Cuban had a seemingly inexhaustible supply of fishermen who were willing to buy stolen, top of the line equipment.

"The guy who owned this boat sure went first class," Spider observed.

By the time Speedo had everything disconnected, they heard a familiar throaty rumble. *Bank Walker* was approaching so they untied the boats and towed the Edgewater back out into the narrow channel.

Manny was at the helm of *Bank Walker* guiding the clumsy looking trawler down the channel. As he pulled up next to the Edgewater, he was steering the boat with one hand and had a Twinkie in the other. One of the main reasons he was fifty pounds overweight was his fetish for Twinkies. A local pilot, who flew regular charters to Palm Beach, brought him two cases of Twinkies at least twice a month.

Speedo tied the Edgewater to *Bank Walker* and Manny lowered a cable from the electric winch. Speedo removed the engine cowling and attached the hook on the cable to the lift ring on the engine. Using the winch, the three men easily removed the five feet tall, five hundred eighty-three pound Yamaha engines.

Within twenty minutes both engines were on the stern deck of *Bank Walker*.

Spider and Speedo towed the Edgewater back to the hiding place in the mangroves. They tied the bow of the Edgewater to the trunk of a large mangrove, with numerous rope burns from previously stolen boats. They used some branches to further camouflage the boat until they were satisfied no one would find it. Then they got in their skiff and left Hole in the Wall. They decided to return Monday to remove the electronics and the T-top. They figured they would make between one and two thousand dollars from the sale of the fishing equipment, electronics and T-top.

As the two boats headed to Sandy Point, Manny called Chino and said, "I'm with the boys, we got them items you want. I'll bring them with me tomorrow."

"OK, but I got to stay here a couple more days. Call Calico Jack and have him hold 'em."

"You the boss. Consider it done."

Chino used a variety of places to hide boats and engines, including numerous private homes in Freeport. Business had been good and his warehouses were full, so he decided to store the engines at Calico Jack's house. Occasionally, Chino used Calico Jack to do a variety of jobs.

Rodney "Calico Jack" Rackham was a small-time criminal who could be trusted, to a point. He was always broke and would do almost anything for fast money. He lived in a large, sparsely furnished house he inherited from his mother when she passed away and he owned a large bed Dodge Ram 1500 truck. He used the truck to make deliveries for Chino, including engines.

Rodney claimed to be related to John "Calico Jack" Rackham, an infamous pirate who operated out of Charles Town, later named Nassau, in the early 1720s. Rackham was best known because of two members of his crew: Anne Bonney and Mary Read gained notoriety as the only two documented female pirates in the New World. They each hid their gender, dressing and fighting as men alongside other crewmembers.

Manny called Calico Jack and said, "The boss wants you to hold somethin' for a couple of days. Meet me at the old government dock west of McLeans Town tomorrow at two."

With their work done, Spider looked at Speedo and Manny and said, "It's time to P-A-R-T-Y. I'll call Effie and let her knows we be comin'." He called his girlfriend and when he was done he told his friends, "She gonna have two of her girlfriends join us."

"Yea, Bro, it's P-A-R-T-Y time," Manny and Speedo said.

Effie's girlfriends turned out to be very cute twins who recently moved to Sandy Point and just celebrated their eighteenth birthday. Effie rolled a couple of joints and everyone got high and the three men partied with the girls until the wee hours, smoking dope, drinking beer and making love.

VIPER BOB

chapter 14

At 7:30, Melody Edwards woke up, relaxed after a wonderful night's sleep aboard their yacht. Melody was an exceptionally attractive woman and whenever she entered a room, any room, she immediately became the center of attention. Her auburn hair and soft, green eyes showcased her sensual, high cheek boned face.

Melody was born in a small town in northern Alabama and raised on a farm where her mother and father struggled to make ends meet. She came from humble people who grew up in the heart of two belts: the Cotton Belt and the Bible Belt. Her mother was very religious. Every Sunday the entire family went to the small Methodist church, two miles down the dusty road from their farm, which was the center of their religious and social life.

It seems as though farmers, the world over, are protective of their daughters, but none more so than Melody's mother and for good reason. Her mother knew all the local farm boys saw Melody as a prize and they were going to chase after her daughter. She knew Melody was going to need all the help she could get to stay on a straight and narrow path.

Like many girls in her early teens, Melody's figure blossomed overnight. In the summer of 1967, she was transformed from a cute young girl to a voluptuous woman. Thirty-five years later Melody was still a very attractive, voluptuous woman.

She met Bob Edwards on April 17, one week before his forty-eighth birthday. Even though they were both in their forties and carried some painful scars from recent divorces, it was love at first sight. Six months after their first date, they stood in front of a preacher saying, "I do, ya'll."

After ten years of marriage, their love was still as passionate and exciting as it was the night they met.

Bob Edwards was infected with the drive and imagination of an entrepreneur from a very early age. He spent thirty years in the electronics industry, starting five companies each more successful than the previous. Three years after they were married, Bob did two things that became milestones in their life. In 1996 he bought one of the first production models of the Dodge Viper RT/10, a sports car with a V-10 engine that could go 170 miles an hour. Melody loved the white car with twin racing stripes so much she started calling him Viper, and soon everyone else did, too.

Two months later Viper started his fifth company. Six years later, it employed three hundred people and he took the company public. Half the employees and a third of their business was in Europe, so Viper and Melody divided their time between London, where they had a house and California. They spent so much time flying around the world when someone asked where they lived, Melody would jokingly reply, "We live on a blue and white Boeing 777."

Melody was proud of her husband and his numerous accomplishments. However, one of the happiest days of her life was when he said, "I'm going to retire." His travel schedule was grueling and he felt like he was in a perpetual state of jet lag.

"It's not worth killing myself and if I don't stop now, that's what'll happen."

On September 10, 2001, at the age of fifty-six, Viper retired. He wanted to spend the next couple of years unwinding. His vision was for them to buy a yacht and spend a couple of years cruising the Caribbean, where they could relax in the sun, scuba dive and pursue his favorite pastime of fishing. Viper and Melody spent the next three months looking for the perfect yacht that would become their home for the foreseeable future. They wanted something that was comfortable, roomy and seaworthy which meant a large yacht, but small enough so they could handle it themselves.

It didn't take long for them to find exactly what they were looking for: a 68-foot Ocean Alexander motor yacht with three staterooms, in-suite bathrooms complete with roomy showers. The three staterooms were on the lower level along with the engine room.

The yacht had twin Detroit Diesel V8 engines, two generators to provide electricity, two air conditioning systems to cool and clean the air, and a reverse osmosis water maker that converted seawater into the best drinking water money could buy. It was a completely self-contained, floating utility company. This yacht could take them anywhere they wanted to go in the Caribbean.

However, what really sold them on this particular yacht was the huge kitchen and spacious living room/dining room. The kitchen, called a galley on a yacht, had every conceivable appliance Melody could think of. Two people could comfortably work in the galley at the same time. The living room/dining room, called the main salon, was eighteen feet wide and twenty-six feet long with large windows along both sides and across the entire back. Two weeks after viewing it, they bought the yacht. For the next three months, their life was transformed into blissful chaos.

Like most new yacht owners, Melody and Viper wanted the interior to reflect their taste. After a two-week shake down cruise in The Bahamas, they put their yacht, newly christened *My Melody*, into a shipyard. It would be in the yard for a month of remodeling in preparation for their first Caribbean cruise.

In early February 2002, the work was completed and they left Palm Beach on their dream cruise. Their first stop was Walkers Cay in The Bahamas, and after a month, they went south, visiting numerous places in the Far Out Islands of The Bahamas. They arrived in Georgetown, The Exumas in mid-April and after two weeks they prepared to leave The Bahamas and travel eight hundred miles southeast to the Virgin Islands. There were only a few islands along the way where they could refuel so Viper planned their route carefully.

They left the sparkling turquoise waters of Georgetown at 9 o'clock on a beautiful Wednesday morning. The first fueling stop was two hundred and forty miles away at Providenciales, better known as Provo to the residents of the Turks and Caicos Islands. They arrived in Provo twenty-four hours later and stayed just long enough to clear in and out of Customs and take on eight hundred gallons of fuel. From Provo they went down the western side of the Turks and Caicos Islands, turned southeast, and went down the north side of Hispaniola.

Hispaniola is a large twin-nation island with Haiti on the west side and the Dominican Republic on the east side. Viper didn't want to stop at Hispaniola for two reasons. Haiti is a poor country that has been in chaos for almost two hundred years, since gaining independence in 1804 from the French. There were numerous stories of Haitian criminals hijacking yachts and killing the people onboard. His second concern was the Mona Pass, which lies on the east end of the island between the Dominican Republic and Puerto Rico. The Mona Pass is only forty miles wide, but it is one of the most treacherous passages in the world.

The water in the Atlantic Ocean generally travels north up the eastern side of North America. When it reaches Iceland and Greenland it circles across both islands, then turns south and goes down the western side of Europe. When it reaches Africa, it circles back toward America and travels three thousand miles across the seventeen thousand foot deep Atlantic seabed. The first land it reaches is Hispaniola and Puerto Rico, where the water is forced through the narrow, shallow Mona Pass.

Sailors have reported waves as high as thirty feet in the pass and on mild days, the swells can be six to ten feet high. Boaters have waited for weeks until the pass was calm enough to make the crossing safely.

Every thirty days, the moon completes a lunar cycle as it goes from a new moon, to first quarter, then a full moon and finally third quarter. During the new moon and full moon phases, the oceans experience what's called a spring tide, which lasts four or five days. During this time the delta between high and low tide is the greatest. During the first and third quarter moon phases, the ocean experiences a neap tide, which also last four to five days, when the delta between high and low tide is the least.

Viper planned to reach the Mona Pass on Friday morning, May 3rd, one day before the moon entered the third quarter phase and the first day of the neap tide. With the tides at their calmest, he hoped to have a good crossing. As they approached the Dominican Republic, Viper started getting radio reports from boats traveling north that just crossed the Mona Pass. They reported the seas were one to two feet and the Mona Pass was as flat as a pancake.

His planning paid off. They crossed the Mona Pass in daylight and mild seas, reaching the southwestern tip of Puerto Rico at eleven that night. They anchored in a large bay outside of Bocaron. The next day they took on fuel and continued to the U.S. Virgin Islands, arriving in St. Thomas that evening.

They spent two months in the Virgin Islands and divided their time between the U.S. and the British islands. On the British side they anchored at Peter Island, Norman Island and Virgin Gorda. Viper dove the numerous shipwrecks in the area, like the RMS *Rhone*, a British mail boat that sank during a hurricane on October 29, 1867. Most afternoons, they would take their 27-foot Edgewater, which they towed behind the Ocean Alexander, and go for a sunset cruise, drinking wine and watching the sun disappear into the emerald green ocean.

In July they left St. Thomas and spent a month relaxing on the Dutch side of St. Maarten, visiting numerous jewelry stores in Philipsburg, and enjoying the wild nightlife in Simpson Bay. On August 1, they said their good-byes and went further south, spending a month visiting St. Kitts,

Antigua, Guadeloupe and Dominica in the Leeward Islands. They anchored in coves at the smaller islands and enjoyed the company of the friendly locals during cocktail hour at the waterfront taverns.

September 1st, they dropped anchor in Marigot Bay, St. Lucia, the location for numerous movies. It was the most beautiful bay either of them had ever seen. They continued south to the Windward Islands, visiting St. Vincent, Bequia, Carriacou, and, finally arriving in Grenada, where they planned to spend three months. From their slip at Spice Island Marina, they could see the American University, where U.S. soldiers rescued American students during the 1979 Communist uprising.

They began their return trip in November, visiting their favorite islands as they went north. They spent Christmas in St. Maarten where they met Chuck and Alice DuPont, an American couple who had been cruising in the Caribbean for five years. Chuck was born and raised in a small town outside of Nashville, Tennessee, just ninety miles from where Melody grew up. On Christmas Day, Chuck and Melody told their favorite stories about growing up in the Deep South, as the two couples drank Bloody Marys until they were bleary eyed.

Now, almost two years and six thousand miles later, they were docked at Walkers Cay where their cruise had begun. As Melody quietly slipped out of bed and got dressed, she looked at Viper and thought, *I won't wake him just yet, I've got plenty to do and he can use the sleep.*

Melody was going to fly to Palm Beach that afternoon while Viper and his son took *My Melody* to St. Simon's Island, Georgia. Then, in about a week, Melody was going to drive to Georgia where they planned to spend a couple of months.

Melody went to the galley and made a pot of coffee. As she glanced out the window she thought, *what a gorgeous morning. The guys are going to have perfect weather for their trip.*

As she waited for the coffeemaker, she sensed something wasn't right but couldn't put her finger on it. Call it woman's intuition, but Melody's instincts were good and she couldn't shake the feeling. When the coffee was ready she poured a cup but she still hadn't figured out what was wrong.

She went forward to the pilothouse and opened the portside door. As she looked outside she realized what was wrong.

Their 27-foot Edgewater powerboat wasn't there.

She thought, *Well, maybe Viper or Robert moved it last night when they were getting ready for today's trip.*

Robert, who slept in the forward guest stateroom, was usually up by now. Melody went down the stairway and knocked on his door.

"Did you or your dad move the Edgewater last night?"

"No," he replied, "it's where we always keep it."

Melody said, "No, it's not."

"That's impossible. I saw it last night at eleven, just before I went to bed."

"Well, come and look for yourself," was Melody's reply.

And he did. "Wow, the Edgewater's gone. We'd better wake up Dad," he said.

Melody went down to the master stateroom. "Viper," she asked, "did you move the Edgewater last night?"

Viper was in a deep sleep and he didn't understand her question but he responded, "Sure it's outside, tied up to the boat."

"No, it's not," she said. Viper woke up instantly. He quickly got out of bed and went to look for himself. All three stood on the deck and stared at the spot where the Edgewater had been every day for the past two months, since their arrival at Walkers Cay.

Viper said, "What the hell's going on?" He walked toward the bow and picked up the dock line that secured the Edgewater to *My Melody*, still tied to the cleat. He looked back toward the stern and saw both dock lines dangling from the aft cleats.

They stood outside in a state of shock. "This is Walkers," Melody said. "Nobody's ever had a boat stolen from here!"

It took a couple of minutes for everyone to accept the fact the Edgewater had been stolen.

"It's not just a boat, it's our Edgewater. It's traveled six thousand miles with us all over the Caribbean," Viper said.

Their Edgewater had taken them on more than a hundred fishing trips, as they caught dolphin, wahoo, tuna, snapper and grouper. Robert caught his first wahoo in the Edgewater. It took them to remote places where they went diving for lobsters and snorkeling off the beautiful coral reefs of the Turks and Calicos islands. It had been in six fishing tournaments with Viper and his fishing team winning two.

Their Edgewater took Viper and Melody on countless sunset cruises around Charlotte Amelia Harbour in St. Thomas and beautiful Morris Bay on the west side of Antigua, up and down the Intercostal Waterway in Palm Beach, to lunch at the numerous waterway cafes. She took Viper and Melody trolling in the deep Atlantic waters, off the coast of Florida and The Bahamas.

She took them to remote islands throughout the Caribbean, where she sat quietly as Viper and Melody made love on a sandy beach or on the soft helmsman seat behind her center console.

No, Viper thought, *she isn't a boat, she's much more than a boat, she's better than a good friend, she's a member of our family and we take care of our family.*

Melody and Robert, who were standing next to him, were startled when Viper angrily stated, "Someone kidnapped our Edgewater and I'm going to get her back. I swear to God, I'm going to get her back!"

VIPER BOB

chapter 15

Viper got off *My Melody*, rushed down center dock, turned left, went past the fuel dock, the marina office and the dive shop. He turned left again onto the north dock and went to slip North-8, stopping in front of a 27-foot Century boat with a cuddy cabin and *Lone Star* painted on the transom.

"Ahoy, Captain, anybody aboard?" Viper asked. A slender man with light brown hair stepped up from the cabin and replied, "Hi Viper, how you doin'?"

"Not good. Somebody stole our Edgewater last night," Viper said to Ed, owner of the boat. "Can you take me up and look for the bastards? Maybe they're still in the area."

Ed Worthington, a long-time resident of Ft. Worth, Texas, kept a boat at Walkers Cay and flew to the island a couple of times a year in his Cessna 210. Ed was an accomplished pilot, who held a couple of *Guinness Book* flying records.

Ed said, "Sure, but I don't have a lot of spare fuel. I hope you know where to look."

Viper said, "All we can do is give it our best shot." And with that he went back to *My Melody*, got a VHF radio and a pair of gyroscopic binoculars. When he got to the airstrip Ed was already completing his pre-flight checklist.

Ten minutes later the two men taxied down Walkers' cement and asphalt patchwork runway and took off toward the southwest. They flew over Grand Cay and Big Grand Cay, hoping someone who attended the birthday party last night used the boat to get home. But, that was not the case.

They continued down the outer island chain with a bright morning sun burning behind them and a pale blue sky with puffy, white clouds all around them. Viper was using the gyro-binoculars to look at every boat in the crystal clear waters of the Little Bahama Bank. They checked every boat, but to no avail. Every time they saw a boat, Viper would push a button on the binoculars and the gyro would stabilize the lens, allowing him to examine the boat.

They went past Carter Cay and then banked to the south and went over Great Sale Cay, past Barracuda Rocks and back toward Walkers. They searched every island in the area, looking at every waterway. The Edgewater was nowhere to be found.

They searched the area for almost an hour when Ed said, "Viper, we're getting low on fuel. I think it's time we go back to Walkers."

Viper agreed. Reluctantly, they flew back to Walkers, disappointed they hadn't found the boat or a single clue to its whereabouts. Ten minutes later they landed the Cessna and parked opposite the small gray building that announced they had arrived at Walkers International Airport.

A group of locals were gathered at the airport waiting for the morning flight from Freeport. Randy Morales was standing with the group watching as Viper and Ed took off to search the area. He thought, *You fools, you don't have a snowballs chance in hell of findin' that boat. It's gone. Long gone.*

Meanwhile, Melody was two hundred feet from the airport terminal, in the one room police station, filling out a stolen boat report. On her way to the police station, Melody passed Randy and said, "Hi Randy, how are you today?" He said, "Fine. I'm sorry to hear about your boat. Good luck findin' it." Melody took it as a positive statement but Randy knew better.

While the two men were flying high over the Little Bahama Bank, Corporal Blackstone, a large and friendly police officer, was taking Melody's statement. He was compassionate, but business like, as he guided Melody through the events of the past few hours. He meticulously recorded all the information about the boat and motors from the boat's registration, which Melody had given him.

He got the serial number for the gray Yamaha engines, the Hull Identification Number and the Coast Guard registration number for the 27-foot Edgewater. His report was two full pages. When he was done, Melody read it and said, "It's correct to the best of my knowledge."

Blackstone smiled at her, but thought, *There's almost no chance these people is gonna find their boat. Things like this ain't supposed to happen at Walkers and the people on* My Melody *is well liked by the locals and the other fishermen who visit the island.* In the two months they had been on the island, Blackstone only heard good things about them.

As Blackstone was finishing his report, Ed and Viper were returning from their unsuccessful search. Viper went directly to the corporal's office where he and Blackstone discussed the theft. Blackstone added some additional information to his report and then asked Viper to read the police report, which he did. When Viper and Melody were satisfied the report was correct, she signed it, and they left the Corporal's office.

Dejected, they walked down the hill and back to their yacht.

Viper was confident the Edgewater was not in the eastern part of The Bahamas, so the next logical place to look was the western side. Freeport, on Grand Bahama Island, was the largest city in the northern Bahamas and was the best place to base their search. Freeport was located on the south side of Grand Bahama Island, forty-seven miles southwest of Walkers. But for *My Melody* to get there, they had to go around the west end of the island and then turn to the southeast. There was a shorter and more direct route, but *My Melody* drew five feet of water and the other route went across banks with less than five feet of water. This meant the route Viper had to take was eighty-one miles.

By noon *My Melody* was ready to depart for Freeport and Viper had a decision to make. If they went directly to Freeport they would arrive around 7 o'clock and sunset was at 6:57 p.m. Viper was well aware of the unpredictable problems a large yacht can encounter entering a narrow channel and docking in a marina after dark. He decided to play it safe and spend Friday night at West End and continue to Freeport Saturday morning.

The marina at West End is situated on the northwest tip of Grand Bahama Island and has been a popular resort area for over fifty years. In the 1960s, some U.S. businessmen built the first luxury hotel and casino at West End. Every week thousands of tourists made the fifty-mile trip from Palm Beach to gamble and relax at the luxurious resort. As larger and grander resorts were built on Grand Bahama Island and elsewhere, the resort fell out of favor with the fun loving tourists. In the late 1990's, a group of investors tore down the hotel and built a luxurious boutique hotel and marina complex on the one hundred and fifty acres of sandy white beach surrounding West End.

My Melody arrived at the West End marina just after five o'clock. By the time the yacht was docked, Viper knew he made the right decision. If he had gone directly to Freeport he would have entered the narrow, shallow channel with a setting sun. As the sun begins to set it cast shadows and makes it very difficult to read the water or spot coral heads lurking just below the waters surface.

Instead, at sundown, *My Melody* was comfortably resting at the end of the center dock at West End. Melody prepared dinner while Viper and Robert washed the yacht. Then everyone relaxed and enjoyed their traditional strawberry daiquiri, but tonight they were made with a double shot of rum.

After a mentally exhausting day, everyone onboard the yacht was ready for a quiet evening and by nine, everyone was in bed, sound asleep. As Viper fell asleep, he reviewed his search plan and was eager to get started.

He planned to leave West End by 8 o'clock in the morning, which meant they would have *My Melody* tied up at the marina in Freeport no later than 1 o'clock. They had visited Freeport on numerous occasions and he planned to stay at Lucayan Marina, which was less than five miles from downtown Freeport.

Viper decided to make Lucayan Marina their base of operations while he searched the northern Bahamas. Freeport had a large airport with numerous private charter airplanes. Also, it was headquarters for the Royal Bahamas Police Force for The Abacos.

VIPER BOB

chapter 16

SATURDAY
OCTOBER 11, 2003
SANDY POINT, THE BAHAMAS

Saturday morning Spider, Speedo and Manny were bleary eyed and exhausted from last night's party with Effie and the twins. But, they managed to leave Sandy Point by 10 o'clock on *Bank Walker* to make the four hour trip to McLean's Town on the east end of Grand Bahama Island.

By two o'clock, *Bank Walker*, with the three men and the two engines, was at the remote dock where Calico Jack was patiently waiting. Manny maneuvered *Bank Walker* up to the seawall and the dilapidated wooden dock while Calico Jack backed his truck up to the boat. Using the winch, they lifted the engines off the boat and into the spacious vinyl-lined truck bed.

Calico Jack covered the engines with a blue tarpaulin and tied all four corners to clamps in the bed of the truck. When everything was ready, Calico Jack, Spider and Speedo drove to

Calico Jack's house in Freeport. They drove around to the back of the house and moved the engines inside. It took all three men to lift the six hundred pound engines and carry them into an empty bedroom.

They left Calico Jack's house and went directly to the Jungle Room to have a few beers and wait for Manny. The job had gone off without a hitch and in a couple of days Chino would advance them a thousand dollars to cover the fuel they bought and the money they agreed to pay Randy.

When Chino told Spider he wouldn't be back for a couple of days he said, "I'll give you four thousand dollars when I return if you want your cash now, or five thousand dollars when I sells the engines."

Since neither man needed the cash Spider said, "If you gives us a grand to cover our expenses, we can wait for the rest." Chino agreed and Spider thought to himself, *Not a bad weekend. We each picked up seventeen hundred bucks plus we'll get another thousand from the sale of the fishing' tackle and the electronics, plus we had a great party.*

R andy Morales called Speedo Sunday afternoon. Speedo told Randy, "We ain't getting our money 'til the engines are sold but the boss is gonna cover your three hundred dollars. So, come to the Jungle Room tomorrow and you be paid."

Randy breathed a sigh of relief. For a moment, he thought, *they gonna screw me out of my money. After all, who you gonna call when a thief gets cheated by another thief?*

"Great, I'll take the mornin' flight and should be there by eleven."

"When you gets to the airport, take a bus to the Jungle Room, it only cost a dollar," Speedo said.

Monday Spider and Speedo went to the Jungle Room at 10:30. Randy got there an hour later and saw Spider and Speedo drinking beer at the end of the bar. A third man was sitting with them but when Randy joined them Calico Jack left. Spider said, "What's up, Bro?" Randy said, "Everything's cool, my man."

Speedo ordered three beers. They moved to a table where Randy told them everything that happened on Walkers since Friday morning. He ended with, "Nobody knows nothin'. We be good." Spider said, "See Mon, I told you. We bad."

A few minutes after 3 o'clock, Randy left the Jungle Room and took a taxi back to the airport for the return flight to Walkers. He thought, *I got more cash in my pocket today than I've had in months.* The combination of the excitement of getting away with a major crime and having over three hundred bucks in his jeans aroused and pleased him. *When I gets back to Walkers I'm headin' straight to Nicole's apartment and we're gonna P-A-R-T-Y all night.*

chapter 17

Early Saturday morning, as Viper and his family were leaving West End, a fisherman from Grand Cay arrived at Admiralty Marina in Freeport.

James McArthur lived and worked in Grand Cay but he was born in Freeport. Like many of the locals, he moved back and forth between Grand and Freeport. When there was no work available on Grand or Walkers they looked to Freeport for employment.

The twenty-five year old fisherman had an easygoing personality, like many Bahamians. However, there was a serious side to him only his wife, Gerry, and his best friends knew. His favorite pastime activities were watching reruns of Hawaii Five-O and writing poetry.

McArthur had all 283 episodes of Hawaii Five-O and was a dedicated fan of Jack Lord. The series had been on the air for twelve years beginning in 1968 and ending in 1980. McArthur bought 175 episodes that were digitally re-mastered and recorded or traded with other enthusiasts for the remaining 108 episodes.

Most evenings after dinner he and his family gathered around their TV and watched one or two episodes.

McArthur dreamed of the day he would take his wife and son to Hawaii and visit all the places McGarrett and Danno caught bad guys on the Big Island.

One evening his wife was teasing him about his addiction to Hawaii Five-O and said, "Baby, you're more crazy 'bout that show than you is about me. But, that's OK, cause I love you."

"You know what? I'm gonna call you Five-O," Gerry said.

McArthur laughed and replied, "Yea, Five-O. I likes that."

McArthur's poetry reflected the feelings of a complex and compassionate man. Many of his poems describe the rugged Bahamian lifestyle. He wrote most of his poetry while he was alone, fishing for snapper and grouper. The quiet coves and the solitary Little Bahama Banks were the perfect place for the introspective fisherman-poet to get in touch with his inner self.

Five-O was a religious man who thought of the Ten Commandments as a blueprint for how he should live his life. His strong views on morality and justice were also evident in his poetry. His favorite poem, titled *Little One*, was inspired by the powerful feelings he experienced when his son was born three years ago.

Five-O owned a twenty-two foot Mako powerboat he used for fishing and diving for lobster and conch. The boat's hull had been leaking for several months and two days ago he got caught in a strong storm, causing more damage to his boat and making the leak worse. He decided it was time to get it fixed. Saturday morning he left Grand Cay at seven and went to Admiralty Marina in Freeport. Admiralty's workshop specialized in fiberglass and its prices were the lowest on the island. As Five-O was waiting to speak with the service manager, he saw a high school buddy, Alphonso "Burt" Reynolds.

Burt came over and gave Five-O a low-five hand shake. Burt said, "Hey Bro, what's up?"

Five-O told his friend about his leaking hull. Burt pulled him over to a corner of the building and asked, "You hear 'bout the boat that got heisted from Walkers?"

Five-O looked at Burt and said, "No Mon, when did that happen?"

"Friday, real early in the mornin'," was Burt's reply. Five-O was surprised, not because Burt knew about a stolen boat, but because one was stolen from Walkers. The island had a reputation for being a safe haven. The island's sole business was tourism. The visiting fishermen and scuba divers brought thousands of dollars worth of equipment and boats worth up to three million dollars to the island to use and enjoy during their vacations. If they were concerned about their boat or equipment being stolen while at Walkers, they might go elsewhere. Vacationers are finicky and once an island develops a negative reputation, it's very difficult to reverse it.

Business throughout the Caribbean dropped off dramatically after the September 11, 2001 attacks but Walkers seemed to recover faster than most, and now it was business as usual. Many of the locals suffered for the past two years and none of them wanted to see the tourist business slow down again. Everyone on Grand Cay relied on Walkers directly or indirectly for jobs, including Five-O.

He continued talking to Burt, occasionally going back to the theft, trying to get the names of the men involved.

"Last night I was having a beer at the Jungle Room and overheard two dudes talkin' 'bout a boat some fishermen heisted from the Marina at Walkers," Burt said.

Five-O was eager to get back to Walkers and find out what was being done to find the stolen boat. Five-O talked with the service manager for Admiralty Marine about the repairs and he agreed to bring his boat back Tuesday to have the work done.

During the forty-seven mile ride back to Walkers, Five-O thought about what he was going to do. *I have two choices and I needs to consider each one carefully. Although Burt didn't give me the names of them thieves, he did say the two men was involved with a drug gang.* This made Five-O weigh his options very carefully.

My safest choice is to go home and say nothin' to nobody, including Gerry, he thought. Most of her family still lived in Freeport. If Five-O provided information to the police and the gang found out, they could easily get back at him by going after Gerry's family. Five-O knew this had happened before and he had no doubt it was a real possibility.

His other option was, *I can go to the police and tell them I overheard someone talking 'bout the crime and not give them Burt's name.*

By the time he arrived at Walkers Cay, he decided to talk to Roland "JR" Watson, the Customs officer for the island and a good friend he knew he could trust.

After telling JR everything he heard, and his concerns about the gang, JR said, "You need to go to the police and tell them what you heard. Don't give them your buddy's name. Tell them you be afraid for your family."

"Would you come with me?" Five-O asked.

JR agreed.

The government offices at Walkers are located in a rectangular shaped, one-story block building adjacent to the airport. The Customs office is fifteen feet wide by twenty feet deep and is the largest of the three offices. All merchandise coming into Walkers must be cleared by Customs and many of the items are not claimed immediately, and the office doubles as a storage facility.

Next to Customs are two offices about one-third the size of the customs office. They are the police station and the immigrations office. Corporal Blackstone, the sole police officer on Walkers, was not in his office.

JR called his house and told him, "Blackstone, I has a man from Grand who gots information about the boat that was stolen yesterday."

Corporal Blackstone arrived fifteen minutes later and listened to Five-O's story. He said, "I understand your concerns 'bout your wife's family but without your buddy's name, this information is useless."

Five-O replied, "I may be the only person my friend told this to and if the police question him, he'll know I told you, so I can't risk givin' you his name."

Corporal Blackstone filled out a police report and told Five-O to read and sign it. Then Blackstone asked, "Would you be willin' to go to Freeport and tell your story to the owners of *My Melody?*"

Five-O thought for a minute. He looked at JR who nodded his head and said, "That be a good idea." Five-O agreed to go if they paid for his airline ticket.

Corporal Blackstone opened a file cabinet, removed the stolen boat report and got the telephone number for *My Melody*. He called the number but there was no answer. He left a detailed message and told Five-O, "When I hear from them, I'll call you."

Five-O left the police station and went home to tell his wife everything that had happened. After Five-O left Blackstone's office, the policeman sat in his chair and tried to figure out how he could use this new information. Blackstone's instincts told him something besides his buddy's name was missing from Five-O's story. He wondered if Five-O was somehow involved in the crime.

In a theft like this, a local person usually provides the crooks with critical information and acts as lookout. In the theft of a boat, the dock master, or one of his staff, is considered a "person of interest."

Blackstone thought, *Five-O could have been the local person. But if he be involved, why would he talk to the police? Maybe there was a disagreement and Five-O didn't get his share of the money?*

Oh well, Blackstone thought. *Half of police work is patience and like we always say, you can run—but there's nowhere to hide in The Bahamas.*

He pondered, *how much effort should I put into this case.* His pride was hurt. This was the first boat ever stolen from Walkers and it happened on his watch. Another factor he needed to consider was, *How concerned are the owners?* He thought, *They're wealthy, but that don't make 'em good people.*

He knew of at least three cases where owners had arranged to have their boat stolen so they could collect insurance money. But, the Edgewater was almost new, and he knew from the boat's documents there wasn't a loan on the boat. He couldn't think of a good motive for the owner to arrange for his boat to be stolen.

Then, he thought, *I left them a message. If they don't call me or if they say they be going home to file an insurance claim, I won't waste any time on the case. After all, hundreds of foreign registered boats are stolen each year in The Bahamas and no one will blame me if this case goes unsolved.*

Corporal Blackstone adjusted his oversize body in the undersize chair. He thought, *If the owner continues to look for the boat I'll do everything I can to help him.*

My *Melody* was comfortably docked at the Lucayan Marina by 1 o'clock. Viper's son washed the salt off the boat from the thirty-mile trip and Viper and Melody went to the pool bar at the marina to have a drink and try to put some fun back into their life.

They drank double rum punches and told Navaro, the bartender, and Cleo, the cook, their tale of woe. The combination of Navaro's heavy hand and their lack of sleep from worrying about the stolen boat lowered their alcohol tolerance. It wasn't long before both of them couldn't walk a straight line. At 5 o'clock, they wandered like lost sheep down the dock and back to *My Melody*. They fell asleep and day two passed quicker than either of them thought possible.

VIPER BOB

chapter 18

SUNDAY
OCTOBER 12, 2003
FREEPORT, GRAND BAHAMA ISLAND

Sunday morning Viper and Melody woke up with hangovers, but they actually felt better. Melody suggested to Viper, "Why don't you call Corporal Blackstone and see if he has any information?"

When Viper hung up from his conversation with Blackstone, he told Melody and Robert about the tip Blackstone received from a local man named McArthur. Viper said, "Blackstone suggested we fly McArthur to Freeport, so he can meet with his friend and try to get some more information."

Viper agreed to the suggestion since there were no other leads and the prospects of finding the boat were looking more grim each passing day. Viper knew, after three or four days, the likelihood of solving a crime like this dropped dramatically.

"Right now," he said, "this McArthur person is the only hope we have of finding the Edgewater."

Blackstone told Viper, "I contacted the Freeport Police Headquarters and Detective Inspector Jamison wants to meet with you and McArthur. I'll call him and tell him when McArthur will arrive."

Viper went to the marina office and spoke with Alonzo Hudson, the dock master. Alonzo, like most people in the marina, heard about the boat theft.

Viper asked him, "Can you suggest a pilot? I want to charter an airplane to search for the Edgewater."

Alonzo made a few calls and within fifteen minutes, Viper was speaking with Ricky Johnstone, a native of Freeport who operated a charter service. Business was slow this time of year and Ricky agreed to take Viper anywhere he wanted to go.

That afternoon Ricky flew Viper and Robert in his twin engine Aztec around Grand Bahama Island for almost two hours, searching for the Edgewater. They flew up and down the Grand Lucayan Waterway, searching the honeycombed canals. Hundreds of boats of all size and color were docked behind the pink, yellow and lime green houses, where affluent Bahamians and Americans lived.

The search produced no sign of the Edgewater. Ricky returned to the Freeport airport and dropped off Viper and Robert. Then, he flew to Walkers to pick up James McArthur. Thirty minutes later, McArthur was standing at the entrance to the flight service building at Freeport airport.

McArthur introduced himself and said, "Everyone calls me Five-O." Viper and Detective Inspector Jamison asked him to tell them what he heard and where he heard it. He retold his story about meeting a friend who may have seen the thieves.

Inspector Jamison had spent the past sixteen years tracking down the worst criminals in The Bahamas. He was as tenacious as a pit bull. The five-foot, ten-inch tall man appeared to be quiet and easygoing. This was a technique Jamison perfected over the years to disarm criminals and get them to open up and talk to him.

Jamison suggested Five-O call his friend and invite him to a bar to shoot pool and drink some beer. Five-O would try to get him drunk and reveal more information about the crime or the name of the thieves. Everyone agreed to the plan, since there weren't any other leads.

Five-O called Burt Reynolds and told him, "Hey, Bro, it's Five-O, I'm back in Freeport. How's about we gets together for a few beers and shoot some pool?"

"Yea Bro, I'll meet you at the Jungle Room."

Five-O had been there numerous times and replied, "OK Bro, I be there 'bout eight tonight."

Inspector Jamison reminded everyone, "We don't have much time." He told Five-O to call his cell phone as soon as he had some information. He said, "Five-O, that'll give you all night to get me something to work with." Jamison reemphasized how critical time was in this case. "If the boat isn't already in Haiti, or sunk, it will be soon. We need to move fast, otherwise, we'll never find it."

Inspector Jamison had investigated hundreds of stolen boat cases over the years. This was one of the few cases where the owner stayed involved and was willing to spend money to find his boat. Jamison thought. *Who knows? This might be the one in a thousand case where we find the boat, or better yet, catch the criminals.* He wanted to catch the thieves but more importantly, he wanted to break up the organization that funded this lucrative, black market business.

Viper drove Five-O back to Lucayan Marina to tell Melody and Robert what was happening.

Melody was excited and continually interrupted Five-O, peppering him with questions about his mysterious school friend and where he thought their boat might be. He stayed aboard *My Melody* for nearly an hour. Then Viper drove him to a hotel where he checked in and prepared for the meeting with Burt.

As Viper was driving Five-O to the Grand Oasis Hotel, Spider and Speedo were on their way back to Mores Island from Freeport. It was late Sunday afternoon, and they planned to return to the Edgewater Monday morning and remove the electronics and the T-Top. Raul, their Cuban-American contact in Miami, told them, "I think I can get you amigos about one thousand dollars for the electronics and T-Top, and five hundred dollars for the fishing gear."

They took their skiff to the northwest side of Mores Island and anchored in back of Ellison Braithwaite's house. Ellison was due to return home today, after selling their catch of fish, lobsters and conch. Ellison planned to take a couple of days off to rest and make some repairs to *Lady Gertrude*. Speedo was anxious to get home and spend a couple days with his wife, who was pregnant with their second child. Inez hadn't seen Speedo in a month and she was eagerly waiting for her husband to come home.

Inez was a good wife and a great cook. She told him, "I learned how to cook from Momma, and I learned about sex from watchin' the local dogs."

That night, Inez cooked Speedo his favorite dinner of fried grouper, dirty rice and cole slaw. Later that night, her husband was howlin' like one of the local dogs in heat.

The next day was Monday October 13, Hero's Day, a national holiday in The Bahamas honoring the founders of the country. The event is marked with festivities throughout The Bahamas. On the east end of Grand Bahama Island, thirty miles from Mores Island, hundreds of people gather to watch parades and attend the celebration at McLeans Town. Most of the residents of Hard Purchase, the small town on Mores Island where Spider and Speedo lived, planned to go to McLeans Town early in the morning. Spider and Speedo planned to work on the Edgewater and then go to McLeans Town later.

Before returning from Freeport they had made arrangements with Manny Pender to store the electronics and T-Top with the fishing gear that was already at his house. Once everything was safely hidden, they would return to Mores Island, pick up Inez and join the celebration at McLeans Town.

VIPER BOB

chapter 19

S pider and Speedo stayed up late Sunday night and didn't get up until 9 o'clock Monday morning. Inez made a hot breakfast of eggs, sausage and grits and by 10:30, they were in the Whaler heading to Hole in the Wall and the Edgewater. They had all the tools they needed to remove the electronics and T-Top. Spider estimated it would take two hours to remove everything and another hour to take it to Sandy Point and store it at Manny's house. Then they would return to Ellison's house, get Inez and go to McLeans Town and join the Hero's Day celebrations. As they finished breakfast, Speedo told his wife, "Be ready 'bout 1:30, Sugar."

Spider and Speedo left Ellison's house and walked to the lagoon where their Whaler was anchored. They got in the boat and went to Hole in the Wall.

As they passed the government docks at Hard Purchase, Viper was seventy miles away, parking his rental car at the Grand Oasis Hotel. Five-O and Jamison were waiting in the lobby and saw him as he entered the hotel.

"How'd the meeting go with your friend?" Viper asked.

"I already told the Inspector, I didn't get no names," and he paused, "but I might know where they took your boat. My friend thinks they either took it to Mores Island or Eleurethra."

"Why those two islands?"

"He thinks the dudes who stole your boat is from Mores Island, and if they was gonna strip it, they would most likely take it there."

Five-O continued, "And if they ain't gonna strip it, then they gonna sell it to the drug smugglers, and those boats are taken to Eleurethra before they go down to Haiti."

"What do you think about these two islands?" Viper asked Jamison.

"Well, it makes sense and it's all we got," was Jamison's reply.

"OK," Viper said, "I'll call Ricky." When Ricky answered his phone Viper said, "Hi, Ricky, this is Viper. I want to charter your plane ASAP."

"OK, when do you want to leave?"

"I'm on my way to the airport, I'll be there in ten minutes."

"I'm at my plane and it's ready to go. All I needs to do is file a flight plan. Where we goin'?"

Viper replied, "Mores Island and then Eleurethra."

Twenty minutes later they were airborne and Ricky was speaking to Viper over the airplane's intercom.

"Mores Island is sixty-five miles southeast of Freeport; we'll be there in fifteen minutes. It's a small island, four maybe five miles long and a couple miles wide. Eleurethra is one hundred and thirty miles southeast of Mores Island. It'll take about forty minutes to get there."

"If we spot the boat, can we land on either of these islands?" Viper asked.

"Mores Island has a strip that's OK to land on. I take tourists and supplies there once or twice a month. Eleurethra is a long, crooked shaped island about seventy miles long with three airstrips. There's one at John Cistern, a town on the northern tip, Rock Sound in the middle, and Free Town on the southern end."

For the next ten minutes the four men sat quietly in the Aztec looking down at the crystal clear water of the Little Bahama Bank on their left, and the deep blue waters of the Atlantic Ocean on their right. From five thousand feet they couldn't see the Florida coast, but they could see the haze hanging over the Palm Beaches, seventy miles to the west.

As they approached the north end of Mores Island, Ricky descended to three thousand feet and banked to the east. He planned to circle the north end of the island and then the south end. Circling the island was the most effective way to search a small island.

He reduced the speed of the twin-engine plane to one hundred and twenty miles an hour—and then descended to one thousand feet as he circled the island. As they crossed the center of the island Ricky banked the plane to his left, giving Viper and Five-O a better view.

Both men were straining their eyes trying to look at every mangrove tree on the island as they flashed below them.

A thousand feet below the airplane, Spider and Speedo were unscrewing the T-Top when they heard the plane. They looked up through the mangrove trees and saw a black and white twin-engine plane as it passed over them. They stood still and watched as the plane banked to the north and began circling around.

On the first pass over the island, no one in the plane saw anything. Ricky banked the plane and began to make a large sweeping circle to the north for the second pass. The Aztec had four rows of seats with a seat on each side of the craft. Ricky and the co-pilot were in the front row, Viper was in the third row and Five-O was in the last row. Viper and Five-O were able to move left and right, looking out either side of the plane. Ricky and the co-pilot were concentrating on flying the plane, while Viper and Five-O were searching the water and island below for the boat.

Suddenly Five-O shouted, "Stop! Stop! Go back—go back. I seen somethin' in the mangroves."

"How 'bout I go around, again Five-O, cause I don't think you want me to stop at five hundred feet," Ricky said over the intercom.

As the plane turned to make another pass, Spider and Speedo realized it was searching for something, most likely the Edgewater. Their hearts were racing as Spider grabbed the bowline of the Whaler and pulled it underneath the mangroves to hide from the plane.

Ricky banked to the north, and prepared to circle across the north end of the island for the second time. As the plane reached the east side of the island, everyone saw a shiny piece of white metal in the top of a large clump of mangrove trees.

The plane completed the second pass and Ricky dropped the plane to three hundred feet and circled to the northwest again. As soon as the plane passed over Hole in the Wall the second time, Spider and Speedo pushed the Whaler out of the mangroves and raced out the small cut. Spider made a violent turn to his left and another to his right, putting them in the narrow channel. They went northwest going in the same direction as the airplane.

Viper was busy adjusting the gyro-binoculars while Five-O was hollering, "I seen it, I seen the boat!" Everyone on the plane was too busy or excited to notice the small boat race out of the mangroves and out the channel.

The plane circled the island two more times, dropping lower and lower as they passed over the hiding place where the Edgewater was camouflaged. On the fifth pass, Ricky was flying fifty feet above the mangroves. He slowed the plane to seventy knots per hour, ten knots over the Aztec's stall speed.

As they passed over the boat Viper saw the familiar ice blue and white hull of his Edgewater, hidden under a large mangrove tree. Everyone on the plane was shouting and talking at the same time.

Confident they had done the impossible, Ricky climbed to one thousand feet and prepared to land on Mores Island.

Viper smiled, *Forty-five minutes ago no one believed I'd find the Edgewater.* He eased back in his seat.

You bastards. You thought you were so smart. Well, I've found my boat. Next I'll find you. I'll follow you to Hell, if I have too.

Spider and Speedo looked at each other. For the first time in their lives they were afraid they might get caught and sent to Fox Hill prison. After removing the electronics and T-Top, they had planned to tow the boat into deep water off Mores Island and set it on fire, destroying their fingerprints and any evidence.

They never expected the boat would be discovered. But it had, and now they only had a few minutes to get rid of any evidence linking them to the crime.

As the plane prepared to land, Spider raced back to the Edgewater. Speedo jumped aboard the boat, quickly wiping the gunwale, center console and seats with a rag.

Speedo jumped back into the Whaler and said, "I did the best I could Bro, but I'm not sure I got everythin'."

"I know Bro, but we gots to get out of here."

They left Hole in the Wall and raced back to the government dock.

chapter 20

Ricky guided the Aztec onto the airstrip and taxied to an abandoned airport building. There were no welcoming signs and in fact, Viper got the distinct feeling they were not going to be welcome. Five-O called Inspector Jamison on his cell phone and he answered on the third ring. Hero's Day was one of the few holidays Jamison had off, but in reality, CID detectives were never off duty.

Jamison listened to Five-O, as he excitedly told him they were on Mores Island and they found the boat. Jamison told him to stay at the airport and he would have the local police officer meet them.

The group waited impatiently as the minutes passed. It seemed like an hour before Private Dollar arrived at the airstrip, but it had been less than fifteen minutes. As the officer brought his Jeep Wrangler to a halt, everyone began talking to him at once. He recognized Ricky as the pilot who brought supplies and visitors to the island.

He looked at him and said, "Jamison told me there may be a stolen boat on the island. What did you see and where did you see it?"

Ricky gave Private Dollar the approximate location of the boat and introduced him to Viper. Then, everyone climbed into the jeep and headed for the government dock.

The people on Mores Island seemed oblivious to the four visitors as they passed amongst them. Everyone saw the airplane circle the island five times and they assumed the plane was searching for something. When Private Dollar arrived at the government dock with the four men, the locals knew this had to be a criminal matter. So, they ignored the group, not wanting to get involved.

Spider and Speedo arrived at the government dock just as the police Jeep pulled up to the dock. Spider recognized Private Dollar and Ricky. He didn't know the other two black men or the white man. Their hearts sank as they watched the men get into a boat and head toward Hole in the Wall and the Edgewater.

"We gots to call Chino and tell him they found the boat," Spider said.

It took the group less than ten minutes to find Hole in the Wall and the engineless blue and white boat.

Viper looked at the boat and said, "Yep, that's my Edgewater."

"It looks like the crooks was gonna come back and strip the top and electronics. By now, they know we've found it. On an island this small, news travels faster than a coyote chasing a road runner," Dollar said.

By the time the group returned to the government dock with the Edgewater, the only residents who didn't know what the airplane was searching for were the people thirty miles away at McLeans Town attending the Hero's Day festivities.

Private Dollar called Inspector Jamison and told him they found the Edgewater. Jamison spoke with Viper, who agreed to send the airplane to Marsh Harbor to bring a CID detective and fingerprint expert to Mores Island to dust the boat and file a report.

Viper instructed Ricky to make the trip to Marsh Harbour. Thirty minutes later he returned with his two passengers. It took the fingerprint expert an hour to dust the boat. When he was done he told Detective Clarke, "I've got a number of good prints."

CID Detective Sergeant Clarke told Viper, "It looks like the thieves tried to wipe the boat clean but they didn't do a very good job. We've got at least six good sets of fingerprints. If we catch these crooks, there's more than enough evidence to convict them."

Viper replied smugly, "We found the Edgewater. We'll find the thieves."

While the boat was being dusted for fingerprints, Sergeant Clarke wrote a one-page police report. As Clarke wrote up the report, he thought, *Why did this guy bother to search for his boat? He could have bought a new one for what he spent searchin' for this one.* He knew Ricky charged three hundred twenty-five dollars an hour for the Aztec, which was a comfortable and fast airplane. *Oh well, at least the guy travels first class and he got a great tour of the northern Bahamas,* Clarke thought.

Viper reviewed and signed the report. Then the officer got Viper's fingerprints so they could disqualify his prints.

Before leaving the island, Viper asked Private Dollar if he could recommend someone to tow the Edgewater back to Lucaya. Dollar recommended Ellison Braithwaite and offered to drive Viper out to Ellison's house. On the way he explained Ellison owned a large fishing boat and was only home for a few days. Viper met with Ellison and explained what happened and what he needed done.

Ellison said, "Yes sir, I could tow your boat to Lucaya. But, that'll take a lot of gasoline and gasoline is expensive."

"I spent a lot of money to find my boat and I don't want to lose it again or have it mysteriously catch on fire," Viper replied.

"Would it be possible for you to tow the Edgewater to Lucaya tomorrow?"

Ellison agreed to tow the Edgewater Tuesday morning and said, "I'll need a thousand dollars." Viper thought for a moment and calculated the expenses. "I figure you'll burn about one hundred gallons of fuel and it'll take six hours to tow it over and four hours to get back to Mores Island. I'll pay you eight hundred dollars. That's four hundred dollars for the fuel and four hundred dollars for your time."

Ellison looked at Dollar and back at Viper. "I know you been wronged by some of our people and I'm willin' to help you. But I can't take my boat one hundred and forty miles for four hundred fifty dollars. I hope you don't think all Bahamians is bad people, but that ain't a fair price."

"OK, Ellison I'll pay you one thousand dollars on one condition."

"And what might that be?"

"I want you to get my boat now, tow it back here, keep it behind your house, and guard it tonight."

Ellison agreed and Viper said, "I'll see you tomorrow at Lucayan Marina."

Ellison had planned to take his family to McLeans Town that afternoon for the Hero's Day festivities. Now he would have to get up at 4 o'clock in the morning, so he decided to stay home and get some rest.

Ellison was a good man who always obeyed the law, God's first, then man's. He knew many of the young men, and probably his son-in-law, made extra money stealing things and he strongly suspected Spider and Speedo had stolen the boat. They disappeared Thursday night and showed up at Mores Island on Saturday, without telling anyone where they had been.

Ellison knew Spider would never admit to stealing the boat, so it made no since to confront him. How ironic he thought: *Viper might be payin' a relative of the thieves to return his boat.*

That didn't make Ellison feel very good and he asked God to forgive his son-in-law.

As Hero's Day was drawing to a close, Spider and Speedo sat in Ellison backyard looking at the boat they had stolen three days ago. The Edgewater sat behind Ellison's house, much higher in the water without the twin Yamaha engines.

They drank beer as they stared at the boat and laughed at the irony of the Edgewater. It was nervous laughter because they were concerned. They hadn't expected anyone to come looking for the Edgewater, much less find it at Hole in the Wall. The boat had been well camouflaged in the mangroves and should have been impossible to find.

One of their friends was on the dock that afternoon and told Spider, "Someone in the plane spotted the top of the radar unit." The three-foot long white metal tube, mounted on the T-top, had given away the boat's location.

Their fingerprints were on the boat, and the police had their prints on file at headquarters in Nassau. If Spider and

Speedo were questioned, their explanation would be they'd found the abandoned, engineless boat and went aboard to look for any identification of the owner. They didn't find any, so they were about to notify Private Dollar when they saw him returning to the government dock with the boat in tow.

They knew the police wouldn't believe their story but they couldn't come up with a better explanation. Worst case they would be arrested and spend a couple days in jail before Chino arranged for their bail. Spider and Speedo were best friends and neither would rat on the other.

Spider called Chino's lawyer and said, "Mr. Thomas, this here is Theophilus Dean. They call me "Spider" and I does some work for Chino. He told me to call you. We may need your services and we may need you to post bail. If Speedo and I gets arrested my wife Inez will call you."

"Make sure she has my mobile phone number," David replied.

Spider called Manny and told him what happened. "Get rid of the fishin' tackle soon as you can. OK, Bro?"

Aside from their fingerprints, the only evidence linking them to the crime was the engines and they were well hidden at Calico Jack's house.

Viper got back to *My Melody* at 6 p.m. and there was already a party, celebrating the recovery of the Edgewater. Inspector Jamison called Melody shortly after receiving the call from Private Dollar confirming they found the boat. Melody prepared a seafood feast of broiled fresh lobster, steamed asparagus and large baked potatoes smothered in butter and sour cream. To complement the meal, Melody served their two favorite wines, La Motte Millennium, a rich Cabernet Sauvignon, and a Merryvale Chardonnay.

After dinner, they continued celebrating and by 11 o'clock, had consumed all three bottles of wine. Melody went to the liquor locker and got three more bottles and the celebration continued until 2 a.m. Finally, everyone retired and planned to sleep late Tuesday morning.

chapter 21

TUESDAY
OCTOBER 14, 2003
LUCAYA, GRAND BAHAMA ISLAND

Inspector Jamison called Viper at 10:30 and said, "I'd like to come by and update you on our investigation. I can be there in about an hour."

Viper sensed the inspector had some important news he wanted to share with him and said, "OK, we'll be here."

Viper went to the galley and was fixing a pot of coffee as Melody joined him. They sat in the main salon drinking coffee, reminiscing about the events of the past three days.

Inspector Jamison arrived just before noon. After he was seated in the main salon he told Viper and Melody, "First, I'd like to review with you what we know, then our assumptions, and, finally, what we're doing. When I'm done, I'll answer any questions you have.

"Your boat was stolen sometime between 3 and 7:30 a.m. Friday, October 10. The engines were removed and the boat was hidden at Mores Island. The thieves removed the GPS receiver, the VHF antenna, all the fishing tackle and approximately half the screws holding the T-Top to the center console.

"Now, I'll review our assumptions about who and why your boat was stolen. We believe the thieves are commercial fishermen who were either working in the Walkers Cay area or had been there recently. They knew or met someone who either worked or lived on Walkers. This person identified your boat and had knowledge about your travel schedule."

He continued, "Let's look at the events of Friday morning. We believe they stole the boat and took it to Mores Island, where they removed the engines. Then, they hid your boat in the mangroves, with the intention of returning to remove the T-Top and the electronics.

"We believe they delayed removing the electronics and top because they were comfortable no one would find the boat at Mores Island. We believe they have used that location on numerous occasions, based on the rope burns Private Dollar found on the mangrove tree your boat was tied to. We also believe one or more of the criminals either lives or used to live on Mores Island.

"We believe the thieves have contacts, probably in south Florida, who buy electronics and fishing tackle and resell it in the Miami and Ft. Lauderdale area. It's almost impossible to trace these items, because they are usually sold directly to fishermen so they never get to pawnshops or one of the many flea markets.

"Regarding the engines," Jamison continued. "We believe they transported the engines to Freeport, sometime Saturday or Sunday and are still in the Freeport area. We believe the fishermen who stole your boat are associated with a Freeport drug gang that deals in stolen boats and engines.

"Since the engines were the first thing they removed, we believe that was the primary purpose of the theft. They may or may not have a buyer for the engines. In either case, they would need to bring the engines to Freeport for the buyer to inspect and take possession of the engines.

"Now, let me update you on our investigation. I'm leading the investigation on Grand Bahama Island and we're questioning all the likely suspects. Private Dollar is interviewing people on Mores Island and Inspector Clarke is questioning people in Marsh Harbour. We've contacted the Law Enforcement Division of Florida Fish and Wildlife, the U.S. Coast Guard and D.E.A. and gave them the serial numbers of the engines and a description of the fishing tackle. Finally, we faxed a description of the engines and fishing tackle to all members of the Royal Bahamas Police Force and instructed them to be on the lookout for your property.

"That's the status of our investigation," he said. "Do you have any questions?"

Viper said, "I'm impressed, Inspector. It sounds like you have all the facts correct. Your assumptions seem to be based on good logic and your plan appears to be solid. I don't have any questions. Melody do you have any questions?"

"No, but I'm pleased with what you've done so far. Thank you, Inspector."

"Thank you, but all of this is possible because of what you did. You spent your time and money to recover your boat, providing us with fingerprints and enough evidence to link the criminals to the stolen boat. We appreciate what you've done and we've made this a priority case," Jamison responded.

Melody walked over, gave him a hug, and said in her soft Alabama accent, "I really hope you catch the bastards who stole our boat!"

"We're doin' everything we can," Jamison replied. He could sense her emotion and realized this wasn't just a theft to these people. It was an invasion of their privacy and they were angry.

As the Inspector was meeting with Viper and Melody, Private Dollar was busy questioning anyone on Mores Island he thought might know something about the Edgewater. He focused his investigation around the docks where most of the fishermen anchored their boats.

If anyone knew anything about how the boat got to Mores Island or who stole it, they weren't talking. Private Dollar had recently been transferred to the island and he was just beginning to develop useful contacts among the residents. He didn't want to alienate the residents because this was neither the first, nor the last crime that would be committed on this remote island.

As Tuesday drew to a close, Private Dollar was frustrated because he didn't know anymore about the stolen boat than when he found it yesterday. The people of Hard Purchase were tight lipped and protected each other. Most of the residents suspected one of their own stole the boat and brought it here.

Some people secretly suspected Spider and Speedo for a variety of reasons. They knew *Lady Gertrude* had been fishing in the Walkers Cay area for a couple of weeks. They were near Walkers the morning the boat was stolen and Spider and Speedo were members of the crew.

Viper met with Assistant Police Commissioner Blackstone Tuesday afternoon. Prior to his meeting, Viper did some research on the Commissioner. He learned he was a man of high moral character and had a good record with the Royal

Bahamas Police Force. Under his supervision they had done an excellent job of reducing crime on Grand Bahama Island.

The meeting was very cordial and Viper told the Commissioner, "I have friends who know the Prime Minister. If it would help the investigation, I'd be happy to have one of my friends call the Prime Minister."

Commissioner Blackstone had no desire to get Nassau involved in an investigation on his island. He told Viper, "Before we ask for any help, give us a couple of days to see what our men can do."

Commissioner Blackstone didn't like private citizens doing police work, particularly a foreigner. But that's exactly what Viper had done by finding his boat and Freeport's Top Cop respected him because he chose to stay and find his boat. That's why Blackstone put his best men, Detective Inspector Jamison and Detective Sergeant Rolle, on the case. He was confident they would break the case.

Before the meeting with Viper, Jamison met with the commissioner and updated him on the investigation. "My guess," he said, "is one of the drug gangs is responsible for the boat theft."

Everyone knew the drug dealers were active in the area, yet violent crimes including murder, kidnapping, and assault had declined over the past couple of years. Ever since the mysterious disappearance of Lucifer "Big Dawg" Cockburn, the drug gangs were far less violent and created fewer problems for the police.

The Police Commissioner didn't like Big Dawg and he didn't grieve over his demise. He was an evil person who enjoyed hurting people. Sometimes that included tourists and innocent locals. He was a suspect in at least a dozen murders. That's the kind of guy they didn't want, or need, in Freeport.

Commissioner Blackstone thought, *Whoever took over from Big Dawg is a real smart businessman.* He suspected David Thomas was either the new leader or a partner with the leader. The police didn't have any hard information, but David was the attorney for most of the drug related cases and the few boat thefts that made their way to the Magistrates Court.

Most of his clients were able to pay their bail, so the bad guys were in and out of jail quickly. The commissioner liked that. His jails were less crowded, less violent, and easier to administer. The commissioner thought, *That's enough about Viper's boat and the drug gang. I've got more important issues to attend to.*

As Private Dollar was wrapping up his unproductive day, Five-O was in his hotel room in Freeport preparing to meet Burt again at the Jungle Room. When Viper met with the police commissioner he announced a five thousand dollar reward for information leading to the arrest of the person or persons responsible for stealing his boat.

Five-O was determined to get the name of the men who stole the boat or find out who had the engines. Five thousand dollars was more money than Five-O could earn in two months of fishing. It was probably more than the thieves earned stealing the boat.

Five-O sat on his hotel bed and thought, *How would McGarrett on Hawaii Five-O handle this? How would Hawaii's Top Cop conduct an undercover meetin' with an unsuspectin' witness?*

Then he remembered a Hawaii Five-O episode, *The Ways of Love,* where McGarrett went under cover as a prison inmate to get information. In that episode, McGarrett said, "Some of our best work is luck," a quote that became famous to millions of Hawaii Five-O fans. As Five-O sat on his bed, he thought,

If I'm gonna get the information I need to claim the reward, I have to get Burt to talk. To do that, I'm going to need to get him drunk and get lucky.

Five-O was no saint. He committed numerous misdemeanor crimes as a teenager. When he was fifteen, his family lived in Freeport where he was a member of a local gang. The Posse was a group of five teenagers that stole beer and cigarettes from grocery stores and gas for their boats to go fishing and diving.

However, six years ago he gave up his petty criminal ways and concentrated on improving himself. Jack Lord as Steve McGarrett and James MacArthur as Danny "Danno" Williams had a positive and lasting effect on the young Bahamian man and in an example of life imitating art, a small-time criminal was converted into a law-abiding citizen.

Tonight Five-O needed to play it cool and get some useful information from Burt. If he didn't get any information tonight he would have to go back to Grand Cay tomorrow without the reward money.

A friend once told him if he wanted to drink and stay sober, he should eat a pasta dinner and drink at least two large glasses of milk. Before leaving the hotel, Five-O ate a plate of spaghetti with clam sauce and drank three glasses of milk.

He took a taxi to the Ghetto and told the driver, "Let me out a block from the Jungle Room." The Jungle Room was located off Mall Drive, on the fringe of the roughest, crime infested area in Freeport. All of Freeport's criminals, either lived in the Ghetto, or operated their business and social life out of it.

On various occasions, CID assigned undercover agents the task of penetrating the criminal center of the island. No one ever succeeded, mainly because the small group of crooks knew each other too well to allow a stranger to enter their world.

Five-O stopped at a bar down the street from the Jungle Room and had a beer to settle his nerves. He finished the beer and walked to the Jungle Room. He saw Burt Reynolds sitting at the bar, talking to a tall, young girl, who was obviously very attracted to the handsome dark skinned Bahamian.

Five-O joined them and Burt introduced him. "Hey Bro, this here is my main woman. Yolanda, this here is Five-O."

Yolanda was about five feet six inches tall with short black hair and beautiful black eyes. As she spoke to Five-O, Burt was running his hand up and down the inside of her thigh, and she was enjoying it.

Burt was obviously enjoying Yolanda and the attention she was giving him. But as soon as Five-O suggested they play some pool, Burt was off the stool and heading for table number three, his lucky table. Burt thought, *Yolanda's my good luck charm and my favorite table is open. I'm goin' to clean Five-O's clock.* He was eager to get started, and said, "OK Bro, let the games begin."

They played the first two games for one dollar a ball and Burt was hot, winning both games. Five-O bought a couple rounds of beer for the three of them and spent a lot of time talking to Yolanda. Burt smiled, *Yolanda's crazy 'bout me.* He thought, *Five-O, you be wastin' your time, if you think you gonna get anywhere with one of my women.*

By 10 o'clock, Burt was fifty dollars ahead, bleary eyed, and drunk. Yolanda got tired of watching the two men shoot pool and joined one of her girlfriends at the other side of the bar. She was engrossed in girl talk and completely lost track of what the men were doing.

Five-O decided this was the perfect time to pump Burt for some information.

"Hey Bro, you heard anymore 'bout the boat stolen from Walkers?"

Burt was concentrating on making the five ball in the side pocket. "Yea, they found the boat yesterday at Mores Island and there's a lot of heat comin' down."

"That's pretty heavy, Dude. That's one of the few boats ever been found."

He waited until Burt was concentrating on his next shot and asked, "Hey Bro, I heard back on Grand the owner is offerin' a reward. Maybe we could make some serious money."

Burt raised his pool cue and looked around to make sure no one was listening to them. "Mon, you got a death wish or somethin? Them dudes that heisted that boat work for a bad dude, a very bad dude."

Five-O instantly saw his opportunity and whispered, "You means they work for Chino?"

Burt nodded, yes, as he looked around to make sure no one could hear them.

"What if we could give the cops some names, so no one knows it come from us?"

Burt said to Five-O, "No Bro, there ain't no reward worth crossin' Chino's people. The risk be too great."

Five-O was about to say something when Burt continued, "Chino wouldn't think twice 'bout taking us off shore, pop our ass with a pistol, and feed us to the sharks."

Burt shivered at the thought and told Five-O, "No way Mon."

Five-O continued to push the idea and asked, "What if we could each make a couple thousand bucks?"

Burt thought long and hard. That was enough money to get his attention. After a few seconds, he shook his head and replied, "No Mon, I ain't interested."

They played two more games and Five-O tried a couple more times to get the name of the thieves but Burt wasn't giving up any more information. Finally, Five-O decided it was time to focus on the pool game. He won the last two games, reducing his loss to thirty-five dollars. He told Burt he had to be somewhere early in the morning, so he needed to leave.

"I'm gonna give it up tonight and go back to my room. I'll see you around, Bro."

Five-O walked a couple of blocks before he found a taxi and went back to his hotel, where he fell asleep, disappointed he wasn't going to get the reward money.

He thought, *I be callin' Viper tomorrow mornin' and tell him I weren't able to get no more information and I be goin' back to Walkers on the mornin' flight.*

VIPER BOB

chapter 22

WEDNESDAY
OCTOBER 15, 2003
FREEPORT, GRAND BAHAMA ISLAND

Detective Inspector Jamison sat in his second floor office at police headquarters on East Mall Drive. The CID office was twenty feet wide and thirty feet deep. There were four government-issued metal desks in the room. Jamison and three other detectives who worked closely together shared the office. Detective Sergeant Rolle worked most cases with Inspector Jamison and sat directly across from him. They had worked together for the last three years and Jamison liked and respected him. Rolle and Jamison learned early in their careers that CID officers worked crazy hours. After all, criminals don't have 9 to 5 jobs and neither do the cops who chase them.

Sergeant Rolle spent Tuesday night with a surveillance team watching a local drug dealer's house located in a subdivision on the north side of Freeport. They took pictures of a lot of people entering and leaving the house, which meant there would be a lot of work to match names to all the faces.

Rolle left the surveillance team at 3:30 a.m. and went home to get some well-needed sleep. Just after 11 o'clock, he walked into the main entrance of the two-story police building and slid his security card in the reader. The lock clicked, he opened the door and walked up one flight of stairs. As he entered his office, Jamison was on the phone. He looked up at Rolle and flashed the *V* for victory sign.

Jamison continued talking on the phone, while he scribbled some notes. When he hung up, he looked at Rolle and said, "We just got a break in the boat theft."

He continued, "That was Queenie Rackham. Her brother-in-law, Calico Jack, has got two engines at his house and he's real nervous about them. She and Skinny, Calico Jack's brother, were at his house Monday."

Jamison said, "Let's move the surveillance team to his house and see what happens for the next twenty-four hours."

"OK," Rolle replied, "I'll drive over to his house and figure out how to deploy the team." Within an hour the team switched locations and was taking pictures of anyone who came to Calico Jack's house.

During the day, a couple of people came over, but it was generally quiet. A couple of times, Calico Jack came out the front door and looked up and down the tree lined street then went back inside his purple and lime green colored house. He was obviously very nervous as he looked around the neighborhood.

As the surveillance team was watching Calico Jack, back on Walkers Cay, Corporal Blackstone was busy dialing for dollars, calling friends and contacts in McLeans Town. He was stationed there for two years and his local knowledge was extensive.

No one saw anything suspicious on Monday or Tuesday. More than five hundred people visited McLeans' Town on Monday to attend the Hero's Day festivities. It would have been easy for someone to slip in or out of town without being noticed.

On Mores Island, Private Dollar continued to question people for any information that would help identify the criminals but he was not having any luck.

He spoke with Ellison Braithwaite, who towed the Edgewater to Lucaya the day before. He said, "I got no ideas who stole the boat."

As he spoke with Dollar, Ellison prayed to God Spider and Speedo weren't involved. He saw the fingerprint powder all over the boat and it was obvious the police had the thieves' fingerprints.

As Wednesday drew to a close, Detective Rolle and the surveillance team were watching Calico Jack's house, their only lead in the case. When Jamison and Rolle had some time to talk, Jamison explained why Queenie called him.

He said, "I busted Queenie 'bout six months ago for possession of cocaine. I made a deal with her in exchange for her cooperation. I let her off and she agreed to work for us. She and Skinny have three young kids and she was willing to do anything to stay out of jail. I called her this morning and told her I needed information about the stolen boat and engines. She told me Calico Jack had two engines in his house."

Jamison continued, "She and Skinny were going with Calico Jack to McLeans Town for the Hero's Day parade. But, when they got to his house, he said he couldn't go. Before they left his house she went to the bathroom and that's when she saw two big outboard engines lying on the floor in one of the bedrooms."

"Well, it looks like she's delivered our first break in this case."

"Yea, the chances are one in a million those are not the engines we're looking for," Jamison said.

Rolle agreed with Jamison, *There's no reason for Calico Jack to have a couple of engines in his house.*

Jamison said, "I spoke with the boss and he recommended we watch the house tonight and see who shows up. We'll either raid the house about noon tomorrow or we'll arrest anyone who tries to move the engines."

VIPER BOB

chapter 23

Chino had been living in The Bahamas almost five years and was comfortably settled into a life far better than anything he could have hoped for in Haiti. He had been leader of the Freeport drug gang for two years and controlled the black market for stolen boats and engines on Grand Bahama and the Abacos Islands.

He was sitting at a corner table in the Jungle Room talking on a pre-paid cell phone to one of his former gang members in Haiti. He was joking with the gang member, who was preparing to bring a load of marijuana and cocaine to Sandy Point. Chino said, "No shit! You still be using the same route to Sandy Point I used six years ago."

Chino always used pre-paid cell phones because it was more difficult for the Bahamian police or the U.S. DEA to trace calls on them. To further confuse anyone who might be trying to listen to his phone conversations he replaced his cell phone every week.

Chino had worked hard since taking over the gang and had made numerous improvements in the businesses. One of the first things he did was put Manny in charge of teaching the local fishermen the best techniques for stealing boats. Consequently, they were successfully stealing around two hundred boats a year. His lawyer provided bail and legal services for anyone caught selling drugs or stealing boats for him. Using his knowledge and contacts in Haiti he improved the drug smuggling and distribution business.

He increased the number of teams selling drugs in Grand Bahama from five to ten and was in the process of doubling the teams in The Abacos to four. His retail drug business averaged two thousand dollars a night per team, which meant he was taking in twenty thousand dollars per day in Grand Bahama and expected The Abacos to bring in eight thousand dollars per day.

In two years, he had grown the retail drug business from two million to more than nine million dollars a year. Of course, there were numerous expenses. Annually he spent about half of the income for legal services, bail, cost of drugs, pushers' commission and miscellaneous expenses. His total operating expenses were about five million per year. Chino was making a forty percent net profit, which amounted to over three million dollars per year.

He invested his profits wisely over the past couple of years. Through dummy corporations David Thomas formed, Chino owned two waterfront apartment buildings that catered to tourists, plus the Jungle Room Bar and Grill, where he conducted most of his business. He lived in a modest apartment, with a state-of-the-art security system, and drove a three-year-old Honda. He kept a low profile and attracted as little attention as possible.

The Freeport police thought Chino was a low-level gang member so they didn't waste their time on him. Chino had a small group of police officers on his payroll. Their contact was Manny, so none of them knew Chino was the leader. They provided him with a treasure trove of information about drug busts and criminal investigations.

VIPER BOB

chapter 24

WEDNESDAY
OCTOBER 15, 2003
FREEPORT, GRAND BAHAMA

Basil Cromwell owned and operated a hardware store in Nassau. He was married to a nagging British wife who spoke in a high-pitched, shrill voice and had two daughters who took after their mother. His one and only passion in life was fishing. Almost every Sunday, Basil would take his 28-foot Boston Whaler powerboat, along with a case of Kalik beer and go fishing from dawn to dusk.

In four years he put over one thousand hours on his engines and it was time to replace them. Basil went to MarineWorld, the Yamaha dealer in Nassau, and they quoted him thirty thousand dollars for two new Yamaha 225 horsepower four-stroke engines, plus, two thousand dollars to install them.

As a businessman, Basil hated to take that much money out of his business. A friend told him he could buy two slightly used engines for around eight thousand dollars and he knew a mechanic who would install them for fifteen hundred dollars.

Although his friend didn't specifically tell him the engines were stolen, Basil assumed he was not going to receive a warranty. He weighed his options and decided to take a chance, hoping he could save twenty thousand dollars and asked his friend to set up the deal. Two days later his friend called and said, "A man's gonna call you this afternoon 'bout them engines."

At 4 p.m., a man called Basil. He said, "I gots two Yamaha four stroke engines and I want ten thousand dollars for the pair." Basil told him he was interested, but he could only pay six thousand dollars. They negotiated for a few minutes and agreed on eight thousand dollars. Basil agreed to fly to Freeport the next day to inspect them and finalized the sale. Then he called Bahamas Air and booked a round trip ticket to Freeport, departing Thursday on flight 321 at 12:00 o'clock, arriving at 12:45 p.m. and returning on flight 328 at 7:45 p.m. In less than twenty minutes Basil had his airline tickets booked and he called the Jungle Room Bar and Grill and left a message for Manny that he would arrive at the Jungle Room about 1 o'clock, as he had been instructed to do.

Chino called Manny and told him a buyer would be coming tomorrow to inspect the engines and for Manny to make sure everything was ready.

Chino told Manny, "He be comin' to the Jungle Room at 1 o'clock and gonna ask for you. Take him to see the engines. Then bring him back to the Jungle Room. He's gonna pay you a four thousand dollar deposit. Then tell him when you bring the engines to Nassau on Saturday you gonna collect the other four thousand dollars."

"I wanna get them engines out of Freeport as fast as possible. That's why I want you to deliver them right away."

Manny said, "I understand. One of our friends at police headquarters called and said CID is looking real hard for them engines." Chino replied, "The safest thing to do is leave them engines at Calico Jack's house. Movin' them could attract attention. I only want to move them when the buyer agrees to the deal."

Manny immediately called Calico Jack and told him, "We got a buyer for them engines. We be comin' to your house tomorrow around 1:00 o'clock. After we make the deal I'll bring a couple guys to help load the engines into your truck. Then, I wants you to drive to McLeans Town and we gonna put them on *Bank Walker*."

VIPER BOB

chapter 25

THURSDAY
OCTOBER 16, 2003
FREEPORT, GRAND BAHAMA ISLAND

For the past twenty-eight hours Sergeant Darrell Rolle had been in charge of the surveillance team watching Calico Jack's house. Rolle spent most of the last two days in the back of a white, non-descript Dodge van. His back was sore and he was tired of drinking cold coffee and eating stale donuts. It seems like cops all over the world survive on the same diet.

Last night he was in the van with Detective Corporal Shirley Cooper. As Rolle was pouring himself a cup of coffee she asked, "Have you heard the story about the truck driver and the coffee shop?" Rolle replied, "No, but I think I'm goin' to."

The detective continued. A truck driver stopped at a roadside coffee shop for lunch, and ordered a cheeseburger, coffee and a slice of apple pie. As he was about to eat, three motorcycles pulled up outside.

The bikers came in. One grabbed the trucker's cheeseburger out of his hand and took a huge bite. The second one drank the trucker's coffee and the third wolfed down his apple pie. The truck driver didn't say a word. He simply got up, paid the cashier and left.

When he was gone, the motorcyclists snickered to one another and congratulated each other on being so *bad*. As the waitress walked up, one of the motorcyclists growled, "He ain't much of a man, is he?"

"He ain't much of a driver, either," the waitress replied. "He just backed his eighteen-wheeler over them three motorcycles."

Both detectives started laughing causing Rolle to spill coffee on his pant leg, causing them both to laugh harder. They quickly got control of themselves: they didn't want anyone walking past the van to hear them and blow the stakeout.

At 7:16 a.m., the eastern sky turned from a dark black to a light shade of blue as the morning sun peeked over the horizon. Last night there was a third quarter moon, which provided enough light to see almost everything going on in Calico Jack's house.

At 8:30 a.m., Sergeant Rolle called Inspector Jamison and gave him a summary of the events of the previous night, leaving out the truck driver joke.

"Unless something suspicious happens, we'll raid the house around noon," Jamison said.

Jamison hung up, called *My Melody*, and spoke with Viper to get a detailed description of everything stolen from the boat.

"There were six custom made rods, six Shimano reels, a Penn electric down rigger and a Lindgren-Pittman deep drop rig."

The raid was scheduled for 12:30, but Jamison and Rolle didn't have everything ready until 1:15. Then a team of three detectives and four police officers closed in on the house.

Two policemen and one detective went around to the back of Calico Jack's house and stood ready at the rear door, the same door Calico Jack used six nights earlier when he, Manny and the two fishermen carried the heavy engines into his house.

Jamison used his Motorola police band radio to confirm that Bravo Team was ready. Then he gave the word to proceed with the raid. He had a warrant to forcibly enter the residence and search for two Yamaha engines, six rods and reels, one deep drop rig and one electric down rigger.

As the two teams simultaneously busted down the front and rear doors, Calico Jack was sound asleep. He and his most recent girlfriend were lying naked on a foam mattress where they collapsed earlier in the morning, after smoking a number of joints and making love.

Inspector Jamison and Corporal Shirley Cooper entered the bedroom, saw the naked couple and moved quickly. Jamison rolled Calico Jack on his stomach and handcuffed him while Cooper cuffed the woman, who was sleeping on her stomach.

Sergeant Rolle and three policemen searched the single story house and found two large, gray engines lying on the floor in an adjacent bedroom. Rolle had the serial numbers for the stolen Yamaha engines and confirmed these were the engines they were looking for.

Rolle walked into the bedroom, where Calico Jack and his girlfriend were both naked, sitting on the floor, leaning against a wall. Rolle tried not to let his eyes stray and look at the young girl. She and Calico Jack were having a difficult time waking up. Neither seemed to care they were naked, under arrest and in for a bad day.

Jamison began questioning Calico Jack while Corporal Cooper led the young girl down the hall to the living room. Calico Jack, now more alert, knew the routine the detectives would use. They would question him about the engines for a couple of hours. He would have to repeat the details numerous times, telling how Manny called him on Friday and asked him to keep a couple of engines until he was ready to go back to Sandy Point. He would tell them what time he drove to McLeans Town and step by step, how they took the engines off the boat and loaded them into the back of his Dodge pick-up truck. He would tell them what roads he took as he brought the engines to his house. How they put the engines on an appliance dolly and wheeled them into the spare bedroom.

Calico Jack knew Manny hadn't told him the truth about the engines. Therefore, he couldn't tell the cops what really happened. All he needed to remember was not to mention the two fishermen who accompanied Manny. Calico Jack also knew he would not be getting Manny into any trouble he wasn't prepared to handle.

Calico Jack spoke freely, repeating the story over and over again until the CID detectives were convinced he had told them everything he knew. They continued questioning him, focusing on how two men could move the six hundred pound engines off the boat, and more importantly, how they got them from the truck into the house.

Calico Jack stuck to his story, knowing if he got charged with a crime, Chino would arrange a lawyer and his bail.

For two hours, Jamison and Rolle took turns questioning him.

Meanwhile, Corporal Shirley Cooper questioned Calico Jack's girlfriend. As the four policemen removed the engines, they stole glances at the young girl, who didn't seem to mind them looking at her. One of the corporals was kind of cute and she thought, *I hope he looks me up when this is over.*

Calico Jack was taken to police headquarters and booked for possession of stolen property. He would have to spend the weekend in jail because it was too late to be arraigned. That would happen Monday morning. His girlfriend was released because it was obvious her only crime was her bad taste in boyfriends. Calico Jack knew that within a few hours, everyone involved in the theft would know he was in jail. He also knew if he cooperated with the police in any way, Chino would find out and take him on a one-way boat ride.

VIPER BOB

chapter 26

THURSDAY
OCTOBER 16, 2003
NASSAU, NEW PROVIDENCE

Basil Cromwell got up at 6 a.m. as usual, and went jogging for exactly sixty minutes. He had a routine he religiously followed every weekday. He enjoyed his daily run. It got him out of the house and away from his wife and children while they got ready for school. By the time he returned home, they had eaten breakfast and were on their way to school, leaving the house to him.

He rarely saw his family in the morning and he didn't come home from work until 8 p.m. So, he only had to put up with them for a short time in the evening. Every Sunday he went fishing if the weather cooperated, which it did on most weekends, while his wife and two daughters went to church at St. Jude's Anglican Church.

Basil lived a simple life. If it hadn't been for his fishing, he probably would have died from boredom years ago. But today, he was going to do something truly exciting and completely inconsistent with his lifestyle. He was going to meet with men who were probably criminals and buy two engines that were probably stolen. He had never done anything like this in his life. He was a little scared and very excited. He would remember this day for the rest of his life, reliving it over and over again.

Of course, he would never tell his wife what he was doing. She thought he was going to Freeport on business for the hardware store and in a way he was. This morning as he jogged, there was a spring in his step that hadn't been there in years.

Basil arrived at the hardware store at exactly 8:30, went inside, and got everything ready for business. He took two hundred dollars out of the safe, put it in the cash register, and turned on all the lights.

His two employees arrived every morning at 8:45, clocked in and put on their aprons. By 9 a.m., everyone was ready to assist customers as they came with their barrage of questions. How do I fix this and what kind of paint should I use for that. At precisely 9 a.m., Basil unlocked the doors and turned the sign from CLOSED to OPEN.

At 9:30, Basil left the hardware store and walked three blocks to the Royal Bahamian Bank, where he had been doing business for nearly fifteen years. He went directly to Mr. Atkinson, the branch manager, and told him he needed to withdraw nine thousand dollars in cash.

Jerome Atkinson was an old friend and asked Basil, "What do you need so much cash for?"

Basil replied, "I'm going to Freeport to purchase some close-out merchandise from a chap who has an import business.

"I've arranged for two men with a lorry to remove the merchandise today, so I must pay in cash," Basil explained.

The two friends talked about fishing for a couple of minutes. Basil took the nine stacks of bills and carefully placed them in a compartment in his briefcase and locked it. "Good day, ole chap," said Basil.

Back at the hardware store, Basil took five thousand dollars out of his briefcase and placed it in his safe.

At 10:30, he left the hardware store and drove his white 1995 Volvo station wagon to the Nassau International Airport. At 11:50, he was in seat 4C, waiting for the plane to depart for Freeport.

Basil arrived at Freeport International Airport forty-five minutes later and took a taxi to the Jungle Room. He paid the taxi driver fifteen dollars for the fare and gave him a three-dollar tip. He walked inside, sat down at the bar, and ordered a scotch and water and asked to see Manny. By the time the drink arrived, a large man sat down next to him and asked him, "Is you the man from Nassau?"

"Yes, yes I am."

Manny Pender looked the man over and thought, *Is he a man or is he a mouse?* Basil was five feet five inches tall and weighed one hundred and ten pounds. He let the light brown hair on the side of his head grow long so he could paste it across the top of his balding head. Manny could barely see his dark brown eyes because of his droopy eyelids.

"You're here to buy some equipment?" Manny asked.

"Exactly, ole chap."

"OK, here's how this gonna work. I'm gonna take you to a friend's house where you will inspect the equipment. We guarantee the equipment works. If you wants to buy it, we'll come back here and you pay me four thousand dollars.

Saturday afternoon, I'll bring the merchandise to Nassau and you'll pay me the other four thousand dollars."

Basil was extremely nervous but he was trying to appear cool and confident. He was being asked to leave the bar with a total stranger and go to a house with him. Basil was concerned he might be robbed, or beaten, or killed.

"How do I know I can trust you? How do I know you won't rob me, ole chap?"

Manny looked at him and said, "We can drive to the police station and leave your briefcase there while we go to look at the equipment, if you don't trust me," and he chuckled.

Basil was having second thoughts. *This was a really stupid idea. Why did I agree to do this?* He took a deep breath and thought, *Well, I'm here and it looks like this chap isn't going to let me back out of the deal. So, I better go through with it.*

He looked at the big man and laughed, he meant for it to be a confident laugh. But it didn't come out that way. He said "Right, ole chap, leave my briefcase at the police station, that's a good one."

Manny thought, *Jesus Christ, this guy is stupid. Where did Chino find this one? But hey, he's got balls comin' here.*

"Don't worry, if I wanted your cash, I would have already took it from you."

They both laughed as Manny slapped him on the back.

"OK, ole chap, let's go look at the equipment, I got lots of shit to do," Manny said.

The drive to Calico Jack's house took less than five minutes. As they turned onto Nasen Avenue, two policemen were smashing down the front door of a purple and lime green house. Manny drove past the house without looking or slowing down. He continued down Nasen and turned left on

Explorer Way. He told Basil he forgot to call his associate, who had the engines.

"I'll call him from the Jungle Room," Manny said.

Basil offered his cell phone but Manny refused and kept driving. When they reached the Jungle Room, Manny went to a pay phone and called Chino who was sitting thirty feet away. In a quiet voice Manny said, "As we was approachin' Calico Jack's house, the police was bustin' down his front door." He continued, "If I'd gone five minutes earlier I'd be talkin' to the police instead of you."

Chino said, "Make up an excuse and take the man back to the airport."

Manny agreed, hung up the telephone and walked to where Basil was sitting. Manny ordered a beer for himself and a Scotch and water for Basil and explained to Basil there was a problem.

"I ain't gonna be able to show you the equipment today."

Basil wasn't stupid. He assumed the police raided the house where the engines were being kept. He thought, *Good God, ole boy. If we had arrived ten minutes earlier, I'd be in police custody, instead of having a drink with this hoodlum.*

Manny offered to take him back to the airport and Basil calmly said, "That's OK. I'll finish my drink and take a taxi to the airport. Thanks anyway, ole chap."

Manny insisted on taking him to the airport. He wanted to make sure he left Freeport and didn't go somewhere else, like the police station. After a couple of minutes, Basil agreed. They finished their drinks and left for the airport.

Fifteen minutes later, Basil and Manny arrived at Freeport International Airport. Basil went directly to the airport lounge, where he told the bartender, "Give me a double. No, make it a triple Scotch, ole chap." He had never been more scared in his entire life. He ordered another triple scotch and went to the restroom, where he relieved himself from a combination of nerves and all the scotch.

Basil thought, *My God, ole boy, you could have been arrested and taken to jail. I'm never going to do this again. A couple of engines aren't worth my life.*

Basil had a long wait. The next flight to Nassau was at 7:45 p.m. and he waited impatiently in the airport lounge until it was time to board his flight. While he waited, he called MarineWorld, the Yamaha dealer in Nassau. He ordered two new 225 horsepower Yamaha four stroke engines and gladly agreed to pay thirty thousand dollars for both engines, plus two thousand dollar to install them.

Basil got up Friday morning at 6 a.m. as usual, and prepared to go jogging. As he did, he thanked God he was at home and not in jail. He knew better than to complain to anyone. The people he was with yesterday were definitely not members of the Freeport Chamber of Commerce.

VIPER BOB

chapter 27

Manny's cell phone rang at 6:30 Friday morning. He cursed the damned thing for waking him up. During the next hour he received three more calls. Every caller telling him what he already knew: Calico Jack was in jail for possession of two stolen Yamaha engines and the police were looking for him.

Manny needed some time to make sure everything was arranged before he turned himself in to the police. He had to make sure his alibi was as rock solid as a lie could be. At 8 a.m., Manny made two telephone calls. First, he called David Thomas who agreed to call Inspector Jamison and tell him Manny would turn himself in 9 a.m. Monday morning. Then, he called Chino and they discussed what he needed to do.

Manny wasn't concerned about spending a few days in jail. But he didn't want the police to arrest him today. If he were arrested on a Friday he would needlessly spend three nights in jail because he couldn't be arraigned until Monday morning. If he disappeared for the weekend and turned himself in on Monday, he would spend only one night in jail. That meant he could spend the weekend in more comfortable surroundings.

Inspector Jamison had planned to arrest Manny and interrogate him without his attorney present. However, once David Thomas called and advised him Manny would turn himself in, the interrogation would have to be more civil. Inspector Jamison knew Manny would lay low for the next three days, using the time to firm up his alibi, making it as airtight as possible.

Thursday night Manny moved into one of Chino's apartments in Lucaya, four blocks from the Lucayan police station. Chino arranged for the refrigerator to be full of food and beer. The apartment had cable TV in the living room and both bedrooms plus an attractive young woman to clean, cook and take care of Manny's sexual needs. There was no reason for Manny to leave the apartment. The beer was ice cold, the food was good and the sex was hot.

As Manny sat in the living room drinking a Kalik, watching ESPN Friday Night Boxing, Calico Jack was two miles away in an eight-foot by eight-foot cell he shared with a Rastafarian, who had stolen twenty-six dollars from a tourist.

Calico Jack didn't know any details about the stolen boat nor did he ask Manny any questions. He wasn't the brightest star in the sky, but he knew when not to ask questions and how to keep his mouth shut.

After the Edgewater had been found, Manny made it very clear to Calico Jack, "You never seen them two fishermen."

"If anythin' happens and we get caught, tell the cops we moved the engines by ourselves. We used the electric winch on *Bank Walker* and the appliance dolly at your house.

"There's no need gettin' other peoples involved."

Manny knew Spider and Speedo had too much time they couldn't account for and Ellison Braithwaite was a good friend, but he wasn't going to lie for them.

Manny's story was simple. He received a call Friday around noon from a guy in Marsh Harbour, named Cecil, who heard he was looking for a couple of engines. Manny told him, "I wants a couple of 200 or 225 horsepower Yamahas. I'm lookin' for Saltwater Series or them new four stroke engines."

The caller said, "I gots a pair of Yamaha 225 horsepower four strokes and I'll let 'em both go for eight grand." Manny said, "We negotiated for a couple of minutes and settled on six thousand and Cecil agreed to bring the engines to Sandy Point that afternoon."

As far as Calico Jack was concerned, he was telling the police the truth. All he had to do was forget about the two fishermen.

From past experience Manny knew the best lie was one based on the truth. He knew he and Calico Jack had to give the cops a story that included truthful information that backed up their alibi. He knew they would check out all the information once he was in custody. He would give them a fake name but a real telephone number for the man from Marsh Harbour. Manny's favorite uncle's name was Cecil. He decided that was an easy name for him to remember.

Now Manny had to get a cell phone number he would say belonged to Cecil. That would require a little work. But it was not difficult. He called Chino and told him the story he planned to tell the police. Chino liked it and knew Manny was in for a couple of tough days. Also, Chino knew Manny would never go to prison for this crime.

Chino said, "Call me tonight and I'll have the number of a pre-paid cell phone that will be at the bottom of Freeport Harbor." Manny was confident he had done everything necessary to insure he would spend the least amount of time as a guest of the Royal Bahamas Police Force.

Manny thought, *This is the first boat heist in three years where the boat was recovered and any of our people arrested. Unfortunately, this boat heist is gonna be expensive, both in time and money.*

The Bahamian bail system is very different than the U.S. system. There are no bail bondsmen in The Bahamas. A defendant is required to put up the entire bail in cash or surety and sometimes both. In a possession of stolen property case like this, bail would be six to ten thousand dollars for him and the same for Calico Jack.

Chino's attorney, David Thomas, charged a flat fee of five hundred dollars to handle a bail hearing. Chino would pay David his fee, plus the bail for both men. In addition, Chino had advanced one thousand dollars to Spider and Speedo for the engines now in police custody.

Damn, Manny thought, *this is no way to run a criminal operation. This boat heist is gonna put us fifteen to twenty grand in debt to Chino.*

As Manny sat on the couch drinking a cold beer, he thought, *Spider and Speedo are gonna have to steal four maybe five boats to settle the bill with Chino. Well, at least he doesn't charge interest on the loan.*

VIPER BOB

chapter 28

The mood aboard *My Melody* had been festive all weekend. The fact they recovered the Edgewater was good luck. Recovering the engines was nothing short of a miracle but one bad guy sitting in jail, and a second turning himself in this morning, could only be described as divine intervention.

Of the three hundred plus boats stolen each year in The Bahamas, about one in a thousand are recovered. Fast-acting owners usually find those boats within a few hours after they're stolen. In most cases, once the thieves remove the engines and anything of value, they immediately sink the boat.

Viper was aware of these facts and knowing this made him even more pleased with his accomplishments. His boat had been missing for three days, which was a long time. The engines were recovered five days after the theft and two criminals were on their way to prison. The bookmakers in Las Vegas would have given odds of a million to one against all three things happening.

Viper knew the only way he could search the vast expanse of The Bahamas, and its seven hundred islands, was to use an airplane. He admitted he had been lucky to find the Edgewater but he never would have found it if he hadn't tried.

In August, before leaving Palm Beach, Viper installed a radar system on the Edgewater. It was the three-foot horizontal arm of the radar system they spotted, not the boat. If he hadn't installed the radar, he probably wouldn't have found his boat.

While he was pleased two crooks were in jail, he wasn't satisfied. He wanted to catch all the crooks involved in stealing his boat. Only when the other crooks were caught would he feel satisfied.

But that would have to wait for another day. Today he and Melody were going to the police compound to identify their engines. The police already verified the serial numbers; this was merely a formality.

Inspector Jamison called Viper and made arrangements for him to claim the engines. Then, Viper called MarineWorld and arranged for them to pick up the engines and reinstall them on the Edgewater.

At 8 a.m., David Thomas drove to the apartment where Manny was staying. The maid prepared breakfast as they discussed what Manny was going to tell the police. Then David drove him to police headquarters. They arrived at the two-story complex at 9:30, where Inspector Jamison met them in the lobby and immediately placed Manny under arrest.

Once the formalities were over, Jamison and Rolle took Manny to an interrogation suite and took his statement. Then they questioned him for two hours. David was present during the entire process. Manny remained calm as he repeated his story over and over. They questioned him repeatedly about how two men could move a five hundred eighty-three pound engine off Calico Jack's truck, onto an appliance dolly and into the bedroom.

He told them it was hard work. "There be scratches on the engines to prove how hard it had been to move them," Manny explained.

Finally, David insisted they wrap up the interrogation. "Manny's told you everything he knows and you're just harassing him."

Inspector Jamison, who was playing the good cop, told David, "There are a couple of glaring holes in Mr. Pender's story. I believe they had help getting the engines into Mr. Rackham's house. I want to know who helped them."

Sergeant Rolle added, "The telephone number he gave us is a pre-paid cell phone, so we can't determine the owner." He said, "This sounds like a story he made up and spent the weekend getting the facts to fit his story."

David looked at Sergeant Rolle and said, "Can you prove any of that?" David was getting a little more aggressive with the two detectives and said, "You don't have a shred of evidence to connect my client to the theft of those engines. He bought them and now he's lost six thousand dollars. That's the extent of my clients' involvement in this unfortunate crime."

Rolle said, "Mr. Thomas, we believe Mr. Pender is a major player in the theft of numerous boats over the past three years. He's going down for what he's done. If he agrees to tell us who else is involved, we're willing to cut him a deal."

Jamison added, "We don't really want Manny. We want the guy who runs the operation."

David responded to Jamison, "Manny can't give you the name of someone he doesn't know. The only person he met was Cecil. He's told you everything he knows.

"Now let's wrap this thing up, and get my client in a cell. He has nothing further to say to you. I better not hear you pulled him back in here to interrogate him without me being present."

Jamison and Rolle knew they were not going to get anything out of Manny without some incriminating evidence. They already compared his fingerprints to the ones found on the boat and they didn't match. The pre-paid cell phone was a dead end because there was no way to identify who or where the phone was purchased and the man named Cecil was nowhere to be found.

The information Manny gave them was useless. Unless someone gave them new information, all they could charge Manny with was purchasing stolen property. He probably wouldn't get any hard time for that.

Jamison and Rolle decided to put Manny in a six-man cell with two snitches. They hoped to get a jailhouse confession or at least some new information. At 1 o'clock, Manny was escorted to the cell that would be his home for the next twenty hours.

Manny sat down on a bed and surveyed the thirty by thirty foot cell he shared with five other men. He knew two of his cellmates. They immediately asked what he was in for. Manny stuck to his story.

He said, "I bought two Yamaha engines from a guy in Marsh Harbour. The engines were hot and I got caught with them. Now, I'm short six thousand bucks." He claimed he didn't know they were stolen, but admitted he got a very good deal on the two engines. "They're probably worth twenty grand," he said.

Manny assumed the police had at least one snitch in the cell. He had no intention of saying anything that would incriminate him. The two men, who knew Manny, understood he was not someone to mess with. Manny sat calmly on his bed and waited for the hours to pass. Tuesday morning, he would be taken to the Magistrates Court where he would be arraigned, post bail and be free by 2 o'clock.

David Thomas did a first-class job of greasing the legal skids, to get Manny in and out of jail as quickly as possible. David was already working on his defense and told him, "You won't be charged with grand theft because the cops don't have any evidence linking you to the theft. There's no proof you knew the engines were stolen."

Manny was a cautious man though and as he sat in his jail cell, he thought of how things could turn against him. *The weak link is Calico Jack. He's a small-time criminal who never graduated to more serious and more profitable crimes,* and that worried Manny. *There had to be a reason he never moved up in the criminal food-chain.* Today was the first time Manny had given that any thought.

He thought about Spider and Speedo and knew they would keep their mouths shut. The cops had no reason to suspect they were involved in the crime. Manny and Chino were the only people who knew they stole the boat. Or were they?

He thought, *Wait a minute. Didn't they mention a kid from Walkers, who tipped them off and acted as lookout the night they stole the boat? Well, I need to look into that loose end tomorrow.*

Manny laid back on the gray and white striped jailhouse mattress and rested his head on the yellow, stained pillow. He thought about what he needed to do tomorrow. As far as

Manny was concerned, this was the only night he would spend in jail for this crime.

At 1 p.m., as Viper and Melody arrived at the police compound, Calico Jack walked out of police headquarters. At 9:30 a.m., Calico Jack was in Magistrate Court 1, where he was charged with one count of possession of stolen property. Immediately after the hearing David Thomas posted the six thousand dollar cash bail.

"I spent four nights in jail, just 'cause I kept two engines for a friend," Calico Jack told everyone.

Calico Jack did everything he was supposed to do and nothing more. He never mentioned the two fishermen and he was confidant Chino would take care of him.

He heard, via the jailhouse grapevine, Manny was turning himself in this morning. He might even see Manny before he got out on bail today.

VIPER BOB

chapter 29

M anny was awake at 7 a.m., when a trustee brought food to the six prisoners. All the prisoners wore blue dungarees and light blue cotton shirts.

Breakfast was boiled fish, grits and a cup of coffee, served in a metal bowl and cup. The only utensil they were given was a plastic spoon. Manny sat on the edge of his bunk and ate in silence.

The previous afternoon, two inmates tried to get Manny to talk about his crime in more detail. One of the men told Manny about the crimes he committed, and freely admitted he was guilty. Manny kept his mouth shut and listened to them.

Manny assumed they were working for the cops. Therefore, he wanted to learn everything he could about them. He wanted to tell Chino everything about them once he was out of jail. Who knows, one day they might try to infiltrate Chino's business.

At 8:45, Manny and three of the six prisoners were handcuffed, chained together, and taken to a van. They were driven to the Magistrates Court two blocks away on Mall Drive. Manny was not surprised that the two men who confessed to him yesterday were not going to the Magistrates Court. After breakfast they were taken to another jail cell. Now he was sure they were jailhouse snitches.

Court began promptly at 9 o'clock, as it always did everywhere in the British Empire. When the British governed The Bahamas, everything had to be done according to procedures. Manny thought, *What a joke these people are, with their proper attire, silly wigs and arrogant attitude.*

He was led into Courtroom No. 2, where Magistrate Percevile Crosswhite presided for Her Royal Majesties Court. Manny sat down with the three other defendants and waited his turn, which didn't take long. By 9:15 the bailiff was reading the charges: Possession of Stolen Property.

The Magistrate asked in a totally uninterested tone, "How do you plead, Mr. Pender?"

David Thomas was standing next to Manny as he said in a loud, firm voice, "Not Guilty."

For the next few minutes, the prosecutor, the Magistrate, and David discussed his bail. Finally the Magistrate said, "Bail will be six thousand dollars." The discussion was over.

David informed the court his client was prepared to post bail. Then he proceeded to the clerk's office and handled it. No one in the legal system was surprised. All of David Thomas' clients seemed to have plenty of cash to post bail.

Manny looked at David and gave him a quick smile and sat down, as the next man stood up to have his case read. By 10 a.m., all four men were being led back to the van and returned to their jail cell.

At noon the same trustee who brought breakfast came to the cell with lunch, which was boiled fish, rice and a cup of coffee.

"What's for dinner, Pops?" Manny asked the trustee, who was in his late sixties.

The trustee, who looked like he had spent most of his life in prison, replied, "Our Tuesday night special is, let me see, oh yes, boiled fish, dirty rice and a cup of coffee."

Manny looked at the old man and saw what Manny called the thousand-mile stare. Men like him had completely given up on life outside of prison. They were totally institutionalized. He could tell by the way they shuffle their feet, moving in a slow, steady beat, almost like a soldier marching, but much slower. Their eyes had no shine; they were dark and empty like a black hole. Their shoulders slouch forward, as if they were trying to protect themselves from being attacked.

As Manny ate his boiled fish and rice and drank a cup of coffee, he thought, *I could lose some weight if I stayed in here for a week or two.* Then he decided, *No, that's not a good idea, I'd miss my Twinkies.*

At 2:15, Manny walked out the revolving door of police headquarters and thought, *How appropriate, revolving doors at the police station.* He got in the passenger side of David's car, shook hands, and said, "Thanks for getting' me out so fast." David smiled and replied, "That's my job and I aim to please.

I'll take you back to the apartment." He asked, "Is there anything I need to know about, while you were in jail?"

Manny told him there were two snitches in his cell.

"I got lots of good information about them. I knows where they live, and names of their relatives."

David asked, "What are their names?"

David knew one of the men. The other was a new name to him. He thought, *Well, that's useful information. I certainly don't want any jailhouse snitches for clients.*

VIPER BOB

chapter 30

TUESDAY
OCTOBER 21, 2003
POLICE COMPOUND
FREEPORT, GRAND BAHAMA ISLAND

Inspector Jamison and Sergeant Rolle were busy working a multiple homicide case this morning. For the moment, the stolen boat investigation was put on hold. Jamison didn't have enough time to make an appearance at the Magistrates Court this morning, when Manny was arraigned. He knew with an attorney like David Thomas he would be out on bail after lunch.

As Manny was leaving the Freeport jail, Viper and Michael, a mechanic from MarineWorld, arrived at the police compound and took custody of the two Yamaha engines. They were unable to get the engines Monday because MarineWorld's truck was in the shop all day. The previous weekend, MarineWorld hauled the Edgewater out of the water and took it to their shop, where they would service and re-install the engines.

Michael said to Viper, "The engines are in much better shape than I expected."

"Yea, I figured they would be all banged up. Well, I'm glad they took good care of my engines for me.

"How long do you think it'll take to get them back on my boat and running?" Viper asked.

"Oh, I need to check everything out and make sure nothing inside was damaged. There are a couple of parts I'll need to order. It'll take at least two days for them to get here from Nassau. We should have her back in the water and running by Monday, at the latest."

"That's great. We want to do a little fishing while the weather's good."

"Yes, sir," Michael replied. "That'll be no problem." And with that, Michael used the hydraulic winch to load the engines in his truck and take them back to MarineWorld. He thought to himself, *I can't figure that guy out. He would have been better off not looking for his boat. His engines have eight hundred hours on them, and the hull is beat to shit. With the money he's spent plus the insurance money, he could buy a new boat and engines.*

But Michael had to admit, *I'd never steal anything from Viper, he's not a man to mess with.*

"What would you have done if you hadn't found your boat at Mores Island?" Michael asked Viper.

"After Mores Island I was going to Eleurethra. If it wasn't there, then I was going to charter another plane and search Haiti, Jamaica and Cuba."

"The only place they could have hidden my boat, where I wouldn't find it, was at the bottom of the ocean."

Michael thought, *He should be a little more careful, he's messing with some very, very bad dudes. If he doesn't watch out, he might wind up at the bottom of the ocean.*

In the past two years several boats had been stolen from MarineWorld's compound. A year ago, someone drove a large truck through the chain link fence surrounding the compound. They stole a trailer with a 34-foot Contender and three new Yamaha engines that was worth two hundred and fifty thousand dollars.

The police never found the thieves or a single clue as to who committed the crime. Shortly afterward, the owners of MarineWorld installed lights, night vision cameras, plus they hired armed guards with pit bull dogs to guard the compound at night.

Michael heard one of the owners say—they were forced to spend over one hundred thousand dollars a year on security because if they didn't, they'd lose their insurance.

In addition, they were starting to lose Yamaha sales. Many people wouldn't buy Yamaha engines because they were the drug dealers' engines of choice.

Viper told Michael, "About ninety percent of the three hundred boats stolen each year in The Bahamas, had Yamaha engines." Viper said he learned that from the police commissioner.

Michael figured the number of boats stolen each year was closer to four hundred. He should know. He was one of the mechanics who worked part-time for Chino, removing engines from stolen boats.

He thought, *Wouldn't it have been ironic if I removed the engines from Viper's boat, and now I was putting them back. If Viper knew about my other job, he'd have a heart attack.*

VIPER BOB

chapter 31

Manny and Chino were sitting at a small table in the corner of the Jungle Room talking about how Manny was going to beat the stolen property charges.

Chino said to Manny, "I ain't worried 'bout the possession of stolen property thing. I'm worried about Calico Jack cuttin' a deal with the police. That means the only way we be sure you're safe is if Calico Jack disappears. So, I'm thinkin' Calico Jack meets with an untimely, deadly accident."

Manny liked Calico Jack and was trying to think of another way to solve the problem. Unfortunately, Calico Jack was not very bright and he wasn't a very good criminal. So, Manny had to admit Chino's solution was the only sure way to solve his problem and protect the organization. Chino said, "In the jungle..." he paused, "room, only the strong survive." Both men laughed and had another beer.

"Here's what we do. I'll tell Calico Jack you guys need to steal some boats to repay me for the bail and attorney fees," Chino said.

Manny chimed in, "OK, so I'll take him with me to do a job. Instead, when I gets a couple of miles from Freeport, I'll knock him unconscious. Then I'll tie a rope around his legs and attach a couple of cement blocks to weight him down, and toss him in a couple thousand feet of water."

Chino said, "That sounds good." And he thought, *Hmm that sounds familiar, too.*

"So, when you want to do it?"

Chino answered, "No rush, how about in a couple of weeks? We don't want to move too fast, that would be too obvious."

"OK," Manny replied. "Now, let's have something to eat, all this work has made me hungry." They laughed and told the barmaid to get them two large rib eye steaks.

Just as they were ready to eat, Calico Jack came in and asked if he could join them. "Of course you can, Bro," Chino said.

"How about havin' a steak with us?" he said, and winked at Manny.

Calico Jack was afraid Manny was mad at him for giving the cops his name. But Manny told him, "No problem, Bro, there was nothin' else you could do. You had to tell 'em somethin' and besides, our mouthpiece will beat this wrap."

Calico Jack breathed a big sigh of relief. He was sure Manny was going to break his neck. He sat down and finished a beer while he waited for his steak. By the time it arrived his stomach began to relax.

For the first time since his arrest he was able to enjoy a meal. He realized how hungry he was, having eaten boiled fish and grits or rice for five straight days.

He finished his steak and asked Chino if he could have another. Chino called the barmaid over and told her, "Give our Bro another steak, and hurry."

"How about another round of beer," Manny said to the girl. She rushed off, not sure whether to give the cook the food order first, or get the beers. She decided since Chino told her to get another steak she would do that first. Then she'd get the beers.

Calico Jack looked at Manny and Chino, as he finished his third beer in two gulps. He was still a little concerned Manny or Chino might be secretly mad at him.

"Hey Mon, I needs to pay you back the six grand for the bail money. What you wants me to do?"

"Right, but you also owe me five hundred for David Thomas, so it's sixty-five hundred. But who's countin' among friends?" Chino said, as he jokingly slapped him on the back.

Manny looked at Calico Jack and said, "Hey, I got an idea. How 'bout you and me steal a couple of boats and that'll settle both our debts?"

Chino smiled and said, "That works for me. But let's wait three or four weeks before we put you guys back to work. The cops are gonna be watchin' you pretty close for a while."

By the time Calico Jack's second steak arrived he was feeling much better. His stomach was almost normal and the constant headache he had for the past six days was starting to go away. It looked like Chino and Manny were accepting the whole thing as a bad break and they were ready to move on.

"Hey Mon, this steak tastes great," he said to no one in particular. Then feeling bolder, he said, "Hey barmaid, bring me and my friends another round of Kalik, and hurry, we be thirsty." He looked at Manny and said, "Mon, this is great. All we need is a couple of women and we could celebrate being out of jail."

Chino looked at Manny and smiled.

"Calico Jack, I guess after spending four nights in jail you must be pretty horny. You didn't get down on all four and bark like a jailhouse bitch for any of the brothers while you was in the slammer, did you?"

"Shit, no way, Mon. I ain't no girlie man. None of them boys was dumb enough to fuck with Calico Jack."

Then he took a drink of his beer and said, "Yea, I been four nights without a woman. When them cops busted me I be layin' up with Lawanda all night." He closed his eyes and remembered the young, naked seventeen-year-old girl's hot body.

He sighed and said, "Yea, I wish I knew where Lawanda was."

Chino got up and said, "I be right back." He walked into the bathroom, closed the door, took out his cell phone and dialed a number. On the second ring a girl answered. He told her, "It's Chino. Send two young, sweet beauties to the Jungle Room and hurry."

Ten minutes later two young girls, one black and the other white, walked into the Jungle Room. Everyone stopped what they were doing and looked at them. The black girl was about eighteen and her jet-black hair shimmered in the light. Her long legs were covered with black leather, skintight pants that were tightly stretched across her firm, round buttocks. She wore a white see-through lace blouse, and she didn't wear a bra—she didn't need one. Her breasts were round, with nipples the size of silver dollars.

Latoya walked over to the table where Chino was sitting. Her friend, Sharleen, followed close behind. Sharleen was as beautiful as Latoya, but as different as night from day. Sharleen had creamy white skin and her platinum blonde hair was shoulder length. The combination of her 38-D breasts and her twenty-one inch waist showcased her hourglass figure. She had long legs, too but instead of showing them off, they were partially covered with a multi-colored blue and red sarong, with patches of white clouds, making the pattern look like a Bahamian sunset. She wore a matching top that barely covered her ample breasts, to the delight of everyone in the bar.

Chino invited the two girls to join them. The barmaid rushed over to get their order, asking Sharleen and Latoya, "What can I get you, honey?"

Latoya said, "I'd like something strong and stiff, the same way I likes my men." Choruses of howls were heard in the bar. The barmaid suggested, "Rrright. How 'bout a sloe gin fizz?" Everyone at the table busted out laughing.

"I would like a double Scotch on the rocks," Latoya said.

Latoya sat down next to Calico Jack and his heart skipped a beat, then another. He couldn't say a word. He'd never been this close to a woman as beautiful as Latoya. Finally, he was able to look her in the eyes and said, "Hey, they call me Calico Jack."

Latoya smiled and said, "Ohhh, now, that's original, Sugar.

"Hey, Calico Jack, nobody's ever used that pick up line on me before. But, that's OK darlin', you're doin' good. My name's Latoya." She leaned over and kissed Calico Jack on the cheek and he almost fainted.

While Latoya was talking to Calico Jack, Sharleen moved around the table and leaned against Manny. She rubbed her breast against the back of his head and said, "What does a girl have to do to get a seat around here?

Manny stood up and held his chair out for her. Meanwhile, the waitress patiently waited for Sharleen's order. Sharleen took her time, knowing every man in the room was watching her. She put her left foot on the chair and ran her hands up her leg, smoothing out her black mesh stocking. Then, she eased herself into the chair slowly and sensuously. Whatever Sharleen did, she made it look like she was having an orgasm.

All eyes in the room stayed fixed on her, until she opened her pouty, red lips and said to no one in particular, "I think I'll have," she paused for a moment, "a purple passion. And make it in a tall glass! I feel very passionate tonight."

Manny rolled his eyes back in his head and smiled at Chino. Then, he thought, *What a guy, we're going to kill Calico Jack in a couple weeks and Chino just bought him the most gorgeous black woman on the island. After tonight Calico Jack will do anything for Chino. When the time is right, killin' him is gonna be real easy.*

chapter 32

For two weeks Viper and his family kept busy working on the Edgewater and their yacht. In addition, they enjoyed the numerous activities and restaurants in Freeport and Lucaya.

Someone once described a boat as a hole in the water where you throw money. If that's the case, Viper had two holes in the water, where he was throwing money on a daily basis.

Viper's boats were insured. But he believed in large deductibles, which meant two things: It substantially reduced his annual premium, and he didn't file insurance claims for small, frivolous damages. Viper took good care of his boats because he knew from experience a properly maintained boat could protect your life in an emergency.

Almost every day, Viper and Robert went to MarineWorld and did minor repairs on the Edgewater while Michael worked on the engines. It took a week longer than Michael expected to get the missing parts. They didn't have them in Nassau so they ordered them from Yamaha's warehouse. Friday afternoon, Michael installed the twin engines and today they were going to put the boat in the water and do the sea trials to verify all the systems operated correctly.

The sea trials took most of the morning. When Viper, Robert and Michael returned to Lucayan Marina, it was time for lunch. Viper invited Michael onboard *My Melody* and they talked while Melody made her famous Cheeseburger in Paradise. It was made with lettuce and tomato, Heinz 57 and French fried potatoes. A big kosher pickle and a cold draft beer completed the meal, just the way Jimmy Buffet sang it.

Michael was amazed as he sat in the main salon, talking with Viper and Robert. The salon was much larger than he expected and it was not furnished like a typical yacht. Melody took great pride in making their yacht look and feel like their home.

The main salon was eighteen feet wide and twenty-six feet long. The rear of the salon had two, floor to ceiling glass windows, trimmed with tan mahogany. A double sliding glass door was in the middle of the two windows and led out to the cockpit. On both sides of the salon were eight-foot wide by four-foot high picture windows.

A fourteen-foot L-shaped sectional sofa made of ultra soft white leather was against the starboard wall. The sofa curved to the left and extended six feet, along a wall that separated the main salon from the galley. The wall had a floor to ceiling mirror that made the salon look much larger than it actually was. Opposite the couch, on the port side of the salon, was the dining area with a modern chrome table and four white leather chairs that matched the sofa. The chairs had thick seats and back cushions. When Michael sat on one of the chairs, his body literally sank into the soft cushions.

The floor was covered with snow-white, plush, wall-to-wall carpeting and the walls were decorated with original paintings of the Caribbean. Michael felt like he was in a beautiful home in The Bahamas, not on a yacht. He sat in the salon and enjoyed the spectacular waterfront view.

When Melody brought the lunch tray into the salon Michael though, *What an attractive woman.* He couldn't help staring at her soft shoulder length auburn hair, emerald green eyes and well-shaped figure.

As he watched her return from the galley with the drinks he wondered *what part of the U.S. she was from? She has to be from the South, she definitely has a southern accent.* He guessed she was either from Texas or Georgia. He thought, *She certainly qualifies as a southern belle.*

"Excuse me, Melody, with your accent, I'd guess you're from Texas or Georgia. Am I right?"

Melody smiled and said, "What accent?"

Everyone laughed and she continued, "You're very close, I was born in a small town in northern Alabama, where I grew up on a farm."

"If you don't mind me saying so, you sure are beautiful."

Melody's cheeks turned a faint red, as she blushed. She'd heard compliments like that all her life, but she always appreciated hearing them.

As they ate lunch the surround sound stereo was playing a soft jazz song by Dorothy Wilson.

Michael asked Viper, "What are your plans, now that your boat's repaired."

"We still have some unfinished business in Freeport. The police caught two of the bad guys, but we still don't have the bastards who stole the boat. We plan to help the police find them and put them where they belong," Viper said.

Michael looked at Viper with surprise, "Why waste your time looking for them? You've got your boat and engines back! Why not forget about it and get back to your fishing? You said you love to fish, don't you?"

Melody looked at Michael and responded, "Michael, the men who stole our boat had no idea who they were messing with. Viper fully intends to see everyone who was involved behind bars and he won't rest until they are."

Michael didn't know what to say. He thought, *You're messing with honest to goodness evil people! Chino and Manny wouldn't think twice about killing them, or anyone who threatened them.*

Cautiously he said, "But, the people who steal these boats are usually involved in drugs and they're extremely dangerous. They won't hesitate to kill people who get in their way."

A strange look came across Viper's face. His eyelids narrowed as he recalled, "At least a dozen people told me I'd never find our boat. When I found the boat they told me I'd never find our engines." He smiled and continued, "Then they told me we'd never catch the crooks. So far, they've been wrong on all counts!"

Viper continued, "Some people have said we were just lucky. I believe you make your own luck. We'll see this thing through to the bitter end."

Michael thought, *You'll find out what bad guys in The Bahamas are like if you continue.* But he didn't say anything to Viper.

When lunch was over, Viper drove Michael back to MarineWorld and paid his bill. He told the owner, "Everything is working great, and we appreciate the fine service. Particularly, the good job Michael has done in such a short amount of time."

As Viper drove out of the parking lot, Michael thought, *Should I call Chino and tell him about Viper's plan to continue looking for the boat thieves or should I keep my mouth shut?*

He was nervous. If Chino found out Michael knew about Viper's plans to continue looking for the thieves, Chino would certainly come after Michael and teach him a lesson about loyalty. Michael was sure it would be a lesson he would never forget, if he survived.

Michael thought, *Damn, I don't want to get involved in this. Viper and his family are nice people. But, I know what's going to happen if they don't leave Freeport and forget about this.*

Maybe the police will discourage Viper, he thought. *Maybe they'll convince him to leave the area and let them handle the case, and then I won't have to worry about Chino.*

Michael decided to wait a few days and see what happened. Besides, Viper and Robert were going to be busy the next couple of days, cleaning the Edgewater.

Viper and Melody were relaxing on the cockpit at the rear of their yacht, watching another beautiful sunset in paradise. As the sun slipped below the horizon, the sky turned from powder blue to a burnt orange, and the clouds changed from a brilliant white to a soft, silver gray. Seagulls were circling above the harbor, looking for one more snack, before returning to their nest in the trees along the sandy, white beaches.

Viper was having his usual evening cocktail, vodka and tonic with lime, while Melody was sipping a gin and club soda with lime. Robert joined them and opened an ice cold Bud Light, which he richly deserved. He spent all afternoon washing and polishing the Edgewater. It didn't look anything like it did a month ago before it was stolen but it was as good as he could do.

The Edgewater had deep gouges in the hull and there was extensive damage to the transom when the engines had been removed. As soon as they got back to Palm Beach, the boat would have to be hauled out of the water in order to do the repair work. For now, it was operational and as clean as Robert could make it. He took great pride in keeping all three of their boats clean. It was a full-time job taking care of a 68-foot yacht, a 27-foot fishing boat, and the 12-foot inflatable dingy they carried on the flybridge.

Viper and Melody decided it was time to return to Palm Beach and get the Edgewater in a yard. In addition to the Edgewater, there were a number of repairs they needed to do on *My Melody*. They began discussing when would be the best time to leave. Viper had watched the weather channel earlier in the day and the forecast for the next three days was calmer seas and five to ten knot winds out of the southeast.

Viper said, "It looks like the Gulfstream is laying down. In a couple days the waves should be one to two feet so I suggest we leave for Palm Beach on Wednesday. That'll give us a day to wrap up everything in Freeport. Also, I've arranged to see Commissioner Blackstone tomorrow."

Melody and Robert agreed one day was plenty of time to get the boats ready. Robert was eager to get back to Palm Beach and meet some new girls, who always migrated south to Palm Beach for the winter.

chapter 33

Tuesday morning Viper and Melody purchased a few items at the grocery store and said goodbye to the store clerks, waitresses and bartenders they met during their month-long stay.

Viper and Robert tested or checked all the systems, making sure everything on the yacht functioned properly. All the systems were operating correctly and they were ready to make a smooth trip to Palm Beach.

As captain, it was Viper's responsibility to ensure everything was seaworthy for the crossing. Once they left Lucaya, if something didn't work, there were no repair shops in the Atlantic Ocean.

The boating community in Lucaya is substantial, with hundreds of boats and twice as many people who make a living, providing goods and services to the yachting community. In spite of its size, it tends to be a relatively close-knit community where everyone knows what everyone else is doing. It's kind of a miniature Peyton Place, and it quickly became common knowledge *My Melody* was departing Wednesday.

It didn't take long for the news to reach the people who spend most of their time at the Jungle Room. Two people took special interest in *My Melody*'s plans. Manny stopped by the Jungle Room Tuesday afternoon and joined Chino for a drink. After checking to make sure no one could hear him, he said, "I hear them people who owns the Edgewater is plannin' to leave tomorrow."

Chino looked at him and asked, "So?"

"I hear they been pushin' the cops to find the men that stole their boat. Those people are a major pain in our ass. If they was to have an accident on their way to Florida, the pain in our ass would go away.

"I think," Manny said, "we should take Calico Jack with us tomorrow morning and follow *My Melody*. When they be far enough offshore, we hijack the yacht, kill Calico Jack and the people onboard. Then we sink the yacht and that damn Edgewater and all our problems will be buried at the bottom of the sea."

Chino thought about Manny's idea. "How you plan to get onboard their yacht? You think them nice white folks, who just had their boat stolen, is gonna open their arms and invite three Bahamians onboard?"

"Hmm, I gots to think about that," Manny said. He ordered another Kalik and pondered how they could get *My Melody* to stop and let them come onboard in the middle of the ocean.

Chino sat patiently and listened as Manny came up with different ways to disable the yacht but Chino easily shot down each idea, explaining why it wouldn't work.

Finally, Chino suggested to Manny, "Bro, it's almost impossible to disable their yacht once they leave the marina. Let's think about leaving the marina with them."

Manny was enthusiastic about this approach. He began pursuing this new line of thinking and quickly came up with a couple of ideas.

Chino and Manny spent about thirty minutes discussing the new ideas and slowly a plan came together they both agreed would work.

VIPER BOB

chapter 34

Viper had an appointment with Commissioner Blackstone at 2 o'clock. He had written a letter of commendation he wanted to present to the commissioner. The letter acknowledged Detective Inspector Jamison, Detective Sergeant Rolle, and Corporal Blackstone in Walkers Cay, for the excellent police work they did in finding the Yamaha engines and arresting the two men.

Viper and Melody arrived at police headquarters at 1:45 p.m., checked in with the desk sergeant and sat on one of three red couches in the lobby. They didn't expect the commissioner to see them at 2 p.m. Viper reminded Melody, "This is the Bahamas, they take their time."

"When do you think he'll see us?" Melody asked. Viper replied, "Between 2:15 or 2:30."

They were pleasantly surprised when the commissioner walked into the lobby exactly at 2 p.m. and greeted them. He invited them to his office, and on the way, asked Viper, "Have you decided when you'll return to the United States?"

Viper told him they were leaving the following morning. He said, "The weather is perfect and the ocean should be as flat as a pancake."

"How long will it take you to make the crossing?" the commissioner asked.

"We should reach Palm Beach in eight hours. When we're towing the Edgewater we cruise between ten and twelve knots per hour. We could go faster but I like to take it easy on my equipment."

Blackstone looked at Melody and asked, "How was your stay in Freeport?"

Melody replied, "Absolutely perfect. We love the island and the people are so friendly. We had dinner at a restaurant on the beach the other night. The fish was delicious and the band was wonderful."

Blackstone responded, "I'll have to introduce you to Mrs. Newbury, president of The Grand Bahama Chamber of Commerce. She loves to hear those kinds of compliments."

After they were seated in the commissioner's office his secretary asked if they would like any refreshments. Viper and Melody declined, as did the commissioner. Viper removed a letter from a manila folder, handed it to the commissioner and said, "I want to compliment you and the Royal Bahamas Police Force for recovering our engines and arresting two of the criminals."

Viper paused, giving the commissioner time to read the letter.

Blackstone was pleased as he read the letter. When he finished, he looked at Viper and Melody and said, "I'm glad we recovered your engines. I want to assure you, we'll continue to look for the people who stole your boat. When we find them they will be punished to the full extent of the law."

"Will you keep Jamison and Rolle on the case?" Melody asked.

"Yes and you have my word we won't rest until everyone involved is in jail," the commissioner said.

Viper and Melody looked at each other and then turned to Blackstone and Viper said, "Thank you, that makes us very happy."

After a few minutes of small talk Viper said, "Well commissioner we've taken up far too much of your time. We really should be going."

The three stood and the commissioner replied, "I'm glad we could see each other again before you left. I'll put these letters of commendation in each man's file, plus I'll have a copy sent to them."

"Thank you for your gracious hospitality and the wonderful job your men did," Melody said.

Blackstone's secretary escorted Viper and Melody back to the lobby. They returned the visitor cards to the desk sergeant and left the building. They drove down Mall Drive where banks and restaurants lined both sides of the street, past the casino where they spent Saturday evening drinking and gambling. Viper enjoyed playing blackjack. He had been lucky Saturday night winning more than five hundred dollars. Melody, who was not a patient gambler, fed most of his winnings back into the slot machines.

After they returned to their yacht, Melody asked Viper, "Do you really think they'll find the people who stole our boat?"

"If they haven't arrested anybody within a month, we'll have to return and apply some more pressure."

That wasn't an unpleasant idea, since they both enjoyed Lucaya and Grand Bahama Island.

Melody commented, "There are a lot worse places we could be."

Viper said, "We just need to be careful. We don't want to upset the police and become *persona non grata*. The Bahamas are too close and convenient, plus the fishing at Walkers is great."

Melody agreed, "I want to come back and I don't want to worry about the crooks, or the cops."

By 5 o'clock that evening, Viper completed one final system check and decided everything was ready. Low tide Wednesday morning was at 4:14 a.m., and he couldn't leave Bell Channel on a low tide. Just outside the channel there were a couple of spots with less than five feet of water at low tide. But, there would be plenty of water by 6 a.m., when he planned to exit the channel.

They decided to get up at 5:30, have coffee, and get the yacht and the Edgewater ready to depart. They would tow the Edgewater out of the channel, using a short twenty-foot towline. When they were half a mile outside the channel, they would stop and attach a two hundred-eighty foot towline to the Edgewater and then proceed to Palm Beach.

Palm Beach was seventy-eight miles west northwest of Lucaya. Viper estimated the trip would take eight hours and he expected to arrive in Palm Beach at 2:30, two hours after high tide.

Viper was a cautious navigator. He knew low tide was when many boaters got into trouble. Less experienced captains often underestimated the effect tides and currents have on a boat's performance.

Between south Florida and The Bahamas is the Gulfstream, a fast moving body of water that is twenty miles wide and moves at four to five knots an hour. The current in the Gulfstream is so strong it actually pushes a boat to the north as it travels to or from The Bahamas. If a captain doesn't adjust his course to compensate for the current, he can miss his arrival point by as much as eight to fifteen miles.

When traveling to Florida, miscalculating the current is not critical because Florida's coastline is over three hundred miles long. The worst that can happen is the captain will arrive north of his original destination.

However, when traveling to the northern Bahamas, the current is critical because it can push the boat far enough north that the captain misses The Bahamas completely. If the boat has enough fuel, the captain can correct his mistake by either traveling south, until he finds The Bahamas, or turn west and head back to Florida. Unfortunately, over the years, numerous boats have run out of fuel before reaching land. When that happens the Gulfstream will carry the helpless boat north until someone finds it. In some instances boaters have been carried as far as North Carolina before the Coast Guard rescued them or another boater found them.

Viper had made the trip between The Bahamas and south Florida numerous times and knew how to use the Gulfstream to his advantage.

Tuesday evening as Melody was preparing dinner, Chino and Manny were completing their plans for the next morning. Chino devised a simple, effective plan to board *My Melody* and kill everyone. Manny was impressed with the plan and thought, *This is why Chino is so successful. He keeps things simple.*

VIPER BOB

chapter 35

2 **a.m.**—Manny left the Jungle Room and drove south on Mall Drive to Arawak Marina. A friend kept a 17-foot Boston Whaler at the marina and Manny arranged to borrow it. Earlier in the afternoon, Manny went to the marina, filled the boat with gas, checked the engine and made sure it was operating properly.

2:15 a.m.—Manny started the Whaler, went out the channel and turned west toward Bell Channel. When he reached Bell Channel, he turned left and went to Bell Channel Marina.

2:30 a.m.—Chino and Calico Jack left the Jungle Room. They drove Calico Jack's truck down Mall Drive and turned right on East Sunrise Highway. They drove two miles, until they reached a roundabout where East Sunrise meets Sea

Horse Road. At the roundabout, they went south on Sea Horse Road, until they reached Bell Channel Marina. They parked Calico Jack's truck and walked down to the marina.

2:45 a.m.—In front of the marina was a floating bar, with space on three sides to tie up a boat. Manny tied the Whaler at the floating bar, and waited for Chino and Calico Jack. Music was blasting from a band playing next door at Bob Marley Square. Young men and women were drinking and dancing to the beat of a Soca tune, a modern form of calypso with an up-tempo beat.

2:50 a.m.—Manny had been waiting only a couple of minutes before two men walked onto the floating bar and stepped into the Whaler. Chino untied the dock lines while Manny started the motor and eased the boat away from the dock.

3 a.m.—The third quarter moon provided enough light for Manny to navigate in the dark. They quietly made their way toward Lucayan Marina less than half a mile away.

3:10 a.m.—Manny eased up to Lucayan Marina. He pulled into a slip thirty feet from where *My Melody* and the Edgewater were docked.

A light breeze was blowing out of the east, as the three men stepped onto the deck of *My Melody*. Chino and Manny were relaxed, but they could see Calico Jack was wound up tighter then a spring. He was breathing heavy and his hands were shaking. Calico Jack had broken a lot of laws in his lifetime, but he had never seriously contemplated killing someone. Chino knew Calico Jack was going to be nervous, so he kept him between Manny and himself. That way he could prod him forward and keep a close eye on him.

Chino was wearing a backpack, which he took off when they were on the deck of *My Melody* and removed a glasscutter. It was a simple device that had a suction cup with the glasscutter attached to a four-inch piece of string. Chino attached the suction cup to the glass on the pilothouse door and made numerous circles with the glasscutter, until he cut an eight-inch hole in the glass. He removed the glass from the suction cup and dropped it into the water.

Calico Jack jumped as the glass hit the water, even though it hardly made a sound. Chino reached through the hole in the glass and unlocked the starboard pilothouse door. As he slid the door open, Chino was careful not to make any noise. As the door slid on its track it made a slight grinding sound. Chino stopped and listened to determine if anyone onboard heard the noise. He waited a minute before he continued opening the door until it was wide enough to enter the yacht.

3:20 a.m.—Once they were inside, Chino took three taser guns from the backpack. The Air Taser has a one-time use cartridge that fires two probes up to fifteen feet and are attached to ultra-thin insulated wires.

He kept one for himself and gave one to Manny and one to Calico Jack. Chino moved to the stern of the yacht and Manny took Calico Jack and went forward.

Manny went down the forward stairwell first, with Calico Jack close behind. Five steps down the stairwell there was a landing and a stateroom door. Three steps further down the stairwell was a second stateroom door. Manny pointed to the door at the bottom of the stairs and then to himself. Calico Jack understood, he would enter the forward stateroom and Manny would enter the lower stateroom.

Manny counted to three, using his fingers, and they turned the door handles at the same time. Calico Jack's door opened and he was ready to enter the stateroom, but the other stateroom door was locked. Manny motioned for Calico Jack to go into the room.

Sweat ran down Calico Jack's forehead and dripped off his chin. His hands were shaking and he could barely hold the taser gun steady. If he shot at someone, he wasn't sure he would hit them. He gave a huge sigh of relief when he discovered the room was empty.

As Calico Jack entered the room, Manny slipped up the stairs and stood behind him. Calico Jack was startled when he turned around and bumped into him. Manny could see how nervous Calico Jack was, so he gave him a minute to calm down before they left the stateroom.

They went back up the stairs and found Chino, who was standing in front of a stairwell in the main salon. Chino saw Manny and waited, as they came over to where he was standing. Manny whispered, "One stateroom is empty and the door to the other stateroom is locked. Calico Jack's so scared he's ready to shit and piss in his pants." Chino whispered, "OK, leave Calico Jack here as a lookout. You and me will go below to the rear stateroom."

3:30 a.m.—Chino reached the bottom of the stairwell and Manny was one step behind him. Slowly, he pushed the door handle down and it moved. Both men stood ready to enter the room, once the door was open. Chino walked straight ahead, while Manny went to the left side of the room. Immediately they realized this was the master stateroom. They could see the outline of a king-size bed in the middle of the stateroom.

The room was dark but they could see two bodies lying on the bed. Chino raised his left hand, while holding the taser gun in his right hand, and counted to three, using his fingers. Both men aimed the taser gun at the figure lying in front of them. On the count of three they pulled the trigger.

Viper and Melody were asleep and didn't hear the intruders enter their stateroom. Viper was sleeping on his right side and the probes from the taser gun hit him in the middle of his back. Melody was sleeping on her back, and the probes hit her in the stomach.

Their bodies went rigid as the taser gun discharged 50,000 volts into their bodies. Neither one saw or heard anything. Their bodies were paralyzed for thirty seconds from the taser wave and they would remain unconscious at least five minutes.

Manny found a light switch and turned on the overhead lights, while Chino pulled two pieces of rope from his backpack and gave one to Manny. They rolled Viper and Melody onto their stomachs and tied their hands firmly behind their back. Chino got two more pieces of rope from his backpack and they tied their ankles.

They went up the stairs and prepared to go to the forward stateroom and disable the third person onboard. Before they went forward, they discussed the best way to enter the locked stateroom. Chino pulled a twelve-inch crowbar from his backpack. Calico Jack gladly gave Manny his taser gun and stayed in the main salon, while the two men went down the stairwell to the locked stateroom.

3:45 a.m.—Chino slipped the crowbar between the door and the door jam. He looked at Manny, who raised his left hand and counted to three using his fingers. Chino popped the door open. Manny stepped into the room, his eyes straining to see who was in the room. There were two beds in this stateroom and Manny couldn't tell if there were one or two people in the room. Just then, someone stirred in the bed on Manny's left. He aimed and pulled the trigger.

Manny could instantly tell his shot was on the mark, because the body went rigid as the taser gun discharged 50,000 volts. Chino found the light switch and turned it on. Viper's son was the only person in the room. Chino quickly pulled two pieces of rope from the backpack and tied Robert's arms behind his back and then tied his ankles.

They went back to the pilothouse where Calico Jack was waiting for them. Chino said, "OK. Everybody onboard is unconscious and tied up. Now, let's figure out how to operate this yacht."

Chino and Manny looked over the Helms Station in the pilothouse. They spent five minutes going over the controls and discussing what needed to be done to navigate the yacht. The three men had over forty-five years of combined experience on boats but none of them had ever operated a yacht this complicated.

Finally they decided to go forward and get Robert to help them. They assumed he did most of the work on the yacht, and would be the most knowledgeable.

When Manny and Calico Jack entered Robert's stateroom, he was awake, but had no idea what happened to him. He was on his stomach, and he didn't understand why his arms and legs were tied.

Manny rolled him over and said, "I'm going to untie you and if you do anything stupid, I'm going to shoot you again." Then he added, "Do you understand me?" Robert's mouth was dry and he couldn't make a sound, so he nodded his head.

Manny untied Robert's hands and feet. "Don't try nothin'." Robert was still dazed but he knew his life was in danger. He did what he was told.

Viper, Melody and Robert had discussed numerous times what they would do if anyone boarded their boat and kidnapped them. They agreed they would cooperate with their captors until an opportunity to escape presented itself. Since most hijackers killed everyone onboard a yacht, their only chance for all of them to survive was for one or more of them to escape and go for help. Robert obeyed his captors and prayed his parents were all right.

Manny took Robert to the pilothouse. "Show me how to start the generator and the engines." Robert said, "First, we start the generator, then we unhook the two shore power cords."

Manny said, "OK, start the generator. We'll get the power cords." Once the generator was running and the power was switched from the dock to the generators, Chino and Calico Jack disconnected the shore power cords. They brought them onboard, while Manny and Robert waited in the pilothouse.

Once the power cords were onboard, Manny said to Robert, "OK, that was good, what do we do next?"

Robert looked at Manny and asked, "What do you want to do?" Manny said, "We want to go out Bell Channel."

Robert looked at him and asked, "Why?" Manny punched Robert in the face, and the blow broke his nose. Blood was running out his nose and tears ran down his face as he staggered back against the Helm Station.

Manny looked at Robert and said, "I didn't say you could ask any questions. Show me how to start the engines, or I'll bust you in the nose again, motherfucker."

"All you need to do is turn these two ignition keys and the diesel engines will start up."

Manny looked at him with a cruel expression and said, "Good, now you understand how things work. Keep your fuckin' mouth shut, don't ask any questions and answer me when I talk to you." Robert nodded in understanding.

"Where are the keys for the Edgewater?" Robert pointed to a wooden box above the computer monitor on the Helm Station. "We keep the keys in there."

Calico Jack reached in the box and took out the keys and Manny led Robert back down the stairwell to his stateroom.

Once his hands and feet were tied, Manny closed the door and went back to the pilothouse.

Chino had been outside on the forward deck when Robert was showing Manny what to do. He re-entered the pilothouse said, "OK, here's the plan. You guys take the yacht out the channel and head south. I'll follow in the powerboat and I'll tow our dingy. It should take about twenty minutes to go six miles in a boat this size. I'll come along side and join you. We'll kill the three of them and then we'll sink the yacht."

"While the yacht is sinking, we'll soak the Edgewater with gas and set it on fire. Then, we'll take the dingy back to Arawak Marina and go have breakfast," Chino said.

Manny asked Chino, "How we gonna sink the yacht?" Chino answered, "A yacht this size has large hoses that feed seawater to the engines to keep them cool. We'll cut both hoses and water will pour into the engine room. It'll sink like a rock."

4:10 a.m.—Manny started the engines while Chino and Calico Jack went outside and untied the dock lines.

Viper woke up before Melody. The first thing he thought about was his splitting headache. His hands and feet were tied, so he realized they were being kidnapped.

Many boaters carry a tool called a Leatherman, a mariner's version of the famous Swiss Army knife, except it has tools that are appropriate for boating and fishing. It has everything from screwdrivers and knives to fingernail clippers. Viper kept his Leatherman in the top drawer of the dresser next to their bed. He quickly began thinking of a way to get the Leatherman. He slid off the bed and turned backwards, so he could use his hands to open the drawer. As he slid the drawer open, he listened for any sounds of someone coming down the stairs. He had heard multiple voices, so he knew there was more than one person onboard.

With the drawer open, Viper began feeling around for the canvas case he kept his Leatherman in. *Thank God for old habits*, Viper thought. He always put the Leatherman in the left front corner of the drawer. It only took a few seconds to locate it.

He closed the drawer and slithering like a snake, back onto the mattress. He rolled over on his left side, opened the case, and removed the Leatherman.

Viper thought, *That was the easy part. Now I've got to open the blade and that's going to be a real challenge with my hands tied behind my back.*

The Leatherman is designed like a pair of pliers. The handles fold up so it can be easily stored in the canvas case. Once Viper got the handles straight, he used his fingernail and tried to pry open one of the blades. Then he could cut the rope and free himself.

As he was trying to get a blade open, Melody started to wake up. Viper felt her stir and whispered, "Melody, you need to be quiet. Don't make a sound. Trust me."

After a few minutes, Viper realized he was not going to get the blade out. He couldn't get a fingernail on the side of the blade in order to pull it out so he decided to use the Leatherman like a pair of pliers and cut the rope.

He struggled to get the pliers around the rope that bound Melody's hands. He finally succeeded and slowly worked the handles back and forth. He was starting to make some headway when he heard a commotion above. He heard his son's voice as he answered a question from one of the men. He heard a smack and realized someone just hit his son.

Viper redoubled his effort to get loose and deal with these kidnappers. It didn't take much guesswork to figure out his family's fate unless he did something quickly.

Viper continued cutting the rope on Melody's hands. His progress was painfully slow and it took him five minutes to cut the rope. Finally, the rope separated and Melody's hands were free.

"Take the Leatherman and cut my rope."

Melody took the Leatherman and easily opened a blade and cut the rope. As she was cutting the rope, the generator started and they could hear the shore power cords being brought onboard.

The diesel engines roared into life and they could feel the yacht moving. The kidnappers were going to take their yacht somewhere. Viper was certain they would take them to the open waters of the Atlantic Ocean which were just a few miles off the coast of Grand Bahama Island.

VIPER BOB

chapter 36

WEDNESDAY
NOVEMBER 12, 2003
LUCAYAN MARINA
LUCAYA, GRAND BAHAMA ISLAND

While Viper and Melody were freeing themselves, Manny and Calico Jack were busy getting ready to take the yacht out of the slip. Manny located the depth sounder, the GPS and turned them both on. He was ready to leave the dock.

Chino tapped on the pilothouse door and asked if they were ready to leave the dock. Manny gave him a thumbs up and Chino untied the two remaining dock lines and threw them on the yacht.

4:15 a.m.—Manny eased the yacht out of the slip. Once he was clear of the forward pilings, he kept the port engine in forward and put the starboard engine in reverse. This maneuver caused the yacht to rotate to the right, which

Manny had to do in order to clear the rock seawall across the canal from the yacht.

Manny slowly maneuvered the yacht out of the marina and into Bell Channel. Five minutes later they were outside the channel and in one hundred feet of water. He moved the throttles forward, and soon the yacht was traveling at sixteen knots. Manny was impressed the big yacht could cruise at this speed. This was almost twice as fast as *Bank Walker* could go.

Manny went up to the flybridge where there was a second Helm Station and settled into the captain's chair, as he took the yacht due south. Everything was running smoothly. Manny told Calico Jack, "Go forward and check on the boy. Then, go aft and check on the husband and wife. If they say anything, hit 'em, and tell them to shut the fuck up."

"What do you want me to hit 'em with? I ain't got nothin'."

Manny looked around, but didn't see anything on the flybridge Calico Jack could use as a club. "Find somethin' in the kitchen or use your fist. I don't care, just make sure they be tied up and they be quiet."

4:30 a.m.—Calico Jack went to the forward stateroom where Robert was lying face down on the mattress. His face and the pillow were covered with blood. When Calico Jack entered the room, Robert was quiet and didn't say a word. Calico Jack, looked at him and said, "I see you has learned your lesson. Keep your mouth shut, be quiet and you won't get hurt." Robert was tempted to say something, but didn't.

As Calico Jack was leaving the forward stateroom, Viper and Melody were preparing to deal with the kidnappers. They weren't sure how many kidnappers were onboard. They heard at least two, possibly three voices.

Viper kept a Mini-14 rifle and a cloth bag with two clips filled with ammunition underneath their mattress. One clip, known as a banana clip, held thirty rounds and the other held ten rounds. He took the banana clip out of the bag, inserted it in the rifle and chambered a round. He left the ten round clip in the bag. He thought, *With thirty rounds I'll either kill them or they'll kill me. Either way I won't need the other clip.*

Viper placed his hand on the doorknob and was ready to open the stateroom door when he heard someone coming down the stairs. Viper motioned for Melody to lie down on the floor, beside the bed. He stepped to the opposite side of the stateroom and raised the rifle to his shoulder. There was no way he could miss when the person stepped through the door. He hoped only one person was coming to check on them. If a second person was on the stairs, he could easily fire into the stateroom, and it would be difficult for Viper to return fire but he had no other choice. If Viper stood near the doorway, he would be directly in the line of fire.

4:32 a.m.—The door opened and a tall black man walked in the doorway. Viper exhaled, and squeezed the trigger twice. The rifle spit two bullets in quick succession.

Calico Jack couldn't figure out why his chest hurt. As he entered the dark room, he saw two rapid flashes from his left. His chest started burning—and he thought, *What the fuck's happenin'?*

He tried to call out to Manny but his lungs were on fire and he was having trouble breathing. Before he could make a sound something struck him on the head as Viper hit him with the butt of the rifle. Calico Jack saw a flash of light, then he fell to his knees. He was out cold and blood was oozing from his chest. Both bullets hit his chest within four inches of each other. The first bullet passed completely through him. Miraculously it didn't hit any vital organs but it did cause internal bleeding. The second bullet struck higher, hitting his left lung and tearing a hole, the size of a dime, in it.

Viper looked up the stairs to see if there was another kidnapper on the stairs. He couldn't see anyone as he stood at the bottom of the stairs. He strained to hear any voices, but all he could hear was the deep throated droning of the big Detroit Diesel V8 engines.

He thought, *The engine noise must have covered the sound of the rifle shots.* Viper waited about thirty seconds, just to be certain no one was waiting in the main salon for the man he shot. But, someone was surely expecting him to return and Viper decided it was time to go up and deal with whoever was on his yacht.

First, he took the rope the kidnappers used to tie his hands and feet, and tied up the bleeding kidnapper. Then, he asked Melody to get a scarf. Viper put the scarf in the kidnappers mouth, wrapped it around his head, and tied it so he couldn't talk.

He told Melody, "Stay here while I make sure the main salon and galley are clear." Melody nodded her head as Viper continued, "If no one is up there, I want you to come up the stairs and go to the aft doors. If anything happens to me, I want you to grab a cushion off the couch and jump in the water. Those cushions will float and we can't be more than a mile or two off shore. It'll be daylight soon, so you'll be OK." Again, Melody nodded.

He picked up his rifle and cautiously started up the stairs. He crept up the eight steps. When he got to the third step he had a clear view of the main salon and the galley. Thank God, no one was there. As he reached the top step, he raised the rifle to his shoulder and swept the main salon. No one was in the room. He quickly stepped into the galley, the rifle still at his shoulder. No one was in the galley either. Next he stepped into the pilothouse. It was empty, too.

Viper walked back to the stairs and motioned for Melody to come up. She did and he pointed to the rear doors. Melody hesitated; she didn't want to leave her husband alone. Viper gave Melody his, *Don't give me any shit,* look!

She loved this man and trusted him, and now was not the time to argue with him. She went to the rear of the salon, crouched down and waited next to the door.

Viper walked back through the galley and into the pilothouse. On the port side of the pilothouse were two stairwells. One led down to the forward staterooms, and the other led up to the flybridge. *My Melody* had two Helm Stations the yacht could be operated from, one in the pilot-house, one on the flybridge. He checked the autopilot and saw it was not on which meant at least one kidnapper had to be at the Helm Station on the flybridge steering the yacht. What he didn't know was if a third kidnapper was up on the flybridge, or below in one of the forward staterooms.

Time was running out so he had to make a decision. Should he check the forward staterooms for more kidnappers and get Robert, or should he go up to the flybridge and confront the kidnapper running the yacht?

Viper decided to go up to the flybridge. Whoever was up there would be expecting his partner to return shortly. The stairwell leading up to the flybridge had seven steps. At the top was a half door and Plexiglas cover, and they were both open. Whoever was operating the yacht was probably sitting in the captain's chair. That meant he would be facing forward and would see Viper as he came up the stairs. Then he thought,

What if two people are up there and I only have enough time to shoot one of them?

Viper thought, *Going up the pilothouse stairs is a bad idea.* Instead, there was a stern ladder leading to the rear of the flybridge. By using it he had a better chance of sneaking up and seeing how many people were on the flybridge. Also, whoever was up there would not be paying any attention to the back of the flybridge.

Viper walked to the rear of the main salon where Melody was hiding. As quietly as possible, he opened the sliding glass door and both of them stepped out onto the rear deck. The noise from the engines was much louder out here. Any noise they made would be virtually unheard. Viper climbed up the ladder and peeked over the top of the flybridge deck. He was well concealed behind the 12-foot inflatable dingy sitting in its cradle at the rear of the flybridge deck. Viper could see the entire flybridge, and no one could see him.

He saw one person sitting in his captain's chair, operating his yacht. He could tell he was a large man by the width of his back and shoulders. *That's OK*, he thought, *he's not going to be in any condition to fight back after I shoot him a couple of times.*

Just then, Viper heard a faint noise coming from behind him. He turned and saw his Edgewater racing up toward them. Then, he saw a flash. He realized a third kidnapper was following them, in his Edgewater, and he was shooting at him.

Viper had to act quickly or he'd lose the element of surprise with the man sitting in his captain's chair. Disregarding the person shooting at him, he aimed his rifle at the man and fired three quick shots.

4:42 a.m.—Manny heard a noise behind him, but he didn't react fast enough. He grabbed the arms of the captain's chair to get up, when he felt a sharp pain in his back, then two more.

The wind rushed out of his lungs and he dropped, like a sack of potatoes, back into the chair.

Everything around Manny was blurry. The noise from the diesel engines seemed to be fading. *Was the yacht slowing down? Why couldn't he get out of the chair?* Manny was lost in his confusion. He couldn't figure out what happened. Slowly, he relaxed in the chair, and his head sagged. He took a short, painful breath, exhaled, and closed his eyes. Then the pain was gone.

4:45 a.m.—As Chino approached the yacht, he saw someone climbing up a ladder leading to the rear section of the flybridge. He knew it wasn't Calico Jack or Manny because he was white. It had to be the owner or his son. Chino grabbed his backpack and pulled out his pistol, and started shooting at the man. He knew he didn't stand a chance of hitting him. The yacht was rocking, as it plowed through the water and the Edgewater was bouncing in the yacht's wake. His shots were meant to warn Manny and Calico Jack. Who knows, he might get lucky and actually hit the bastard on the ladder. Chino thought, *What's with these people? Why can't they quit fuckin' with us?*

None of his shots found their mark and he wasn't sure if Manny or Calico Jack heard him. Chino decided to pull alongside the yacht when the man on the ladder turned around, stepped down off the ladder and aimed the rifle at him.

Chino saw the muzzle flash and then he heard bullets rip past him. The Edgewater was bouncing up and down and moving sideways in the yacht's wake but the yacht was a much more stable platform to shoot from than the Edgewater. The shooter had a much better chance of hitting Chino.

Chino instinctively swerved away from the yacht as the man continued shooting at him. The yacht was still plowing forward at the same speed. Maybe Manny and Calico Jack were OK. Chino realized he couldn't get close to the yacht, so Manny and Calico Jack would have to deal with whoever had gotten loose. Chino decided to slow down, trail the yacht at a safe distance and wait for a signal from Manny or Calico Jack.

He followed the yacht as it continued south at the same speed. Finally, Chino realized something was wrong—very wrong. Manny and Calico Jack must be captured or dead.

There was nothing he could do with a pistol against a rifle, so he turned around and headed back to the marina.

Viper watched the Edgewater as it dropped out of sight. He could no longer see it, but he assumed the boat was following them from a safe distance, watching and waiting.

Damn it, he thought. *This is the second time in a month our boat has been stolen. We must have the most popular boats in The Bahamas.*

Viper waited on the stern deck with Melody for a minute. The man in the Edgewater didn't return or fire any more shots.

Viper hugged Melody, who was visibly shaken from all the shooting. "Stay here, and watch for the Edgewater. If you see it, come get me. I'm going to check the forward staterooms and then go up on the flybridge."

"Are you going to check on Robert?"

"Yes, then we'll check on the guy in our stateroom and the one on the flybridge."

Viper pointed to an area on the aft deck that would conceal Melody. "Stay here where I can see you from the main salon. Keep a sharp look out for the Edgewater."

"You'll hear me shouting if I see it."

Viper raised the rifle to his shoulder and walked through the main salon into the galley. No one was there, so he went forward and swept the pilothouse with his rifle. No one was there, either. He breathed a sigh of relief. Before he went below to check on Robert, he set the autopilot on its current heading.

He turned around and looked at Melody. She was keeping a sharp lookout behind the yacht. She turned, saw Viper, and gave him the OK sign.

He decided not to go below and check the forward staterooms. Instead, he decided to check the kidnapper on the flybridge first. Viper needed to know if he was alive, or had a gun, which meant he was still a danger. He decided to use the rear stairs again. If the kidnapper was alive and had a gun, he would have to turn around to shoot him. Viper could easily shoot him before he got a single shot off.

5:05 a.m.—Viper went to the back of the yacht, out the sliding glass doors, startling Melody. He told her the change in plans and why.

"Keep watching for the Edgewater. I'm going to check on the guy up top. I need to know what condition he's in before I go below."

"OK," Melody said, "but please be careful."

Viper moved up the ladder quickly. He didn't want to give the kidnapper in the Edgewater another chance to shoot at him if he was still back there. When he got to the top of the ladder, Viper looked to see if the man had moved. He was still sitting in the captain's chair and appeared to be leaning slightly forward. Viper quickly climbed onto the flybridge, dropped to the deck and scanned the area behind the yacht. He couldn't see the Edgewater, or any signs of the third kidnapper.

He got up and went forward to check on the man sitting in his captain's chair. The man was motionless as Viper approached him. Viper kept his rifle pointed at the man's head and slowly circled until he was standing beside him.

The man's chest was covered with blood and his chin was resting against his blood soaked shirt. Viper placed the barrel against the man's head and nudged him. Nothing. Obviously, this kidnapper wasn't going to hurt anyone, ever.

Viper saw a pistol stuck in his waistband. Cautiously, he reached down with his left hand while keeping the rifle pressed against the man's head. He pulled the pistol out and stepped back quickly, the man didn't make a sound.

OK, two down, Viper thought. *Let's see how Robert's doing.*

Viper looked down the stairs and into the pilothouse before he descended the stairs. Once he reached the deck in the pilothouse, he looked back into the galley and the main salon. He saw Melody. She smiled, and held up her left hand and made the OK sign.

Viper smiled back and pointed forward. Melody blew him a kiss as he stepped out of sight. He raised the rifle to his shoulder as he started down the stairs. Five steps later, he reached the first landing. He decided to check the VIP stateroom before he went down to check on his son. He didn't need someone sneaking up behind him and shooting him. He opened the door halfway and put his foot against it, so no one could slam the door on his hand. Then, using his left hand he turned on the lights.

Once the lights were on he opened the door all the way and stepped into the stateroom. He swept the stateroom with the rifle. He gave a sign of relief when he saw there was no one in the room. He walked past the bed, and checked the bathroom and shower. They were empty too.

He left the room, closed the door and went down three more steps, until he stood in front of the busted door to his son's room. Quickly he pushed the door open and trusted his luck that Robert was the only person in the room.

5:10 a.m.—Viper stepped into the room, turned on the lights and saw his son lying on the bed, face down, with his hands and feet tied. Viper pulled out his Leatherman and cut the ropes. Robert rolled over and Viper was shocked. His son's face and shirt were covered with blood.

Robert looked at his father and said, "Thank God it's you. I've never been so scared in my life."

Viper smiled and asked him, "Are you OK, because you look like shit."

"My face hurts like hell," he said. "I think my nose is broken." Robert had a thousand questions to ask his father but before he could ask what happened, Viper said, "Do you know how many kidnappers boarded our yacht?"

Robert said, "I saw two and I think there was a third one outside. They brought me to the pilothouse and made me show them where we keep the keys for the Edgewater and how to start the generator. That's when the big guy punched me in the face."

"OK," Viper said, "I shot two of them and one is following us in the Edgewater. Let's go to the pilothouse and call for help."

Viper led the way back to the pilothouse. He walked to the main salon, opened the sliding door, and told Melody to come inside. Together, they went back to the pilothouse. The first thing Viper did was turn on the radar system, then pick up the VHF radio handset and checked that it was on channel 16.

5:15 a.m.—He pushed the transmit button and said, "MAYDAY, MAYDAY, MAYDAY. This is motor yacht *My Melody*. We're an American flagged vessel. We are approximately eight miles south of Freeport, Grand Bahama Island.

Three men boarded our yacht and kidnapped us. We have captured two of the men. The third man is in a 27-foot blue and white powerboat, and may be following us. He has a pistol and has fired at us numerous times."

He repeated the message three times. Then he removed his finger from the transmit button and listened for a response.

A man's voice came over the loud speaker and said, "This is the United States Coast Guard, Group Miami, calling *My Melody*. We have received your MAYDAY transmission. I repeat, we have received your MAYDAY transmission. We will notify the Royal Bahamas Defense Force and we are dispatching an airplane immediately. Do you copy? Over."

"U.S. Coast Guard, this is *My Melody*," Viper said. "I copy and that's the best news I've had today. God bless you. Over."

"*My Melody*, this is U.S. Coast Guard, Group Miami. Please switch to channel twenty-two alpha. Do you copy? Over."

"This is *My Melody*. I copy and am going to channel twenty-two alpha. Over," Viper replied.

"*My Melody*, this is U.S. Coast Guard, Group Miami. What is your exact location and what are your intentions? Over."

Viper looked at the GPS display and said, "U.S. Coast Guard this is *My Melody*. Our position is 26 degrees 26.142 minutes north and 78 degrees 37.931 minutes west. Our heading is 180 degrees and we are traveling at sixteen knots. Over."

"This is U.S. Coast Guard, Group Miami. I copy your location as 26 degrees 26.142 minutes north and 078 degrees 37.931 minutes west. Heading is 180 degree and speed is sixteen knots. Over."

After a brief pause they heard a voice say, "*My Melody*, this is U.S. Coast Guard, Group Miami. We request you reduce your speed and wait at your present location."

Viper looked at the radar screen and didn't see any boats close to them. There was a dot on the screen showing a boat moving away from *My Melody*. Viper assumed the third kidnapper was returning to Freeport. Confident they were safe, he pulled the throttles back, until the diesel engines were at idle speed. Then he replied, "U.S. Coast Guard. This is *My Melody*. I copy your request. *My Melody* is now stopped and will remain at our present location. Over."

Five minutes after the U.S. Coast Guard received the MAYDAY transmission, a HU-25 Falcon Jet took off from the Coast Guard Air Station, in Opa Locka, Florida.

The HU-25 Falcon Jet is a medium-range, fixed-wing aircraft used to perform search and rescue, enforcement of laws, including illegal drug interdiction, marine environmental protection and military readiness. The twin-engine turbofan jet is one of the few aircraft flown by the military services built by a foreign company, Dassault-Breguet of France. It is 56.25 feet in length, 17.6 feet in height, and has a crew of five. Its ceiling at Mach .855 is 42,000 feet and it flies at 350 knots at sea level and 380 knots at 20,000 feet.

5:20 a.m.—"*My Melody*, this is U.S. Coast Guard, Group Miami. An aircraft is in route to your location. Estimated time of arrival is twenty minutes, I repeat, twenty minutes. Over."

Viper put his arms around Melody and Robert. Tears were running down Melody's checks, as she realized they were going to survive this nightmare.

"I thought we were going to die," she whispered to Viper.

"What an incredible feeling, to hear a total stranger say 'This is the United States Coast Guard.' It put chills up and down my spine."

Melody and Robert looked at him and nodded in complete agreement.

"We're going to be fine. Just fine," Viper said.

chapter 37

WEDNESDAY
NOVEMBER 12, 2003
LUCAYA, GRAND BAHAMA ISLAND

Five minutes after turning the Edgewater around, Chino was approaching Bell Channel. He stopped the Edgewater, and climbed into the Boston Whaler he had been towing. He started the motor, untied the towline, and headed for Arawak Marina.

5:15 a.m.—Chino docked the Whaler at Arawak Marina. Manny's truck was in the marina parking lot, but Chino didn't have the keys. He called Patience, one of the barmaids at the Jungle Room, and woke her out of a sound sleep. It was 5:20 in the morning, and she complained briefly but Chino's reply was unsympathetic. "Shut the fuck up. Get your ass outta bed, and come pick me up at Arawak Marina. N-O-W girl," and Chino switched off the cell phone.

5:35 a.m.—Patience arrived at the marina, but didn't see Chino. Then, someone stepped out of the shadows of a building and she recognized him. She drove over to the building. Chino opened the car door and got in the front seat.

"Take me to the Jungle Room," he ordered. He didn't say a word as they drove the short distance to the bar. Patience pulled up to the front door. Chino looked at her and said, "You weren't here and you didn't see me. Got it?"

"I got it," she replied.

5:45 a.m.—Chino opened the car door. As he was getting out, he said, "Now go home and get some beauty sleep. You look like shit."

Patience was more upset about his comment than she was about being rousted out of bed this early in the morning. She hadn't taken the time to put on any make up before coming to get Chino. She thought, *What did he expect from a girl who worked all night, servin' drinks and entertainin' a bunch of drunken assholes?*

Men are bastards, she thought as she pulled out of the parking lot and drove back to her apartment. *Forget I saw you tonight,* she said out loud. *No problem, I'd like to forget I even know you!*

Chino turned off the security alarm, unlocked the front door and went inside the Jungle Room. He poured himself a double shot of Tequila and opened a cold Kalik beer. He drank the tequila and guzzled down the beer. Then, he poured another double shot of tequila and got another Kalik.

His mind was racing as he went through the events of the last two hours. He didn't have any idea what happened to Calico Jack and Manny. He assumed the yacht owner, *What was his name? Oh yea, Viper. What a stupid fuckin' name. Either he or his son must have gotten loose and managed to stop Calico Jack and Manny.*

He could understand someone overpowering Calico Jack, he's dumber than a bag of hammers but Manny's a street-smart guy. He's big, and he's one of the strongest men Chino knew. There couldn't have been a fight he decided, because Manny could kill anybody with his bare hands.

The million dollar question was, were Manny and Calico Jack dead or alive? Well, I'm not gonna find out sittin' here, drinkin', he thought. He needed to decide what he was going to do and he needed to make a decision soon.

Chino decided the best thing for him to do was leave Freeport for a couple of days. He'd go to Nassau and stay at a friend's apartment until he found out what happened to Manny and Calico Jack. Then he would decide what to do.

If either Manny or Calico Jack is alive, they'll call David Thomas for help. All Chino had to do was stay in touch with David, and he'd find out what happened. He decided, *I'll have Julio fly me to Nassau this morning.*

Julio Ramirez had logged over two thousand hours in his Beech 18, a very popular plane in The Bahamas. Over ten thousand were built for civilian and military use from 1937 to 1964. It had two big round engines that would belch lots of smoke when it started-up and make lots of noise during takeoff. It was a favorite of the drug smugglers during the 70s and 80s: They were cheap and could get into and out of short airstrips, had a good range and a fairly high cruising speed.

Julio's Beech H-18 was one of twelve factory-built tail wheel models. The H model was the last in the series, with electric cowl flaps, fuel injected engines, fully enclosed main gear tires and heavy Hartzell three blade propellers. Gross weight of the plane was 9,900 pounds. Julio could carry 318 gallons of fuel and 1,617 pounds of cargo. It had corporate leather interior and seating for up to six passengers.

7 a.m.—Chino spent an hour and fifteen minutes drinking and thinking at the Jungle Room. He called Julio and told him, "I want to go to Nassau as soon as possible."

"I need to fuel up the plane, but I can be ready to take off by eight," Julio said.

"OK, pick me up at my apartment."

Chino got another beer, locked up the bar, activated the security alarm system and drove to his apartment to pack some clothes.

chapter 38

The Royal Bahamas Police Force is responsible for internal security, while the smaller Royal Bahamas Defense Force is responsible for external security of the island nation. The Defence Force is also responsible for some minor domestic security functions including guarding foreign embassies and ambassadors. Both groups report to The Minister of National Security, headed by a civilian.

Drug smuggling is, by far, the number one crime both agencies deal with. To assist them, the United States government has donated a number of Go-Fast boats to the Bahamian government.

Two of these boats are permanently docked at Lucayan Marina. One is a custom-built, 40-foot, metal hull boat, with three Mercury 250 horsepower engines. Ironically, the government boats are docked less than three hundred feet from where *My Melody* was docked when Chino, Manny and Calico Jack kidnapped Viper and his family.

At 5:15 a.m., Lt. James Hughes, Night Duty Officer for the Royal Bahamas Defence Force, was having a cup of coffee when he heard the MAYDAY from *My Melody*. MAYDAY is the universal term used on VHF channel 16, the emergency and hailing channel, indicating someone is in a life-threatening situation.

Lt. Hughes heard the U.S. Coast Guard respond to the MAYDAY. He switched to channel 22A, along with *My Melody* and the Coast Guard and continued to monitor the distress call. He thought, *What the bloody hell is this all about? It's been years since we've had a yacht hijacked in Freeport.*

As soon as the call was finished, Lt. Hughes picked up the telephone and called a number in Miami, Florida. "United States Coast Guard, Group Miami. How can I help you?"

"This is Lt. James Hughes, of the Royal Bahamas Defence Force. Please connect me with the Duty Officer."

"Yes sir. I'll transfer you immediately."

Next he heard, "This is Ensign Dumas."

"Ensign Dumas, this is Lt. Hughes with the Royal Bahamas Defence Force. I am the Night Duty Officer for Grand Bahama Island. I was monitoring channel 16, when I heard the MAYDAY transmission from *My Melody*."

Lt. Hughes continued, "Sir, I am preparing to dispatch an armed patrol boat to *My Melody* and expect to be on site within twenty minutes."

Captain Dumas said, "We have dispatched an HU-25 Falcon from Opa Locka. Their ETA is twenty minutes. I'll have our airplane secure the area from the air, while your men secure the yacht. As soon as you advise us *My Melody* is secure, we'll begin searching for the powerboat that was chasing them."

Lt. Hughes replied, "Agreed, sir."

The U.S. Coast Guard and the Royal Bahamas Defence Force work together very closely. They frequently hold joint exercises and cooperate on rescue missions. There's an SOP (Standard Operating Procedure) for how the two units respond to just about every conceivable situation, including kidnapping.

Lt. Hughes immediately contacted Sub-Lt. Sweeney who was the Officer-in-Charge of HMBS *Freedom*. The forty-foot Go-Fast boat, also known as *Big Momma*, docked at Lucayan Marina.

"Lt. Sweeney, this is Lt. Hughes," he said. "A yacht was hijacked and three people were kidnapped. You are to proceed immediately to the yacht's location, which is approximately eight miles due south of Bell Channel."

Lt. Sweeney said, "Yes sir, I heard the MAYDAY transmission. Chief Petty Officer Cochran and I are pulling into the marina now. I'll have Big *Momma* ready to go in a couple of minutes, sir. Our ETA is ten minutes."

Lt. Sweeney and Officer Cochran parked their jeep and ran to the slip where *Big Momma* was docked. In less than three minutes they raced out Bell Channel toward *My Melody*. It took sixty seconds for their radar unit to warm up. By the time they exited Bell Channel, they could see two dots on the screen. One was eight miles south of them and the other was just west of Bell Channel. Both boats appeared to be dead in the water. Sweeney pointed to the dot eight miles away, and said, "That has to be *My Melody*."

Cochran turned to a heading of 180 degrees, pushed the throttle to the stops, and headed straight for the dot on his radar screen. The three Mercury engines responded immediately, and five seconds later, Big *Momma* was racing toward *My Melody* at sixty-five knots.

As Sub-Lieutenant Sweeney and Chief Cochran drove *Big Momma* toward *My Melody*, they passed over the exact spot where Chino released the Edgewater twenty-five minutes earlier.

As they raced toward *My Melody*, Lt. Sweeney said, "Our first priority is the people onboard *My Melody*. Once we've secured the yacht, we'll deal with this other boat," as he pointed to the second dot on the radar screen.

Lt. Sweeney took his department issued Uzi sub-machine gun, inserted a thirty-round magazine, chambered a round, and put the safely on. Cochran had a department issued SA80 British assault rifle slung over his shoulder, with a thirty-round magazine, one round in the chamber and the safety on.

When they reached *My Melody* five minutes later, she was quietly sitting in the water. Cochran slowed *Big Momma* as they pulled up to the port side of the yacht. He continued to watch his radar screen, looking for any other boats in the area.

Lt. Sweeney flipped a switched, and a million candlepower spotlight, mounted on the T-Top, lit up the yacht.

"*My Melody*," Lt. Sweeney called over the radio, "this is the Royal Bahamas Defence Force. Do you read me? Over."

"I read you loud and clear," Viper replied.

"What is the status of your vessel?"

Viper replied, "We have two bad guys onboard. I shot both of them. I think one is dead and the other has two bullet wounds in his chest and his hands are tied."

"This is Lt. Sweeney. Permission to come aboard?"

Viper said, "Permission granted Lieutenant. Come along our port side and we'll assist you."

"I copy, *My Melody*. Over," Sweeney replied.

Cochran pulled along side *My Melody* and Lt. Sweeney climbed aboard. Cochran immediately backed away from the yacht, his SA80 assault rifle at the ready. As Cochran was backing away, the U.S Coast Guard announced on channel 16, "*My Melody*, this is U.S. Coast Guard, Group Miami. A Coast Guard rescue aircraft has arrived on the scene. Do you copy?"

"U.S. Coast Guard, this is *My Melody*, I copy. An armed Bahamian Defence boat has arrived also. Over," responded Viper.

As Lt. Sweeney entered the pilothouse, he asked Viper, "How many people are onboard and what's their status?"

"There are three of us. One of the bad guys punched my son and broke his nose. My wife and I are fine," Viper replied.

"I've been tracking you on radar, since you exited Bell Channel. You got here in one hell of a hurry."

There was a faint smile on his face as Lt. Sweeney said, "Yes sir. Our boat's quite fast. Request permission to see the two men and confirm their condition?"

"Follow me. We'll start with the bad guy on the flybridge. The one in the master stateroom is tied up and has two bullets in his chest. I don't think he's going to be a problem."

When Lt. Sweeney saw Manny, he could tell he was dead. He checked his carotid artery and, as he suspected, there was no pulse. Then he and Viper went below to the master stateroom to check on the other kidnapper. Calico Jack was unconscious, but alive.

Sweeney called Chief Cochran on his portable VHF radio and told him, "Contact Rand Memorial Hospital and have them dispatch an Emergency Medical Service team and we'll need a team from the coroner's office. Also, request a CID Detective come to Lucayan Marina. Over."

"I copy," Cochran said. "Sir, I'm in communication with a U.S. Coast Guard HU-25A Falcon. They just arrived and indicate the area appears secure. The only boat within an eight mile radius is the one near Bell Channel. They swept the boat with their infrared sensors and there doesn't appear to be anyone onboard. Over."

Lt. Sweeney turned to Viper and said, "Captain, I request you return to Lucayan Marina. An ambulance will meet us at the marina and some police officers will take charge. Also, there's some paperwork we need to fill out."

Viper said, "Affirmative. Where do you want us to dock?"

Sweeney responded, "Go to the fuel dock. We'll remove the two men and then you can dock your yacht."

"Chief Cochran," the Lieutenant said, "please advise the Coast Guard aircraft and Group Miami, *My Melody* is secure and they intend to return to Lucayan."

"Chief Cochran, do you have the location of the other boat? Over."

"Yes sir. It's about two miles west of Bell Channel."

"Excellent. Pick me up. We'll recover the boat and tow it back to the marina."

Cochran's response was a crisp, "Aye, aye, sir."

As soon as Lt. Sweeney was onboard, Cochran turned *Big Momma*, pushed the throttles to their stops and raced back to the abandoned Edgewater. The sun was starting to paint the edge of the eastern sky a brilliant orange as *Big Momma* cautiously approached the Edgewater. Cochran pulled along side the boat, while Lt. Sweeney visually inspected, then boarded the boat and checked the center console. No one was onboard.

Chief Cochran passed him a towline, which he attached to one of the bow cleats. Then Lt. Sweeney got back onboard *Big Momma* and they towed the Edgewater to the marina.

Sweeney and Cochran were at the marina when *My Melody* entered the channel. Two ambulances were parked at the fuel dock. One ambulance had EMS attendants who were waiting to treat Calico Jack. Another team from the coroner's office were ready to take Manny to the morgue. Inspector Jamison was waiting outside the marina office as Viper eased *My Melody* up to the dock.

It was 6:45 a.m. by the time *My Melody* was tied up at the fuel dock. Viper looked at Melody and said, "This has been the longest three hours of my life and I haven't even had a cup of coffee yet."

Melody hugged her husband, and then gave him a gentle kiss. "I can't believe this happened. I feel like I just woke up from a terrible nightmare."

"Let's wrap up this nightmare, get drunk, and go back to bed," Viper suggested.

"Sounds like a great idea to me," was Melody's response.

The EMS team came onboard first, and checked Calico Jack's vital signs. They were very concerned about one of the chest wounds. It appeared to be a sucking chest wound, which meant at least one bullet punctured his lung.

They put a plastic, occlusive dressing on his chest wounds. Next, they put a cervical collar around his neck to immobilize his head. They were concerned one of the bullets might have damaged his spine so they strapped him on a backboard so he couldn't move his spine and cause further damage.

They started bi-lateral, large bore IVs with lactated ringers to stabilize his blood pressure, to insure he didn't go into shock. Finally, they placed a non-rebreathing high flow oxygen mask on his face, which would help him breathe.

While the medical team worked on Calico Jack, Lt. Hughes called Captain Dumas, at District Seven Coast Guard headquarters in Miami, and requested the HU-25A Falcon take one of the hijackers to Palm Beach County so he could be transported to a trauma center.

There are no trauma centers in The Bahamas. All trauma patients are transported to St. Mary's Hospital in West Palm Beach, or Delray Memorial Hospital in Delray Beach, Florida.

Twenty-one minutes after take off from Freeport International Airport, the Coast Guard jet landed at Palm Beach International Airport. Calico Jack was transferred to Trauma Hawk 1, a helicopter ambulance that would airlift him to the trauma center at St. Mary's Hospital.

Five minutes after Calico Jack was in Trauma Hawk 1 they arrived at St. Mary's trauma center. As soon as he was able to travel, he would be transported back to Rand Memorial Hospital, in Freeport.

A team from Rand Memorial Coroner's Office put Manny Pender in a black body bag and took the body to the coroner's office. Once Calico Jack and Manny were taken off *My Melody*, Inspector Jamison and Sergeant Rolle came aboard.

"We'll be as brief as possible," Jamison said. "I'm sure you folks are exhausted and want some rest. We have some questions we need to ask you and then I'd like to have a doctor examine everyone onboard. If you want something to help you relax or sleep, just tell him."

"Right now," Jamison said, "I want to focus on catching the third member of this group. Can you give me any kind of physical description?"

"No, he never got close enough for me to see him. If he had, I would have shot the son of a bitch."

Jamison replied, "I believe that."

Viper looked at Jamison and said, "When the third kidnapper was following us, I thought I saw a small tender being towed behind the Edgewater."

Jamison asked Viper, "Could we step outside for a minute?"

When they were alone, Jamison said, "You're damn lucky to be alive. There's no doubt in my mind these guys were going to kill you and your family. The two men you shot are the ones we arrested for possession of your engines."

"I figured as much. What I don't understand is why they wanted to kill us."

"As soon as I can talk to Calico Jack, the one you wounded, I hope to get the answer for you," Jamison responded. "I've arranged for Detective Corporal Shirley Cooper to take you and your family to the hospital. A doctor is waiting to see you. If you or you family need anything just tell him and he'll take care of it."

Viper thanked Inspector Jamison. Then he went onboard his yacht and got his wife and son. They left with Corporal Cooper and went directly to the hospital.

As soon as they were gone, a forensic team arrived and started gathering evidence. When they were done, another team cleaned up the blood and had everything almost back to normal before they left. There were four bullet holes that needed to be patched. Otherwise, there was very little evidence of the violence that occurred just a few hours earlier.

When the forensic team was done gathering evidence on *My Melody*, they dusted the Edgewater for fingerprints. They scoured it for clues to the identity of the third person.

When Jamison was finished at the marina, he drove to his office. He met with Rolle, who spent the last thirty minutes with the evidence team. "What have we got?" Jamison asked Rolle.

"We have fingerprints from the Edgewater but nothing else. The lab is comparing the prints against our database. But if this guy has never been arrested, we're not going to get a match."

"Yea," Jamison replied. "One of these days we'll have a complete fingerprint database of all Bahamian citizens. Until then, we have to waste a lot of time looking for a match."

VIPER BOB

chapter 39

Chino sat in the oversize leather chair in his living room, as he waited for Julio. He was teeming with rage. Even though he didn't know what happened to Manny and Calico Jack, he was sure they were either dead or in police custody. He trusted Manny, but Calico Jack was a wimp. It wouldn't take the police long to get a confession out of him, unless Chino did something.

He decided, *if Calico Jack isn't dead and the police have him, I'll have to kill him*. Fortunately, one of his drug pushers, Warren "Disco" Watson, was already in the Freeport jail.

Disco was a mean dude who wouldn't think twice about killing Calico Jack for money. When someone crossed him, he referred to that person as a walking dead man.

Two weeks ago Disco shot a local businessman during an argument over a one thousand dollar gambling debt. Disco was in jail waiting to be arraigned on first-degree murder. Unfortunately for Disco, there were six witnesses to the murder and he didn't have a chance in hell of going free.

Chino saw this as his best opportunity to kill Calico Jack and decided to have David Thomas visit Disco and put a contract on him. Without Calico Jack's testimony there would be nothing linking him to the kidnapping. Also, he would have David meet with Manny, assuming he was alive, and reassure him Chino would cover all his legal expenses and pay him a generous salary for any time he spent in prison.

Chino called David on his cell phone. He answered on the second ring.

"Hello, my friend. We have a serious problem I need you to handle, immediately."

David recognized Chino's voice. "OK," he said, "where are you?"

"Home."

"I'll be right over."

"Hurry. I have an important meeting in Nassau this morning."

"I'll see you in ten minutes," and David left his house. He was cautious and made sure he was not followed. He arrived at Chino's apartment at 7:30 and joined him in the living room. Chino explained what happened and his concern about Calico Jack, if he's alive. David agreed to call the police station and check on Manny and Calico Jack.

"As soon as you've talked to them, call me and tell me what you know," Chino said. "If Calico Jack is alive, go to the jail and meet with Warren Watson. His nickname is Disco."

David nodded his head and said, "I understand." He looked at Chino and asked, "How much do you want me to offer him?"

Chino thought for a few seconds, knowing this was probably the most important decision of his life. No one doubted Disco would be convicted of murder and get the death sentence. If he killed Calico Jack, he'll be convicted of two murders. They can't hang him twice, so this is a way for him to leave his family some money.

Chino looked at David and asked him, "How much is my freedom worth?"

"You're a multi-millionaire. As long as you stay out of prison, you can make millions each year."

Chino nodded his head in agreement and said, "Let's give him two hundred-fifty thousand dollars."

David looked at Chino and said, "A wise investment."

David left the apartment and a few minutes later Julio arrived and took Chino to the airport. Julio parked his BMW Z4 Roadster and went into the flight building and filed a flight plan, while Chino walked to the entrance of the airfield and waited.

Once the flight plan was filed Julio went outside and told Chino, "Let's go, boss." They walked through the security gate, turned right and went to Julio's twin engine Beech 18. In less than ten minutes, Julio completed the preflight check and was ready. He contacted Freeport control and received clearance. They taxied to runway 24 left and took off into a cool ten-knot wind out of the southeast.

Nassau International Airport was one hundred fourteen nautical miles southeast of Grand Bahama Island. Julio's Beech 18 quickly climbed to five thousand feet and by the time the plane was over water they were traveling at one hundred sixty knots. Thirty minutes later the plane was on final approach to Nassau International Airport.

After they landed and parked Chino climbed out of the Beech 18 and went to the flight service building. Julio spoke with a member of the ground crew and then followed him. They spoke briefly and Chino paid Julio six hundred-fifty dollars, which was twice his normal fee for a one-hour charter. Then, Chino took out his cell phone and called his friend, who agreed to come to the airport, pick him up and take him to her apartment, two blocks from the Atlantic Beach Resort.

Atlantic Beach Resort is The Bahamas' playground for wealthy Americans and Europeans who flock there for the pristine diving, water skiing, or just relaxing around the pool. It's a great place to soak up the sun by day, and drink, dance and party by night.

Atlantic Beach Resort is located on Paradise Island on the north side of Nassau Harbour. It's a unique resort that has the world's largest marine habitat, second only to Mother Nature with 50,000 sea animals in eleven lagoon exhibits. Guests can discover the secrets of an ultra-modern resort or take a thrilling ride on one of the five water slides. There are eleven swimming areas and miles of white sandy beach, an innovatively designed casino, full service spa, sports center with tennis and putting course, thirty-eight uniquely themed restaurants and lounges, a world-class marina and haute couture shopping.

When Chino was selling drugs in Nassau, he worked the numerous bars at the Atlantic Beach Resort. Late one Friday night he quit work and decided to go to Dungeon, an exclusive disco club at the resort. He had only been in Nassau a couple of weeks and he decided it was time to have a drink, dance and meet some girls.

Eureka Simone was born and raised in Nassau. The petite beauty was five feet three inches tall with beautiful silky, black hair. She had a small waist and her skin was a light, cocoa brown color, smooth as honey.

Eureka was sitting at the bar in Dungeon with her best friend. She was wearing a floral print skirt and a black and red flowing blouse made of cotton and nothing underneath. As soon as Chino spotted Eureka, she mesmerized him. She and Chino made eye contact as he was walking across the club toward her. They never lost eye contact. A slow song started playing as Chino got to Eureka. He reached out and she gently took his hand. He guided her onto the dance floor and eased her into his arms. Eureka was wearing Wind Song, her favorite perfume, and it instantly became his favorite.

"I hope you have a lot of Wind Song, because I plan to be with you for a long time," Chino told her. Eureka smiled, lowered her eyes and said, "We'll see." She looked into his eyes, ran her tongue across her lips and gave him a warm, sensuous smile.

Their love was as passionate as anything either of them had ever known. When they were apart it produced a burning inside Chino that made him ache to be with her. He wanted to be with her every waking moment. They spent hours making love. Sometimes they made love all night, collapsing in exhaustion in the early morning hours, as the sun began to rise over the sparkling blue waters of Nassau Harbour.

Whenever Chino entered a room, Eureka's heart would skip a beat and then start pounding wildly. She was sure people could see her chest pulsating. Of course, no one noticed her chest pounding, but everyone saw the love struck look on her face whenever the two lovers were together. After numerous love affairs that never seemed to work out, Eureka thought, *I've finally found the man of my dreams. He's handsome, attentive and worships me.*

They spent every spare moment together. Their sex was so wild, explosive and passionate, it sometimes scared Chino. There had never been anyone in his life he could trust. His mother was a prostitute, he hadn't known his father and all the men he hung out with were thieves and murderers. He had no true friends.

Just when Eureka was ready to make a total commitment, Chino started to withdraw, afraid of these new feelings. He had never completely trusted anyone and it seemed as though it was too late for him to learn.

After three months of seeing each other almost daily, she realized Chino was not going to take their relationship any further. One night in October, Eureka told him she loved him with all her heart, but she needed more out of a relationship.

"Chino I have to move on. You're not the marrying kind and I'm ready to get married and start a family." Eureka could see how hurt he was, but she knew she was investing time in a relationship that was going nowhere.

After their relationship ended, Chino focused on selling drugs and making money. He never stopped loving Eureka but he knew he would make a lousy husband. Eventually, they both got over the pain of breaking up and they replaced their love with an awkward friendship. Chino kept close tabs on Eureka and to the best of his knowledge, she never found anyone special, at least, she never got married.

As soon as Chino was inside the Nassau air service terminal he called Eureka. When she heard his voice she couldn't control her excitement, something she swore she was not going to do.

"May I speak with Miss Nassau?" he asked.

Eureka laughed. He called her that the first night they met and she loved it. "This is Miss Nassau, may I ask who's calling?"

"Yes, this is a secret admirer," he said.

"How can I help you, Mr. Secret Admirer?"

"I'd like to come over and show you how wonderful it is to have a secret admirer like me," Chino said in a low, sexy voice.

"I'd love for you to come," she paused, "over. I'm lying in bed wearing nothing but a smile."

"Why don't you put on a robe and come get me at the airport? I guarantee the ride back to your apartment will be one you'll never forget."

All he heard was a click as the phone line went dead. Eureka put on a short robe and drove to the airport. Chino saw her car before she saw him. He walked over and got in the front seat and gave her a soft, gentle kiss.

As soon as they were inside her apartment, Eureka went into the bathroom, opened a cabinet and removed a bottle of Wind Song. She applied small amounts behind her ears, on the inside of the thigh, and around the edge of her breast.

She put the perfume away, walked into the bedroom and slid between the sheets. She couldn't wait for the man she loved to take her to someplace she hadn't been in a long time. Oh, how she loved him. It had been more than six months since she'd seen him. She had a hunger for him that seemed impossible to satisfy and she was more than eager to satisfy all his needs.

Chino was standing at the foot of her bed, facing her and she could see he was completely aroused.

"Well," she said. "Mr. Secret Admirer, come join me and show me how much you admire me."

He climbed into bed, and they were lost for the next hour as they made mad, passionate love. Whenever Chino was with her, he couldn't think of anything but Eureka. Being with her made him forget all his problems.

"I'm going to be in Nassau for a couple of days, maybe longer. Is it alright if I stay here?"

"Only if we make love like this every morning, afternoon and night."

"Hmmm, your terms are acceptable, Miss Nassau."

VIPER BOB

chapter 40

David Thomas called the Freeport Police headquarters and told the desk sergeant he was the attorney of record for Emanuel Pender and Rodney Rackham. He asked the status of the two men and the sergeant said, "Let me put you on hold while I check."

Two minutes later the sergeant told David, "Mr. Rackham is in the trauma center at St. Mary's Hospital in West Palm Beach. Emanuel Pender was taken to the morgue at Rand Memorial hospital."

David asked, "Who is the detective in charge of the investigation?"

"It's a CID case, so you would have to speak with Inspector Jamison," the sergeant replied.

"OK," David said, "put me through to Jamison."

On the third ring Jamison picked up his phone, "CID Detective Inspector Jamison speaking." David identified himself and told Jamison he was the attorney for Mr. Rackham.

"I want to arrange a meeting with Mr. Rackham as soon as possible. I don't want anyone questioning him without me being present. Is that understood, Detective?"

"Mr. Rackham is at St. Mary's trauma center in West Palm Beach. He was in surgery this morning and now he's in intensive care," Jamison said.

"It will be a couple of days before anyone can talk to him. The doctors told me he will recover and should be strong enough to return to Freeport next week."

Inspector Jamison was very disappointed. Calico Jack was unconscious when the medical team took him off *My Melody*, so Jamison was unable to question him. Now, when he'd get a chance to question him, his damn attorney would have to be present. *This isn't going to help me find out the identity of the third man. Now, we'll have to offer Calico Jack a deal to get him to identity the third man*, he thought.

As soon as David hung up, he called police headquarters again and told the desk sergeant, "I'm Warren Watson's attorney. I want to see him this morning."

"What time will you be here?" the desk sergeant asked.

"I'll be there in thirty minutes," David replied.

"OK, I'll have the paperwork ready when you get here. Ask for me, this is Sergeant Smith."

Fifteen minutes later, David left his office on West Mall Drive and drove five blocks to police headquarters. He spoke briefly with Sergeant Smith, who knew David. Ten minutes later he was in an interrogation suite with Disco.

Disco knew who David was and he was surprised he had come to see him. David began, "I have an offer I would like to discuss with you."

"Shoot, I ain't goin' nowhere."

"I have a wealthy client who would like to help you with your current problem."

"I'm listening."

David continued, "I've reviewed your case and it looks like short of a miracle, you're going to hang or spend the rest of your life in Nassau at Fox Hill Prison."

"That's the same thing the public defender told me," Disco said. "I asked the prosecutor if there would be any deals on the table." He said, "With six eye witnesses and your record of violence, I don't think so."

Disco looked at David and asked, "So what does your client want me to do?"

The comment caught David off guard. Disco appeared to be smarter than he looked. David collected his thoughts and said, "My client is prepared to invest two hundred-fifty thousand dollars in a business venture. You and Calico Jack Rackham would be joint partners in the venture. However, if either of you were to die, the other would be entitled to all the money."

"So, where's my partner?" Disco asked David.

The lawyer smiled, "He's at the trauma center in West Palm Beach. He was shot twice this morning."

Disco looked at David, and a smile spread across his face. He said, "What a shame, so my partner's been shot two times?"

David gave a sigh of relief. Disco was very quick on his feet.

"When do you think my partner will be joining me?" Disco asked David.

"I'm not sure, but I think he'll be transferred sometime next week."

Disco said, "Well, I look forward to seeing my old friend," and reached across the table and shook David's hand.

"You will need to contact my wife to make the business arrangements since I can't do much from the jail."

David told Disco, "I'll contact your wife today and have the paperwork ready for her to sign tomorrow."

David left the jail and returned to his office.

E very half hour David called Chino's cell phone and on the fourth try Chino answered. David told his best client about Manny and Calico Jack.

"I had a good meeting with Disco and everything is set. I expect it will be a week before the deal is done."

Chino gave a sigh of relief. "The quicker the better. Call me when everything has been taken care of. I'm going to stay here for about a week and I'll be back after everything is completed." Chino looked across the bed at Eureka. He reached over and placed his hand on her soft, silky thigh. He thought, *Well, there are worse places to be,* and with that, he rolled on top of Eureka and tenderly kissed her lips.

"Excuse me, Mr. Secret Admirer, what are you doing?" Eureka asked.

"Close your eyes and I'll show you, Miss Nassau."

VIPER BOB

chapter 41

THURSDAY
NOVEMBER 13, 2003
FREEPORT, GRAND BAHAMA ISLAND

Viper woke up as the sun was rising over the Little Bahama Bank. He went to the galley and turned on the coffee maker. Ten minutes later, he was relaxing on the flybridge, watching a flock of sea gulls as they climbed into the eastern sky, in search of breakfast. He sat there and reflected on the previous day and how close his family had come to being killed by the boat thieves turned kidnappers.

Drug smugglers began hijacking yachts in the Caribbean in the 1970s. They would kill everyone onboard and use the yacht to smuggle large quantities of drugs into the United States. The problem with large yachts was they could only travel at fifteen to twenty knots. Once the DEA figured out what the drug smugglers were doing, the Coast Guard started checking all large yachts entering Florida waters from The Bahamas and arresting the smugglers.

By the early 1980s, drug smugglers switched from hijacking yachts to stealing fast boats. The smaller, faster boats allowed them to move their product at night across the shallow banks of The Bahamas, evading the Bahamas Drug Enforcement Unit, U.S. Coast Guard and the DEA.

As a result, most yacht owners were no longer concerned about their yachts being hijacked but many captains still carried weapons onboard. Fortunately, there were only a few occasions in the 1990s when a captain needed to use a weapon to protect his yacht.

Viper was one of those captains who carried weapons onboard. When he bought the yacht he purchased a Mini-14 rifle made by the Ruger Corp. and three taser guns. He put one taser gun in each stateroom and kept the Mini-14 under his mattress. He had never expected to use any of them.

A s he finished his first cup of coffee he wondered, *Why did I use the rifle yesterday? If I had used the taser gun the police could have questioned the two kidnappers and gotten the identity of the third man.*

He knew he could have used the taser gun on the man called Calico Jack, who came down to check on him and Melody. *Well, the good news,* he thought, *I didn't kill him. But, I don't think I was any match for the big guy up on the flybridge. He could have easily overpowered me. I'm sorry I killed him, but I'm certain he planned to kill us.*

Viper knew this crazy chain of events that began on October 10 was far from over. He was certain these men didn't kidnap him and his family because they got caught stealing his Edgewater from Walkers Cay.

There had to be something else going on, he thought. *And until I know what was behind yesterday's madness, I won't be able to rest.*

Viper spent the rest of the morning working on the damage done to the yacht the previous day. Two of the three bullets that hit Manny went through him and into a fiberglass panel on the flybridge. One of the two bullets that hit Calico Jack went through him and into the wood paneling on the stairs leading down to the master stateroom. Fortunately, none of the bullets caused serious damage.

Viper decided to repair the bullet hole in the wood paneling first because Melody saw it every time she went to their stateroom. As soon as the hole was filled with wood putty, he applied teak colored stain and unless someone knew exactly where to look, the hole was invisible.

The two bullet holes on the flybridge were a different matter. They were more difficult to repair because the exterior of the yacht was coated with Awlgrip, a thick compound much more durable than paint, designed to protect the exterior of yachts. It's also much more difficult to patch and usually requires an expert to repair it and match the color. Viper decided to find someone on the island to repair the holes on the flybridge.

As he was starting to look for a specialist to make the repairs, Inspector Jamison called. The inspector wanted to talk with Viper about their plans for the next couple of weeks.

"We plan to stay in Lucaya while you catch the third member of the gang. Then we'll return to Palm Beach."

Jamison told Viper he was reasonably confident Calico Jack would identify the third man. He planned to talk with him in a couple of days. He told Viper, "The surgery went well and Calico Jack will make a full recovery from the wounds.

"Calico Jack's a small-time criminal. We plan to offer him a deal and I expect him to cooperate," Jamison said.

"That's great," Viper replied. "Please call me as soon as you have some news."

Viper hung up and walked back to the galley to get another cup of coffee. Melody was working in the galley and immediately noticed a change in her husband's attitude. "So, what's put you in such a good mood?" she asked.

"I just got off the phone with Inspector Jamison. The guy I shot is going to be OK. Jamison will be questioning him in a couple of days. They plan to offer him a deal if he cooperates."

"Does Inspector Jamison think he'll give him the name of the third kidnapper?" Melody asked.

"Yes, that's the only thing he has to deal with," Viper responded. "As soon as they know who he is, they can go after him. You can run, but there's no where to hide in The Bahamas."

Melody looked into Viper's deep blue eyes and said, "I don't think I'll get a good night sleep until they put that animal in jail."

"Hopefully, it will only be a couple of days before they catch him," Viper said. "Until then, I have some work to do and I would love another cup of your coffee, my love." Melody poured a cup of coffee, added sweetener, a splash of cream and handed it to him.

"Hi ho, hi ho, it's off to work I go," Viper sang, as he took the cup of coffee and went back to the pilothouse.

VIPER BOB

chapter 42

FRIDAY
NOVEMBER 14, 2003
ST. MARY'S HOSPITAL
WEST PALM BEACH, FLORIDA

At 8 a.m., Dr. Raj Singh examined Calico Jack and told him, "You're recovering very nicely, Mr. Rackham. We're going to transfer you from the Intensive Care Unit to the hospital ward at the Palm Beach County jail later today."

Calico Jack was weak and any sudden movement was painful, but it was obvious he was going to live.

"How long will I stay there?"

Dr. Singh replied, "I think you'll be well enough to go back to The Bahamas early next week."

Calico Jack was not looking forward to returning to Freeport. He was terrified of spending the rest of his life in Nassau's infamous Fox Hill Prison.

David Thomas made arrangements with Inspector Jamison to call Calico Jack Friday afternoon at the hospital.

"Hello, Mr. Rackham. First, I want to advise you, the police are allowed to record all telephone conversations from the prisoners' ward, except conversations between a lawyer and his client. However, the police have been known to accidentally tape these privileged conversations. I recommend we don't discuss any aspects of the charges against you until we can meet face-to-face."

He continued, "I assume you know Mr. Pender is dead."

"No," Calico Jack replied. "They ain't told me nothin'. You the first person I've talked to."

"I understand the doctors expect you to make a full recovery from the gun shot wounds. I think they're planning on transferring you to Rand Memorial Hospital early next week. Until then, I don't want you to talk with anyone about the events associated with *My Melody*. Not the doctors, or nurses and especially the police."

"I understand."

"Mr. Rackham, the Freeport police are very interested in this case. Hijacking and kidnapping are extremely serious charges. It's in your best interest to follow my instructions to the letter. Is that clear?"

"OK. I won't say nothin' to nobody."

"Good. I'm going to call you every day until you're back in Freeport. I'm going to do everything in my power to make sure you get the best defense," David said.

"Now, is there anything you need or is there anything I can do for you?"

Calico Jack replied, "I can't think of nothin'. But, I gots to tell you, I'm scared, really scared."

"I know this has been a very difficult experience for you. But, we'll work together and get you through this. Now, I've got to go. Don't worry Mr. Rackham, and for God's sake don't talk to anyone."

Monday morning Dr. Singh examined Calico Jack and told him he was healing nicely and he was well enough to return to The Bahamas. "I'll have the sergeant notify the authorities."

Monday afternoon Inspector Jamison notified David Thomas they were bringing Calico Jack back to Freeport Tuesday afternoon. "We're going to put him in the prison ward at Rand Memorial."

David asked, "What time will I be able to see him?" Jamison replied, "He arrives at noon. So, if there are no delays, we should have all the paperwork done by 3 o'clock."

"Thanks, Inspector, and remember, no questioning my client. He's on medication, including painkillers. Also, I would like to see my client at 3:30. Can you arrange that?"

Jamison answered, "I'll take care of it."

Tuesday afternoon David went to the hospital and met with Calico Jack. The first thing Calico Jack said was, "If I goes to Fox Hill, I be a dead man. Mr. Thomas, I got enemies in there."

David said, "I understand your concern. But you need to remember your friend is a very powerful person and you are doing him a tremendous favor. He has many contacts inside Fox Hill, both guards and inmates. He will guarantee your safety and with the weekly salary you'll get, you can live a very comfortable life."

"But, first, they have to convict you, Mr. Rackham. Let me remind you, I'm the best barrister in The Bahamas. They have to beat me before we have to start thinking about Fox Hill Prison.

"However, if we lose, your friend has instructed me to never stop filing appeals and to use every legal remedy to get you out in the shortest possible time.

"In addition," he said, "you have a job for life, once you're back in Lucaya."

David looked at Calico Jack and said, "Handle this right and you'll have a very powerful friend for life."

Calico Jack gave David a weak smile. "I hope everythin' you're saying is true. I'm scared to death and I can't do this alone."

"Believe me, Mr. Rackham," David responded, "you will be well taken care of. You've seen how your friend has taken care of other business associates who had problems with the law.

"His rules are simple." David continued. "Keep your mouth shut and you'll get the best legal defense money can buy. And you'll be taken care of."

Calico Jack looked scared and David could tell he wasn't going to keep any secrets once he got to Fox Hill Prison. As soon as the police had him to themselves, they would work on him night and day until he gave them the identity of the third kidnapper. David estimated Calico Jack would be telling the police everything within twenty-four hours after arriving at Fox Hill.

David expected the prosecutor to move quickly because they had more than enough evidence to prosecute Calico Jack and get a conviction. David was trying every stall tactic he knew. He even tried to call in a couple of favors. Unfortunately, the Prime Minister had taken a personal interest in this case and the people David normally got inside information from were afraid they would get in trouble if they helped him.

Everyone in The Bahamas knows that any government employee who angers the Prime Minister can expect to be transferred to an out-of-the-way island. Police officers have spent eight to ten years in places like Mores Island, Grand Cay or worse, Great Inagua, the loneliest outpost in The Bahamas.

Great Inagua is the southern most island in the seven hundred island chain. There is a large, shallow lake in the center, which abounds with bird wildlife. Half the island is a wildlife sanctuary with guesthouses and camps and Morton Salt Company employs twenty-five percent of the residents in their salt panning facility. Life is very boring at Great Inagua.

The capital, Matthew Town, is sixty-five miles north of Haiti, fifty-five miles northeast of Cuba and one hundred-five miles southwest of The Turks and Caicos islands. But, worst of all, it is three hundred-fifty miles southeast of Nassau, the seat of The Bahamian government. If a government employee was exiled to Great Inagua, there would be no promotions and his career in government service was probably over.

David worked Calico Jack's case as hard as any barrister could, but there was just so much he could do. Because an American family had been kidnapped on their yacht and almost murdered, the media in The Bahamas ran the story as front-page news. The following day the U.S. media picked up the story and it quickly received worldwide coverage. Fox News covered the story and compared The Bahamas to the American Wild West of the 1800s.

Every politician in Nassau wanted this case tried immediately and justice served, which meant Calico Jack found guilty and sentenced to hang. Kidnapping is a very serious crime, no matter what country it occurs in. But when locals kidnap a tourist it decries lawlessness and in The Bahamas that translates into lost tourist dollars.

David knew he had a highly volatile situation on his hands. He was working overtime babysitting Calico Jack. He visited him twice a day, spending most of the time reassuring him everything was going to be all right. Meanwhile, Chino was hiding in Nassau, waiting for Disco to silence Calico Jack.

M ost of the inmates knew Calico Jack was in the prison ward at Rand Memorial. Hijacking and kidnapping are crimes that catch everyone's attention.

One prisoner was particularly interested in Calico Jack. Warren Disco Watson spent Tuesday night working on a plan to get into the prison ward, to spend some quality time with Calico Jack. One of the trustees told Disco the police commissioner had ordered twenty-four hour guards to insure nothing happened to Calico Jack.

VIPER BOB

chapter 43

THURSDAY
NOVEMBER 20, 2003
FREEPORT POLICE HEADQUARTERS
FREEPORT, GRAND BAHAMA ISLAND

Two days after Calico Jack was transferred to the hospital prison ward, Disco was ready to implement his plan to get himself admitted to the hospital. After eating lunch, Disco walked toward the counter where the inmates deposited their trays, eating utensils and water cup. Just before he reached the counter, he dropped a piece of margarine and then stepped on it, slipping and falling on his back. He hit his head on the floor and knocked the wind out of his lungs. Disco really hurt himself but he exaggerated his injuries to make sure he was sent to the hospital ward.

Five minutes later, he was in an ambulance being taken to the prison ward at Rand Memorial where a doctor examined him. As he lay in the hospital bed, he scanned the ward for Calico Jack. The ward was a large rectangular room, sixty feet long and thirty feet wide. Six beds were on each side of the room with privacy curtains around each bed. There was a single door to enter and exit the ward. Just inside the door were two offices. One office was for the doctors to use and the other was for storage. Both doors were always locked, so unauthorized personnel, like inmates or trustees, couldn't get in.

At the opposite end of the room was a door that led to the quarantine room. The door had a large glass window that allowed anyone to look into the room. Calico Jack was in the quarantine and a guard was sitting next to the door.

It only took Disco a few minutes to devise a plan for getting into the room and killing Calico Jack. Disco laid in his bed and pretended he was semi-conscious. After thirty minutes, the orderly left his bedside and exited the ward. It was eerily quiet in the room, as the steady hum of the air conditioners lulled people to sleep. The guard at Calico Jack's door was bored as he read the newspaper and tried to stay awake. Disco decided now was the time to act.

He slipped out of bed and quietly walked toward the glass door. He was a few feet away when the guard looked up and saw him. But he was too slow and too late. Disco grabbed the guard by the throat and jerked him off the chair and threw him on the hard, linoleum floor. He banged his head like a hammer against the floor until blood started running from the guard's mouth and head. His eyes rolled back in their sockets and he was lifeless.

Well, Disco thought, *one more murder charge ain't gonna make no difference to me.*

Calico Jack heard the commotion and looked out the glass window. He could usually see the back of the guard's head or his hat, but neither was visible. Disco stood up and looked at Calico Jack. His eyes were like an empty hole in the ground.

Calico Jack was terrified but he couldn't think of anything to do. He tried to sit up in his bed, but he was frozen with fear and couldn't find the call button for the nurse.

Disco took the door key from the guard's belt, unlocked the door and stepped inside. The door automatically locked when he closed it. He walked toward Calico Jack's bed.

"Wwwwwhat you wants?" Calico Jack asked, in a high pitched voice.

Disco said, "Hi partner." He walked straight to Calico Jack's bed, grabbed his head and, in the blink of an eye, broke his neck. As soon as Disco was sure he was dead, he covered him with the white, sterile-smelling sheet and walked back to the door. He unlocked the door, picked the guard up and placed him back in his chair. He replaced the key chain on the guard's belt, put the newspaper in his lap, and returned to his bed.

Ten minutes later, a trustee entered the infirmary and Disco called him over to his bed. "Hey, Bro, would you tell the doc I'm feeling better and I'd like to get back to my cell?"

The trustee looked around the nearly empty infirmary. He looked at the guard, whose head was slumped forward, resting on his chest and assumed he was asleep. He went to the main door, rang the buzzer and when it opened he walked outside. Two minutes later, the doctor came in and began examining Disco. As they were talking, he glanced at the guard seated by the quarantine room. Instantly, he knew something was wrong.

He told Disco he had to do some paperwork and would be right back. He rang the buzzer, stepped outside and told the guard, "Something has happened to the guard inside. He's either unconscious or dead. He didn't move the entire time I was examining Mr. Watson."

The guard called for reinforcements and when four other guards arrived, they entered the ward. Three guards went directly to Disco's bed and guarded him. One waited at the main door while another moved to the back of the room and checked the guard sitting in the chair. There was blood down the back of his head and neck. He immediately radioed for the doctor to come in and look at the guard. Then, he entered the quarantine room and looked at Calico Jack.

It didn't take a medical degree to see Calico Jack was dead. His head was lying at an odd angle to his body and he was staring at the ceiling. He looked around the room but didn't find anyone or anything unusual.

The guard left Calico Jack and returned to Disco's bed. They handcuffed him, took him out of the ward and returned him to the Freeport jail. Later, he would be charged with two additional counts of murder.

The prosecutor's office got a call at 2:15 p.m. "Mr. Rackham was killed this afternoon. Also, Corporal Ian Wainright, a guard in the ward, was killed. An inmate, Warren Watson, is suspected of murdering both men," the Sergeant told him.

The prosecutor sank back in his chair. "Shit, there goes our best chance of finding the third kidnapper. OK, what have you done with Mr. Watson?" he asked.

The Sergeant replied, "We transferred Mr. Watson back to Freeport jail and put him in solitary confinement. There are a number of guards in here who would love to get their hands on Disco."

"Good work, Sergeant," the prosecutor said. "I'll be over in an hour to talk to the detectives. I assume Inspector Jamison is handling this."

"That's correct, sir."

VIPER BOB

chapter 44

THURSDAY
NOVEMBER 20, 2003
NASSAU, NEW PROVIDENCE ISLAND

Eureka and Chino slept late Thursday morning. They woke up at 10:30 and Eureka suggested, "Let's go to the Atlantic Beach Resort and sunbathe by the pool bar." Chino always enjoyed going to the beach or pool with Eureka, especially when she was wearing one of her string bikinis. He called them, "Two Band-Aids and a cord." The top barely covered her nipples and to describe the bottom as skimpy was being generous. All the men around the pool were mesmerized by Eureka; they couldn't keep their eyes off her. The women looked at her too, but there was a very different look in their eyes. They wondered, *why was God so good to her and not me?* Eureka was a stunningly beautiful woman and Chino knew every man and some of the women wished she was with them.

After three leisurely hours at the Mayan Temple Lagoon, drinking piña coladas, they went back to Eureka's apartment. When they got home Eureka went into the bathroom to take a quick shower, while Chino went to the kitchen and made them a rum and Coke. They met in the bedroom. As Chino put the drinks on the nightstand, Eureka slowly lowered the towel wrapped around her. Chino slid his hands down her back and caressed her firm ass. They were kissing and touching each other when Chino's cell phone rang. He was annoyed as he picked up the phone and said, "Yeah?"

"I have some sad news," a familiar voice said. "Calico Jack was murdered a short time ago in the hospital ward at Rand Memorial Hospital."

"I'm sorry to hear that, David. I'll be back Saturday. I'll call you as soon as I return."

Chino picked Eureka up and gently placed her on the bed and began kissing her with renewed passion. Everything was going according to plan. He would spend one more day with Eureka and have Julio fly him back to Freeport Saturday morning. But, right now, he felt like celebrating. He said to Eureka, "Let's go out tonight and have dinner at the Outback Steakhouse."

"Ummm," she replied. "That sounds wonderful, but what will we do until dinner time?" she asked in a teasing way, as she laid her head back on the pillow, spread her legs and began touching herself.

Chino looked at her and thought, *Damn, she's one of a kind.* He slid his right hand across her thigh and began gently stroking her. Then he took her hard, taunt nipple into his mouth and sucked on it. In one fluid motion, Chino eased himself on top of Eureka and they began making love for the third time that day.

Eureka thought, *Now this is a man who really knows what a woman wants and needs.* She laid back and enjoyed the afternoon, wishing it would never end.

Chino called his pilot and told him to be at Nassau Airport at ten Saturday morning.

"Where we goin'?"

"Back to Freeport," he replied. Chino and Eureka spent the rest of the afternoon in bed. At 8:30, they drove to the Outback Steakhouse. They sat at the bar and ordered two rum and Cokes. Eureka was completely content. Her man had satisfied her every need. Now, she was going to enjoy a drink and then a delicious steak dinner.

Chino sat close to Eureka at the bar and, for the first time in weeks, was totally relaxed. Eureka was the only woman he really felt comfortable around. She didn't want him for his money, she just wanted to be with him. *Maybe, if things were different, I would have married her. But that isn't going to happen,* he thought.

Turning his thoughts to business, Chino smiled and thought, *Calico Jack's dead and there's no one who can link me to the kidnapping of that pain in the ass American.*

Damn, he thought. *That man and his boat have cost me a quarter of a million dollars, plus one of my closest friends.*

The more he thought about Viper, the more annoyed he became. *Who the hell does he think he is?* Chino asked himself. *I've killed drug dealers, like Big Dawg, who are ten times more dangerous than that shit head.*

What the hell kind of a name is Viper, anyway? Chino mumbled to himself out loud. *I ought to whack that bastard, for all the money and trouble he's caused me.*

"What are you talking about, Baby?" Eureka asked. She could see his mood had changed and he was agitated.

"Oh, nothing," he responded, realizing he was getting carried away and needed to calm down. "Don't worry your pretty little head about anything I say, just relax and let's enjoy our celebration." Suddenly, the love and romantic feelings he felt a short time ago were gone. He was back in the world of drugs, murder and paranoia.

The evening was anything but a celebration. Chino's dark mood continued and there was nothing Eureka could do to cheer him up. When they got back to her apartment, Chino made two drinks and flopped on the couch. Eureka went into the bedroom and slipped into a tiny red negligee she bought when she was in Miami last month. She stood in front of the full-length mirror on her bathroom door and admired her figure. She thought, *Girl, you look good!*

She walked into the living room and sat on the couch next to Chino, not saying a word. Eureka knew no man in his right mind could watch TV when she was in the same room, wearing her skimpy red negligee.

Chino was staring at the TV, not paying attention to the show. All he could think about was the man who killed Manny and forced him to spend two hundred and fifty thousand dollars to have Calico Jack executed.

After a minute his rage began to subside. He noticed Eureka and was surprised she was sitting next to him. *When did she sit down on the couch? How long have I been staring at the TV?*

He shook his head, took a long sip of his rum and coke, and turned to face his girlfriend. "Hey Baby, what you been doin'?" he asked.

"Waiting for you to return," she replied.

They both laughed and soon he was back in a fun-loving mood.

Eureka stood up and pretended she was modeling her negligee, as she walked, like a platform model, over to a cabinet on the other side of the room. When she turned around she was holding a tray with a small mirror and a butter knife. On the mirror was a small pile of white powder. She looked at Chino, smiled and said, "Maybe we need somethin' to loosen us up a little bit?"

She walked back to the couch, bent at the knees and set the tray on the coffee table in front of him. The top of the negligee was paper-thin and Chino couldn't help noticing her nipples were hard. Eureka parted her silky legs and Chino responded by looking between them.

She parted her legs a little farther, placed her middle finger on her bottom lip and licked it with her tongue. Next, she dipped the tip of her wet finger into the white powder and raised her finger back to her lips. She slowly sucked the powder off her finger, moving it in and out, very sensually, as she threw her head back and moaned.

That was all Chino could take. He picked up the mirror, cut two lines of cocaine and snorted it. Then, he put the mirror back on the table and stood up. As Eureka watched him, he undid his belt, unbuttoned his slacks, and dropped them to the floor. He was as hard as she had ever seen him in the six years they had known each other. *I need to buy more of these negligees*, she thought, *in different colors, of course.*

VIPER BOB

chapter 45

FRIDAY
NOVEMBER 21, 2003
FREEPORT, GRAND BAHAMA ISLAND

After dinner Thursday night, Viper mentioned to Melody that Inspector Jamison was coming over in the morning to go over the kidnapping, in hopes they could remember any additional details. Viper poured two glasses of red wine and they went over the events of nine days ago but couldn't remember any additional information.

Early the next morning, Viper was on the flybridge, drinking his second cup of coffee and watching the sun as it declared the start of another beautiful day in paradise. Birds were circling around *My Melody* looking for baitfish hiding under the yacht.

The events of nine days ago were still a complete mystery to him and the police. Inspector Jamison couldn't come up with a good explanation why Manny and Calico Jack hijacked the yacht and kidnapped the Edwards family. In addition, the third kidnapper had vanished and nobody knew who or where he was hiding.

Inspector Jamison agreed to put a surveillance team at the marina to watch *My Melody* at night.

"It appears criminals and cockroaches are somehow related," Viper said.

"Yea, they both prefer working at night," Jamison observed.

Because they were asleep when the men boarded *My Melody*, Viper and Melody were unable to remember anything until they came to, hog-tied, in their staterooms. Although Robert was brought to the pilothouse, he never saw the third man because he had been outside. Viper replayed the events over and over in his mind. Shooting the thin man in the chest twice as he came through their stateroom door and shooting the large man sitting in the captain's chair on the flybridge. Neither of them said a word to Viper before or after he shot them.

Viper had closed his eyes numerous times over the past week and saw the third man in the Edgewater, as he followed the yacht. He was standing behind the steering wheel with a pistol in his right hand, shooting at Viper. Viper felt his body jerk in reaction to the gunshots and remembered scrambling up the ladder to safety behind the dingy on the back of the flybridge.

Viper concentrated as hard as he could but there was nothing else he could remember. The man was too far away and none of the lights on *My Melody* or the Edgewater were on. Finally, he gave up, knowing there was nothing else he could remember that would help the police catch the third man.

Viper finished his coffee and went below to the main salon and worked on his laptop computer. Like most captains, he kept a journal of his travels. He began by noting the weather was mild, the temperature was a comfortable 68 degrees, sunrise was at 6:40, visibility was excellent this morning and the seas were two to four foot rollers, moving from the east. The wind was a pleasant fifteen knots out of the east.

At 8 a.m., the phone rang on *My Melody*. Viper stopped working on his computer, walked into the pilothouse and answered the phone.

"Mr. Edwards," a familiar voice said, "this is Inspector Jamison. Something has happened and I would like to come over and see you right away."

"OK, I'll let my wife and son know."

"I'll be there in five minutes," the inspector said.

When Jamison arrived at the yacht, Viper greeted him. He could tell from the look on Jamison's face he was not a bearer of good news. Viper led him inside to the main salon where Melody and Robert were sitting.

Jamison began, "Yesterday, Calico Jack Rackham was murdered in the hospital ward at Rand Memorial Hospital. The man suspected of killing him is named Warren Watson. He's been in jail a couple of weeks, waiting to be arraigned on a murder we believe he committed two months ago."

Viper looked at Melody and could see the renewed fear in her eyes. "What does this mean?" she asked.

Jamison said, "It means the third man involved in the kidnapping has a long reach, much longer than we estimated."

"We believe," Jamison continued, "he is a major player in the drug business. No one else would have the contacts to do something like this right under our nose."

Then, Jamison added, "A local attorney who represents most of the drug dealers visited Mr. Watson four days ago and we believe he gave him the contract to kill Mr. Rackham."

Viper, Melody and Robert were stunned at this information.

Melody was the first to speak. "Do you think they're going to come after us?" she asked.

"We don't know but we're not taking any chances," Jamison said. "We recommend putting all of you in protective custody. You will need to pack some things and come with me. We're moving you to a safe house in Lucaya."

"Hold on," Viper said. "I think we should talk this over before we pack up and run away from this thug."

Melody and Robert looked at Viper. "What are you doing?" Melody asked in an irritated voice.

Viper looked at Jamison and said, "Would you excuse us for a few minutes, I want to talk in private with my family." Jamison nodded and left the yacht.

When Jamison was gone, Viper looked at Melody and said, "I want you and Robert to go. I'm going to stay here until this son of a bitch is caught."

Melody looked at her husband and started to object. Then she saw an expression she'd seen before. It was a look of total determination. Over the years in business, Viper succeeded where lesser men would have failed. Melody knew he was not going to change his mind. She reached over and put his hand in hers and said, "I don't agree. This is a police matter and we need to let them handle it!"

Robert had other ideas. He looked at Viper, as his love for his father swelled in his heart, and said, "If you stay, I stay."

Viper's response was immediate. "No, I'm the only person who's staying. You two are going and that's final."

Robert didn't want this to turn into an argument. He looked at Viper and said, "I assume your plan is to use yourself as bait.

Don't you think whoever is going to come after us has been watching the yacht? If the only person they see is you, they'll know something is wrong and they'll back off."

Viper couldn't argue with Robert's logic but he didn't like it either. "Let's get Jamison back in here and develop a plan."

Robert walked to the sliding doors at the rear of the main salon; opened them and asked Inspector Jamison to join them.

When Jamison sat down, Viper told him, "We're going to stay onboard and help you draw the kidnapper to us."

Jamison looked at Viper and his family and said, "You're crazy, you know that. The people we're looking for are ruthless killers. Drug dealers have no conscious and killing your family means nothing to them."

Viper completely ignored Jamison's comment. "I was thinking, you could have a couple officers stationed nearby," Viper said, "maybe in one of the condos at the end of the dock."

"Besides," Viper continued, "if we go into hiding, you have no chance of catching the third kidnapper. His two partners are dead, so you have no witnesses. We don't want to be looking over our shoulder wondering if he's coming after us. Detective, you can't guard us forever."

Jamison looked at Viper and shook his head. He knew Viper was right. He had not expected Viper to agree to protective custody, but he made the offer.

Before Jamison called Viper, he spoke with the director of the marina and made arrangements for the police to occupy an apartment on the third floor of the condominium. The apartment faced the dock where *My Melody* was tied, plus, it had a commanding view of Bell Channel and the surrounding

Bell Harbour. If anyone approached by water they would spot them before reaching *My Melody*.

Jamison planned to have another team just inside the gated entrance to the marina, hidden in the pool maintenance building. Because chemicals were stored in the twelve by fourteen foot building, there were numerous openings in the walls for ventilation. The officers would have a clear view of the entrance and the rear perimeter of the marina. This meant the two teams would have almost one hundred percent coverage of the grounds.

After a few minutes of spirited discussion, Jamison agreed to Viper's plan. As Jamison left the yacht he smiled to himself. He was concerned about Viper and his family but he needed to catch the third kidnapper, otherwise, Viper was right. Drug smugglers have gang members in Florida who could easily track Viper and his family down and kill them. Because he didn't know why someone was trying so hard to kill Viper's family he had to assume they would follow them to Florida if he didn't catch them.

VIPER BOB

chapter 46

SATURDAY
NOVEMBER 22, 2003
FREEPORT, GRAND BAHAMA ISLAND

Eureka woke at 7:00 o'clock Saturday morning. She was not a morning person but because Chino was returning to Freeport today, she wanted to give him a surprise. As Chino lay sleeping, she slipped into her kitchen and made him a special breakfast.

Twenty minutes later she put a pot of coffee, a quart of freshly squeezed orange juice, a platter of scrambled eggs and four slices of toast on a tray. When everything was arranged to her liking, she removed her powder blue robe and stood naked in the kitchen. She went to her stereo and put her favorite CD, *Sole Provider* by Michael Bolton, in the CD player and adjusted the volume.

The music woke Chino out of a peaceful sleep. He rolled over and found the other half of the queen size bed was empty.

Eureka stood in the doorway, wearing nothing but a smile and a tray.

Chino returned the smile. As she leaned over to place the tray on the bed, he could feel himself becoming aroused again. He looked at the food and his stomach growled. He was really hungry. Then, he shifted his eyes and feasted on Eureka's beautiful face and figure. He asked her, "Does your microwave work, Baby?"

She had a puzzled look on her face. At first she thought she hadn't heard him correctly. Then, he pulled the sheet back and she immediately understood what he meant. She placed the tray on her nightstand and slipped under the sheet and into his strong arms.

As they made love, Michael Bolton's music created a soft, loving feeling inside Eureka she had never known before. When they were finished making love, she curled her body around his, as their breathing slowed to normal. After she caught her breath, she lifted her head, looked straight into his dark brown eyes, and asked him, "Why have you never asked me to marry you?"

Chino was taken completely by surprise and didn't know how to answer her. He thought for a long moment and finally said, "Because in my business, you never know if I'll be coming home."

"But, we've known each other for six years," she said. "Chino, I fell in love with you the night we met and I've never met anyone like you."

Chino knew having a wife and a family in his business was a liability, one he couldn't afford. But he was lonely and he had to admit none of the women in his life made him feel the way Eureka did. Plus, things were different now. He was a multi-millionaire and his true identity was only known by a small group of people.

He said to Eureka, "Heat up our breakfast, we need to talk."

While Eureka was in the kitchen, Chino took a quick shower. Julio was arriving at the Nassau Airport at 9 a.m. to fly him back to Freeport and David Thomas was expecting to meet with him at 10:30. *To hell with them*, he thought. *Let 'em wait.*

Eureka brought the tray back into the bedroom and he joined her on the bed. As he ate the scrambled eggs, he thought about how much of his past and his business he should tell her. Finally, he decided he wouldn't mention growing up in Haiti but would tell her about his business.

"Eureka, Baby," he began, "when we met, I was sellin' drugs."

"I know that."

"Well," he continued, "about two years ago I took over the gang and I've been runnin' it ever since. Havin' a family in this business means trouble for everybody."

She looked at him, finally understanding why they had never gotten married. "I love you, Baby," she said, "and I'm willin' to take my chances."

In a split second, Chino made a decision that would change his life forever. He said, "I've never known a woman like you, Baby. Nobody makes me feel the way you do."

Her eyes filled with tears, as she squeezed his hand. "I love you so much," was all she could say.

They sat on the bed, looking at each other. For the first time in their six-year relationship, they were being honest with one another. Well, almost.

Chino took Eureka's hand in his and slipped off the bed onto one knee, looked into her beautiful eyes, and said, "I love you, Baby."

He paused and Eureka started to say something but he stopped her and asked, "Will you marry me, Eureka?"

She sat on the bed stunned. She never expected him to propose marriage. She would have been happy if he asked her to live with him.

"Oh Chino, you've made me the happiest woman in the world," she said. "Yes, yes, I'll marry you." Tears ran down her cheeks and Chino wiped them with his hands and gently kissed her.

Eureka couldn't believe she was going to become Mrs. Ernest Deal. She thought, *How wonderful that sounds, Mrs. Ernest Deal. She couldn't wait to tell her friends and family.*

Her next thought was, *When?*

"When do you want to get married?"

"I have a couple of things I need to take care of in Freeport."

He paused to collect his thoughts, *Am I actually going to get married? Yes, I am, and I'm going to retire from the drug business.*

With his income from the various business investments, plus the money he had stashed, they could live in the lap of luxury and never work again. He thought, *When I get back to Freeport, I'll figure out how to get out of the drug business. David can help make it happen.*

Chino's thoughts returned to the room he was in and the woman sitting on the bed. He looked at Eureka and realized they were both still naked. He leaned forward and gently kissed her. She let out a soft moan, placing her left hand on his head and pulling him closer to her.

Chino was an hour late. He called Julio and told him he wouldn't be at the airport until 10 o'clock. Next, he called

David and told him he would be at his office around 11:30 and he had some great news to share with him.

Chino and Eureka got dressed a little after 9:45 and she drove her husband-to-be to the airport. On the way, she asked if she could come with him. He told her it would be better if she stayed in Nassau. "I need to make some arrangements and then I'll be back," he said.

"OK, but, Chino," she said in a pleading voice, "hurry back, Baby, I already miss you."

"Don't worry. I'll be back as fast as I can," he said. "Then we'll get married and go on a wonderful honeymoon."

That set her mind thinking in a new direction. She hadn't thought about her wedding or the honeymoon. *Oh dear, there's so much to do, and so little time, where do I start?*

"When can we get married?" she asked him.

"How's next Saturday sound?"

Eureka couldn't believe his answer. She had seven days to make all the arrangements for the most important day in her life. One that, two hours ago she thought would never happen. *What made him change his mind about getting married?* She thought, *I must make one hell of a great breakfast.*

As they arrived at the Nassau Flight Services building, Julio was patiently waiting in the lobby. He had already filed the flight plan for the return trip to Freeport and was ready to leave when Chino arrived.

Julio looked toward the double glass doors as Chino walked in with his arm around a gorgeous woman. As Julio's eyes feasted on Eureka he thought to himself, *No wonder he's an hour late. Hell, I'd be a couple of days late if she was with me.*

Chino stopped and took the woman in his arms and gave her a long, passionate kiss and said, "I'll see you in a week, Baby."

He turned to Julio and asked, "Are we ready to go?"

"We sure is, boss, but are you sure you want to leave her behind?"

Chino smiled and said, "Yea, I know I'm crazy, but she stays."

Twenty minutes later the twin engine Beech 18 was heading northwest toward Grand Bahama Island. As the plane soared high above the turquoise water, Chino was deep in thought. He was excited about getting out of the drug business, but concerned that one of his competitors might use this opportunity to kill him. After all, Chino helped more than one of his competitors retire. In this business, retirement plans didn't include health insurance or pension plans because you usually didn't live long enough to use either of them.

VIPER BOB

chapter 47

SATURDAY
NOVEMBER 22, 2003
FREEPORT, GRAND BAHAMA ISLAND

David Thomas was working on a case scheduled for trial in two weeks. Chino arrived at David's office just before noon. He walked past the empty receptionist desk and into his attorney's office and sat down. David looked up and saw Chino with a big smile on his face. He put his pen down, leaned back in his swivel chair, and said, "You look like the cat that ate the canary."

Chino thought about all the things David had helped him with over the past couple of years. He decided it was appropriate David was the first person to share his good news with.

"I'm engaged to be married," he paused, to let the news sink in and to enjoy the look on David's face.

"I'm getting married next Saturday and I want you to be my best man."

David was stunned. He looked at Chino as he blurted out, "You're doing what?"

Chino was taken completely by surprise at David's response. He thought David would be happy for him. Instead, he seemed to be upset.

For a moment, David had lost his composure and regretted what he'd said. Quickly, he recovered and said, "Chino, I'm shocked, to say the least, but I couldn't be happier for you."

Chino started to relax. For a split second, he thought *David might not be the trusted ally I thought he was.*

"I mean, last week you told me you were going to lay low in Nassau for a while. The next thing I know you've decided to get married. Chino, I didn't even know you had a girlfriend."

Chino leaned back in the chair, "Well, I have to admit I even surprised myself on this one."

"So, who's the lucky lady? And where did you meet her?"

"Her name is Eureka Simone and I met her six years ago, when I first came to Nassau. We've been seeing each other off and on ever since."

"She must be one hell of a woman for you to want to marry her. Thanks for asking me to be your best man. I consider you a dear friend and I'm honored."

Chino said, "I'll have Julio fly us to Nassau Saturday morning. We're going to have a small wedding. Eureka's parents and her sister will be there, plus you. I want you to spend the night and Julio can fly you back anytime you want on Sunday."

"That sounds great, I couldn't be happier for you Chino," he said.

"Now, we've got some work to do, so, let's get that out of the way. Tonight, I want to take you to the Harbour House Restaurant to celebrate."

"Thanks, David," Chino replied. "You're my best and most trusted friend and I appreciate everything you've done for me over the years. There is one other thing I need to tell you," Chino said.

"What's that?" David asked.

"I'm retiring," Chino replied. "I want to get out of the drug business."

"That, my friend, is going to take a little more time," his lawyer said. "With Manny dead, you don't have anyone to assume control of the business, or do you have someone in mind?"

"I was thinking about selling it to my old boss, Edward Knowles in Nassau," Chino said.

David thought about that idea and what a complete disaster Chino's retirement would be for him. Two years ago David purchased the Island Resort Hotel and Casino in Freeport. He arranged a large mortgage, partly because he expected to continue representing Chino. David averaged two hundred and fifty thousand dollars a year from Chino and his drug business. Also, in the past two years David had borrowed a considerable amount of money against Chino's apartments, something Chino knew nothing about.

David needed some time to think. *If Chino retires, I'm a dead man.*

"Have you spoken to anyone else about your plans?"

"Of course not."

"OK, good," David said. "We'll need some time to think this through. Let's meet back here at 6 o'clock. By then I'll have some ideas we can discuss.

"Chino, you really surprised me, but it's the best surprise you could have given me."

David smiled and said, "I love you like a brother and I want you and your bride to be happy for the rest of your life." David thought, *I hope we both live long enough to enjoy what you've earned.*

Chino's car was at his apartment so he borrowed David's car and went to the Jungle Room to have a drink and think. There was something odd about David's reaction to the news he was going to get married and retire. His lawyer was, either really surprised or disappointed. But, he certainly didn't react the way Chino thought he would.

Chino thought, *Well, it looks like it's time to play a little cat and mouse with my friend, David.* He decided to wait until this evening to hear what David had to say before he gave any more thought to his lawyer's reaction. Maybe he read David wrong, but he doubted it. Chino had survived in one of the world's most violent businesses by trusting his gut and his gut was now telling him David Thomas had a problem with Chino's retirement.

While Chino was drinking a beer at the Jungle Room, David was pacing the floor in his private office.

In June of 2001 David decided to buy the Island Resort and Casino and spent three months negotiating the deal. Once the price and terms were agreed upon, he needed an additional three million for the down payment. He flew to Las Vegas and held a series of meetings with some businessmen who had other investments in The Bahamas.

They were prepared to loan him three million dollars in cash but the terms were harsh. They charged him a million dollars in interest and the debt had to be paid off in twenty-four months. David agreed, so with their three million and his one and a half million, he was able to make the down payment and close the sale.

The resort had done well in 1999 and 2000, in part because a rival casino in Lucaya had gone out of business, reducing the competition. However, one month after he took ownership of the resort, terrorists attacked the World Trade Center in New York City.

The tourist business in The Bahamas almost came to a standstill after that fateful day. David struggled to maintain operating capital for the resort, let alone cover the one hundred seventy thousand dollar a month payment to his lenders in Las Vegas. If he had ten clients like Chino who could afford to pay his four hundred-fifty dollars an hour fee, he still couldn't cover his monthly outflow of cash.

That's when David started borrowing money against Chino's property.

In April of 2002, David was getting dangerously close to running out of Chino's assets to borrow against but the tourist business began to improve and in June of 2002, David thought he could see a light at the end of the tunnel.

The negative cash flow reversed itself and in August two things happened. He made the final payment on the four million dollars he owed the Las Vegas businessmen and the resort showed a small profit. At last he had the mobsters off his back and the resort was making a profit. He still owed the local banks more than two million plus interest and it was going to take David three to four years to pay off the bank loans and free up Chino's property.

David sat in his office and thought, *Now, the goose that lays my golden eggs wants to get married and retire. If I allow that to happen Chino will find out about my loans and he'll kill me.*

As David analyzed the situation, he began to calm down. *I have three options. I can have Chino killed. I can have Chino arrested for drug dealing and he'll go to prison. Or I can have his bride killed. The first two mean I'll have to find someone to replace Chino.*

For obvious reasons, it would be easiest to kill Eureka. That would stop him from retiring but would leave Chino alive and on the street to seek revenge against his bride's killer.

David put his considerable talents to work, devising a plan to either kill Chino or have him arrested for dealing drugs.

After an hour of talking to himself and reviewing his options, he decided the best solution was to have Chino arrested for drug charges. David decided to plant five kilos of cocaine in Chino's apartment and then call the police with an anonymous tip.

Chino would be arrested and charged with trafficking cocaine, a very serious offense; making him ineligible for bail. Once the police arrested him, he would stay in jail.

Now that he had a plan to dispose of Chino, he needed to get back to work. He had to devise a plan to sell Chino's drug business to Edward "Blackbeard" Knowles. Blackbeard was a white Bahamian and the major drug dealer in Nassau. Like many Bahamians from Nassau, Knowles claimed to be related to the most notorious pirates who made The Bahamas their headquarters in the 18th century.

David developed two proposals for the sale of the drug business. They were simple in concept but legally complicated. David would suggest to Chino that he go to Nassau and have the initial meeting with Blackbeard. *I am the ideal person to present the deal to Blackbeard. Combining the two drug businesses*

*makes perfect sense but will be complicated, so Blackbeard will need
me to help him handle all the legal matters in Freeport.*

David began to relax. *This could work out much better than I
thought. Chino will be in jail for the next thirty years. Without
access to his money, Chino will be powerless to get back at me. I can
easily assume ownership of his properties. Hell, I can even use his
cash to pay my bank loans off,* he thought.

*First, I need to convince Chino it's in his best interest for me to set
up the deal with Blackbeard,* David thought. *Also, if Blackbeard
thinks Chino's in a position of weakness, he may try to kill him and
take over the business instead of buy it…and that's not a bad idea,
either.*

David needed a couple of days to get the five kilos of
cocaine, then he needed to decide when to plant it in Chino's
apartment. He decided Saturday, the day Chino was getting
married, was the perfect day to execute his plan…what an
appropriate wedding gift.

Chino was a man of action and once he decided to do
something, he moved quickly, but he was also a meticulous
planner. That's why he had been so successful. But, in this
situation it would be Chino's downfall and David decided to
aggressively support Chino until he sprung his trap.

After David developed two plans for the sale of Chino's
business, he spent three hours preparing for his meeting with
Chino. As a successful barrister, he knew presenting a case in
a logical sequence, persuasively, was the key to convincing a
jury, or in this case, Chino. David took a taxi home, showered
and spent two hours practicing his presentation in front of a
mirror until he believed every word of it himself, a unique
skill he had developed over the years.

VIPER BOB

chapter 48

SATURDAY
NOVEMBER 22, 2003
FREEPORT, GRAND BAHAMA ISLAND

Detective Inspector Jamison sat in his two-year-old Ford Taurus talking on his cell phone to Detective Corporal Shirley Cooper. She was in charge of the four to midnight Alpha surveillance team watching *My Melody*. At 4 p.m., she arrived at the third floor condominium at Lucayan Marina overlooking the area where *My Melody* was docked.

The first hour of the surveillance had been quiet. Her partner, Detective Corporal Frank Albury, was perched in a chair watching the dock and Bell Harbour for any suspicious boats or people.

Cooper was catching up on her paperwork when Albury turned and said, "A small skiff came by twice. It looks like they're checking out the area," he said.

"How many people are in the boat?" Cooper asked as she put her pen down and walked toward the window.

"Just one," Frank answered. "I think it's a man. It's hard to tell because he's wearing sunglasses and a sweater with the hood pulled over his head."

"Can you get any close-up pictures of his face? Maybe we can have the photo lab blow up the picture and make an ID."

The boat was a 17-foot Boston Whaler, the most popular workboat in The Bahamas. The black hull and 70-horsepower Yamaha motor weren't any help in identifying the boat. The registration numbers, which are required by law to be placed on the port side of the hull, were not visible. The Whaler was traveling east, which meant the left or port side of the boat was facing away from the condominium. Frank hadn't been suspicious of the boat when it passed by the first time and didn't take any pictures when the left side of the boat was facing them.

The two detectives watched through binoculars, as the Whaler slowly went past the marina. Once it was past the Channel Apartments, the driver made a tight turn to the south and went out Bell Channel. As the boat turned, both detectives were looking through their binoculars trying to get a glimpse of the boat's registration but the driver stayed too close to the shore.

For a split second, just before the boat disappeared into Bell Channel, the port hull was visible. But large coral rocks, jutting out of the water, blocked their view of the registration numbers.

"OK," Cooper said. "I'm going to report the boat and see if anyone else can get a closer look."

She called Jamison and told him about the Whaler.

"I'll get some people over to the other marinas in the area and see if he goes into one of them."

Chino didn't see the detectives in the third story condominium as they watched him go past the marina and out the channel but his gut told him something wasn't right.

Instead of taking the Whaler back to Arawak Marina, he went west, to the Grand Lucayan Waterway. He called Patience, at the Jungle Room, and told her to meet him at the Casuarinas Bridge.

He took the Whaler to a canal just south of the Casuarinas Bridge that was sparsely populated. He went down the canal and found a clump of pine trees growing next to the seawall. He tied the Whaler to the pine trees, turned off the motor and walked a few hundred yards to the bridge. Patience arrived five minutes later and took him to the Jungle Room.

By 6:30, Chino was sitting at a table by himself drinking a Kalik and thinking about what he had to do. He decided he was going to kill everyone on *My Melody*. He was still enraged over Manny's death and the two hundred-fifty thousand dollars he paid Disco to kill Calico Jack. *I'll kill them bastards and then I'll fly to Nassau, get married and retire.* His scouting expedition had been to see where the yacht was docked and the best way to get onboard.

He finished his beer and told Patience to get him another, while he thought about his plan. He would do this job by himself and he would do it as soon as he had a plan and all the details worked out.

Chino thought about whether to tell David. *When he hears the news Viper and his family is dead, he'll know I was the person who killed them. I've got nothin' to lose by tellin' him; he knows too much already. One more murder ain't gonna matter.*

Chino finished his beer and thought, *Time to go to David's. We'll have a few drinks and he can tell me how he thinks I should handle Blackbeard. Depending on how that goes, I'll decide if I want to let him in on my other plans.*

VIPER BOB

chapter 49

Chino finished his beer and gave the key for the Whaler to one of his gang members and said, "I'll show you where it's tied up. I need you to take it back to Arawak Marina."

Patience drove both men to the Casuarinas Bridge and Chino showed him the Whaler. Then, Patience drove Chino to Arawak Marina where he had left David's car. He drove to David's house and joined his attorney for a couple of drinks before they went to The Harbour House for dinner.

David spent thirty minutes explaining how he thought Chino should handle the initial discussion with Blackbeard. He presented two scenarios for structuring a deal. Chino watched David closely, looking for any signs of nervousness or a personal agenda. He was unable to detect either.

When David was finished, he could tell Chino was impressed. Chino asked a number of questions and finally agreed to have David fly to Nassau and meet with Blackbeard. If Blackbeard were receptive, he would present the two business proposals.

Both men finished their drinks and David drove them to the restaurant. The Harbour House was located on the waterfront overlooking Bell Harbour.

David was a bachelor and ate out frequently. He liked the Harbour House and ate there once or twice a week. Chino was a man who lived a simple lifestyle and the Harbour House was not a place he visited frequently.

After dinner, Chino was ready to go to the Jungle Room for a couple of beers. Chino liked David but he could only take so much of his legal talk and his proper British attitude. He declined a cup of coffee and asked David to drop him off at his apartment to get his car.

As they were leaving the restaurant, David congratulated his best client again on his engagement.

Arriving at Chino's apartment, David said, "Don't worry about a thing, my friend, I'm sure Blackbeard will accept one of your proposals."

"He'd be a fool not to," Chino replied, as he closed the car door and walked to his white Honda. While he was driving to the Jungle Room, he replayed the meeting with David and couldn't find anything to suggest his barrister was trying to deceive him. *I need to watch David very closely, I ain't gonna let nobody screw this up. I know I'm being paranoid, but bein' paranoid is better than bein' dead.*

When he got to the Jungle Room, he went to his usual seat at the far end of the bar. He shouted over a Bob Marley song blasting out of the jukebox, "Patience, get me a Kalik." He wanted to wash the taste of the sweet French wine they'd had at dinner out of his mouth.

"And gimme a slice of lime."

Chino decided it was time to come up with a plan for Viper and his family. He needed to decide when and how he was going to get onboard *My Melody. This guy, Viper, is no dummy. He shot Calico Jack and killed Manny. So, I figure he's either got big balls or he's the luckiest motherfucker in The Bahamas.*

He assumed the police would have a surveillance team at the marina watching the yacht. They could easily hide on another boat or in one of the apartments overlooking the marina. In addition, the people onboard *My Melody* had to be wired since the failed kidnapping attempt and Calico Jack's murder.

Chino thought about ways to sneak onboard and kill the three people, and then sneak away undetected. *Difficult*, he thought, *but not impossible.*

As the evening wore on, he switched from Kalik to drinking shots of tequila and a plan slowly began to develop. By 2 a.m., Chino was drunk, but the booze relaxed him and helped him develop the plan. *I'll kill them while they're sleeping*, he said to himself. *You might be smart, Mr. Viper, but I'm one bad dude and in the end I always win.*

It would take him a couple of days to get everything organized. Chino decided he would kill the Edwards' Tuesday night.

Chino left the Jungle Room at 3 a.m. and took a young girl, whose name he couldn't remember, home with him. He felt like celebrating and he had a lot to celebrate: retiring, getting married and killing Viper Edwards.

You gonna pay Mr. Viper, Chino said to himself, as he laughed and grabbed the girl's head and kissed her.

"Yea Baby," he shouted, "you and me is gonna celebrate tonight."

VIPER BOB

chapter 50

In The Bahamas possession of drugs with the intent to distribute is a felony. If convicted, the sentence can be fifteen to thirty years as a guest of Her Majesty at Nassau's notorious Fox Hill Prison and a fine up to one hundred and fifty thousand dollars.

Located in the Fox Hill section of New Providence, the prison has a reputation for being many things. The inmates are the worst criminals in The Bahamas and the guards are equally as tough. Many of the criminals who arrive at Fox Hill in a police van leave in a pine box.

David Thomas was on Bahamas Air flight 324 from Freeport to Nassau. As the plane circled Nassau International Airport, it flew directly over Her Majesty's prison at Fox Hill. *The only thing the criminals learn while they're in Fox Hill*, David thought, *is how to become better criminals, if they survive the experience.*

On more than one occasion, he thought about what he would do if he were sent to Fox Hill. *I'd have to kill myself* was his answer. Many of his clients were in there, but that wouldn't make his life any easier. *Yes, I'm afraid I'd have to blow my brains out. Well, maybe I would overdose on sleeping pills.*

His affluent family would be horrified if he were ever found guilty of committing a crime. His father, Reginald Thomas, had been a barrister for thirty-five years and served Her Majesty's government honorably. He was a great debater and he would have a jury eating out of his hands within minutes after a trial started. He had a deep, baritone voice and the right words just seemed to roll off Reginald's tongue. When he talked, people were mesmerized. They had to believe him.

He's a tough act to follow, David thought. *Maybe that's why I took the path I did. Defending common criminals was something Reginald would never do.* Every time he and his father discussed the law they were on opposite sides. David justified his actions by arguing everyone was entitled to the best possible defense. *Actually*, what David meant was, *the best possible defense money can buy.*

Reginald was unimpressed with his son's apparent noble attitude. He believed a good barrister should share his talents with the other, upper-class members of the community and not waste his talent on dope dealers, murders and street thugs.

"If you associate with trash, you will eventually become trash," Reginald would say. That always signaled the end of their discussion.

How right father is, David thought. *If he knew I used my clients' assets to borrow money he would have a heart attack. Better yet, what would he say if I told him I borrowed three million dollars from*

Las Vegas mobsters. I'm a real hypocrite. I parade around as Mr. Respectability, making people think I'm helping our less fortunate citizens. All the while, I've sold my soul to one of the most, violent, psychotic criminals in The Bahamas. I've betrayed every principle my parents taught me.

How long can this go on? That was a question David asked himself hundreds of times. How ironic his life was. Mr. Respectability was planning to frame one of his clients so he would be sent to jail because David couldn't repay an illegal loan.

I'm pathetic, David said to himself. *I don't have the guts to kill myself and I couldn't handle going to prison. And if that's not bad enough, here I am preparing to sink even lower in the human cesspool I call my life. Way to go, Thomas. Your family, friends and classmates would be so proud of what you've done with your life.*

As David's plane landed in Nassau, Viper and his wife were eating breakfast on the stern deck of their yacht. Melody asked her husband, "Are we going to get out of this mess alive?"

Viper put his fork down, reached across and took Melody's hand. He gently held it, and said, "Absolutely."

"Viper," she said, "we're sitting here like ducks in a shooting gallery. How hard would it be for this guy to sneak into the marina and kill us?"

"It won't be easy," Viper replied. "We've got two teams of police officers watching us and we're keeping watch every night." Each member of the family stood a four-hour watch starting at 7 p.m., and ending at 7 a.m.

When their Ocean Alexander yacht was built, a standard piece of equipment the company installed was a Hailer, used to carry on a two-way conversation with people on other yachts or on the dock. The Hailer was attached to a pair of external speakers, one mounted forward and the other one on the aft section of the yacht.

However, Viper was using the Hailer as a security device. Every night at seven, he turned the unit on and turned the switch to the listen mode, allowing anyone in the pilothouse to hear noises outside the yacht. They could easily hear the sound of a boat approaching the marina or people talking up to one hundred feet from their yacht.

After the aborted kidnapping attempt, Viper contacted a friend in Palm Beach and purchased a pair of night vision binoculars. Whoever was on watch would sit in the pilothouse with the lights out. If they heard a noise, they could use the night vision binoculars to see who or what was making the noise. If anything appeared the least bit suspicious, they could use the yacht's internal telephone system to summon help.

Viper commented on numerous occasions to friends who came aboard their yacht, "We've got every toy a man can own. We installed an Iridium telephone before we departed for our Caribbean cruise in 2002. The Iridium satellite based telephone system works anywhere in the world. Whenever I want to call someone, I simply pick up the phone and dial the number.

"We have a KVH satellite based television system that delivers local and national news, as well as movies on HBO and numerous commercial stations 24/7/365," he would tell them.

The navigation system Viper installed was state-of-the-art, too. He had excellent contacts in the computer industry. He called upon one of them to build a navigation computer with four extra communication ports, along with the standard serial and parallel ports. Using the additional ports, he developed a totally integrated navigation system. He purchased

Nobletec Navigation software and detailed bathymetric maps of the entire Eastern Atlantic Ocean. The maps provided exact water depths, so he could accurately plan his routes. He integrated the Northstar GPS system and the Robertson Simpson AP 20 Autopilot into the custom-built navigation computer.

With this integrated system, Viper could create a route and the system steered the yacht, automatically tracking its position via GPS and making course corrections to adjust for drift. All the captain had to do was monitor the system, watch for other boats, buoys and obstructions in the water. The system made cruising easier and safer.

Viper knew electronic systems were prone to failure and he had a completely redundant back-up system, ready to take over in the event any of the components failed. He also printed a hard copy of his course. If the two electronic systems failed, he would be able to arrive at his destination the old-fashioned way, navigating with a map and a compass. Viper was a cautious man. He tried not to leave anything to chance. When it came to the safety of his family, he was even more cautious.

Money was neither a problem nor a burden to him. He had done well over the thirty years he worked in the electronics industry. He was able to retire at fifty-five with the comfort of knowing he and his wife could do what ever they wanted to do and go where ever they wanted to go.

Now, they had nothing more important to do than help the police catch the third kidnapper. Viper decided, the morning of the failed kidnapping, he would do whatever it took to assist the police, including using his family as bait, so they could catch this lethal menace.

Tuesday was another Chamber of Commerce day in The Bahamas. A mild breeze out of the southeast kept the temperature at a pleasant 78 degrees. The skies were slightly overcast, with the clouds providing just the right amount of reprieve from the warm November sun. The average temperature in Freeport this time of year was 75 to 78 degrees and today was another average day.

While David was busy in Nassau with Blackbeard, Viper was relaxing on his yacht enjoying his wife's company. Across town Chino was busy putting the finishing touches on his plan to kill Viper. The previous day he'd gone to the hardware store, market and a couple of small marine stores to get the things he needed for his plan.

He had everything he needed and now he was busy putting all the pieces together. He spent the morning preparing and double-checking everything and by 3 p.m., was finished. He packed everything in his waterproof backpack, in the order he would need them. When everything was ready, he decided to take a nap so he would be rested and mentally ready to execute (he liked that word) his plan.

Tuesday was turning out to be a great day for everyone. David successfully concluded his meeting with Blackbeard. They agreed on a modified plan, which would be more profitable for David's client in the long run.

Viper, Melody and Robert relaxed on their yacht as best they could, reading books and watching television.

Chino was confident everything would go as planned, insuring his successful retirement.

For the first time in four days, Chino's thoughts turned to Eureka. He called her every day but he usually talked to her answering machine and left a message. Eureka was busy shopping, lunching with friends and doing whatever she needed to do to get ready for her wedding.

When David arrived in Nassau, Eureka met him at the airport and he gave her a briefcase with ten thousand dollars to use for their wedding. He was shocked at how beautiful she was and he quickly found himself jealous of Chino. *How could a vicious criminal like Chino win the heart of such a sweet and intelligent woman? How had she remained single? Why couldn't I meet someone like her?*

David and Eureka went to the airport restaurant and ordered two cups of tea while she told him about her wedding plans. As she talked about how wonderful the rest of her life was going to be, he wondered, *How excited would she be, if I told her one tenth of the crimes her fiancée has committed?*

What would she say if I told her how Chino felt no remorse when he ordered Calico Jack's execution? Or what about the drugs his people sell to school kids? Oh yea, that would stop her dead in her tracks.

Instead, he smiled and listened until it was time for him to leave for the meeting with Blackbeard.

He told Eureka how wonderful it was to meet her and he looked forward to the wedding on Saturday. Then, he left her, glad to be away from her bubbly personality, filled with hope and a wonderful future.

VIPER BOB

chapter 51

TUESDAY EVENING
NOVEMBER 25, 2003
FREEPORT, GRAND BAHAMA ISLAND

Melody always took the seven to eleven watch. She would wake Robert and he stood watch from 11 p.m. to 3 a.m. Viper wanted the third watch because if anything was going to happen, it usually occurred between 3 and 7 a.m. After all, twelve nights ago the kidnappers boarded his yacht around 3 a.m.

Obviously, that was a good time to commit a crime because most of the residents and tourists were asleep. The few people who were moving around at that hour were either going home, full of drugs or liquor after a night of partying, or on their way to work, still half asleep.

For some unexplainable reason, Viper had a foreboding feeling as he prepared for bed. Melody was sitting in a low back deck chair in the pilothouse, drinking a cup of coffee.

Viper turned off the TV in the main salon and came forward to check on her.

They kissed and he told her, "I love you."

She held his hand and asked him, "How much?"

"A bunch," he replied.

"Keep a sharp eye out tonight. I don't know why, but my gut's telling me tonight may be a busy night."

"Is there something you know and haven't told me?" she asked.

"No, but it's been almost two weeks and nothing has happened." He shifted from one foot to the other and continued, "The police haven't come up with a single lead. I think this guy has to make his move sooner, rather than later, that's all. My gut tells me to be extra careful tonight."

"OK, I'll be extra alert. Did you share this foreboding feeling with Robert?"

"No, I didn't. One minute I was fine and the next minute I had this bad feeling. Maybe it's nothing, but my gut instincts are pretty good."

With that said, Viper leaned over and gave Melody a gentle kiss on the lips. "I'm lucky to have you. I love you."

Melody looked at her husband and replied, "Love you back."

David Thomas called Chino as soon as he returned from Nassau. Chino said, "I'll come by your house around nine tonight and you can tell me all about your meetings."

At 8 o'clock, Chino took a shower and got dressed. He wore a pair of black trousers and a black, long sleeve turtleneck sweater. He took a pair of black sneakers he purchased the day before, and carried them to his car, along with his backpack.

When Chino arrived at David's house, David got him a beer and told him about his meeting with Eureka and congratulated him again.

"You're a very fortunate man to have someone as sweet and intelligent as her," he said.

"Thanks, David," was Chino's reply.

"Now, tell me about the meeting with Blackbeard."

Twenty minutes later, Chino ran out of questions. He searched for any evidence his lawyer had a hidden agenda or any secrets to hide. He failed to uncover anything that concerned him. David handled the meeting well and once again, he more than earned his fees.

"Great job, David," Chino said. "Now, I've got some things to attend to. I'll talk to you tomorrow.

"I've got five hours to kill, then I'm going to pay a visit to Mr. Viper." Whenever Chino said Mr. Viper it was with total distain and hatred. "That shit hole killed one of my closest friends and cost me a quarter millions dollars," he said.

"Tonight he's going to pay for killin' Manny."

David was stunned. Why was Chino so obsessed with this guy?

Who knows? Maybe Chino will get caught or killed and that would solve all my problems, David thought.

At 11 o'clock, Melody finished her fourth cup of coffee and woke Robert. She was wired after Viper's warning and wasn't ready to go to bed. She decided to stay up with Robert for a while. She told him about his dad's concern that something would happen, sooner rather than later, and repeated the warning to stay extra alert tonight.

Melody walked aft, stopping at the stairs leading down to their stateroom where Viper was sleeping. Instead of going down the stairs, she opened the salon refrigerator and took out a chilled bottle of Chardonnay. She slid a glass door open, took a wine glass from the hanging rack and filled it half full with the sweet tasting wine. She walked over to the couch and sat down. As she sipped the wine she wondered what would happen. How would this thing play itself out? One thing she knew for sure, as long as the third kidnapper was loose they were not safe.

When Inspector Jamison came to the yacht and told them Calico Jack had been murdered in the prison ward at the hospital, she knew the third kidnapper was capable of killing her family. From that day forward, she believed with all her heart she was in mortal danger. They couldn't hide from this man. He had to be caught before they could be safe.

Robert's watch had been quiet until 1 a.m. when a small boat approached the marina from the east. Robert heard the motor over the Hailer and quickly grabbed the night vision binoculars. He began scanning the channel, but a large yacht docked four slips down, blocked his view. He crouched down and moved as far forward as he could for a better view. A small inflatable dingy came into view and two people were sitting in it laughing and drinking. Robert looked through the binoculars and felt relieved. He recognized Kirk, the captain of a 43-foot catamaran docked nearby, and Cindy, the attractive female mate who worked for him.

Robert relaxed and sat down in the chair, placing the night vision binoculars on the seat next to him. The small dingy was close enough, the Hailer was picking up their conversation. It was obvious they had been drinking because Kirk's words were slurred and Cindy speech was worse. *They must be returning from Bob Marley Square,* Robert thought, as he tried not to listen to their conversation.

He laughed to himself and thought. *What a great life, living on a nice yacht, fishing three or four days a week, traveling from island to island, making new friends and continually seeing old ones. Who can complain? All this and I get paid, too.*

At 3 o'clock, Robert picked up the yacht's internal phone and buzzed the master stateroom. Viper answered instantly.

"I'll be right up," his father said.

Robert told Viper about their neighbors on the catamaran coming home two hours ago. "Other than that, no one came near us," he reported. Then he went down to his stateroom, closed and locked the door, and turned on the TV set, which was suspended from the wall at the foot of his bed. He found a movie and started watching it, but ten minutes later he was sound asleep.

Viper poured himself a cup of coffee and settled into the chair in the pilothouse. As he sipped the Columbian blend he liked, he listened to the sounds of his yacht.

Living on a yacht is very different from living in a house. One thing truly unique about living on a yacht is learning her sounds. Each yacht makes her own special sounds and the owner and crew learn them.

These sounds put them to sleep every night, and the slightest change will wake them out of a deep sleep. When a motor makes a different sound than what the owner is used to, an alarm goes off inside his head almost instantly. A strange noise against the hull can be detected, versus, the familiar sound of a fender rubbing against the dock. Boat owners have learned from painful, and sometimes costly experiences, to immediately check out anything that doesn't sound right.

As Viper sat in the pilothouse, he listened to his yacht. He knew she would warn him if anyone tried to come aboard. Melody and Viper had been living on the yacht for two years and there wasn't an alarm system in the world better at telling Viper something was wrong than his intimate knowledge of his yacht.

As Viper sipped his coffee and listened, Chino was a few miles away making final preparations to kill Viper and his family. He left the Jungle Room just as Viper began the evening's third watch. He drove to Arawak Marina, removed his loafers and put on his black sneakers. He locked the doors on his Honda, opened the trunk, removed his waterproof backpack and slipped it on. Then, he removed two five-gallon plastic gasoline cans. He walked toward the dock and the slip where his friend's black 17-foot Boston Whaler was tied.

The gas cans were heavy, with a combined weight of about seventy-five pounds. Chino set them on the dock in front of the Whaler, removed the backpack and placed it on the dock next to the gas cans.

He climbed into the Whaler and placed the two gas cans in the forward section of the boat. He lifted his backpack off the dock and placed it upright in front of him. He opened the backpack, took three items off the top and placed them underneath the bench seat he was sitting on. He started the motor, untied the dock lines and went out the channel.

Two days ago was a new moon, which meant the night sky was black. There was no moon, only the stars faintly lit up the night. Chino's eyes quickly adjusted to the darkness as he left the marina. It took him five minutes to get outside the channel, where he stopped the Whaler. He removed his sneakers, slacks and turtleneck sweater. He folded them and placed them on the bench seat in front of the backpack. He removed a black diver's wet suit from the backpack and put it on. He checked underneath his seat where he placed his diving mask, snorkel and fins.

He went three miles until he came to the entrance to Bell Channel. He slowed the motor to idle speed, as he crept into the channel and turned toward *My Melody*.

Across from Lucayan Marina is the Channel Apartments and adjacent to the apartments is a large vacant lot. *My Melody* was docked across the narrow canal from the vacant lot.

Chino eased the boat around the bend and stayed close to the seawall in front of the Channel Apartments. He quietly slipped past the apartments. As he got close to the vacant lot he turned the motor off and coasted. When he was straight across from *My Melody*, on the opposite side of the canal, he grabbed the seawall and found a place to tie the Whaler's bowline.

Low tide had been at 2:54 a.m., just before Chino left Arawak Marina. He noticed there was a slight incoming tide as he tied up the Whaler. The dock lights in the marina across the channel were soft and barely lit up the walkway. They weren't strong enough to illuminate the seawall where Chino was.

Chino was having difficulty finding something to tie the stern line to. As he was feeling along the seawall, the boat slapped against the coral rocks just below the surface. It made a deep thud and Chino froze. He held the boat away from the seawall. As he waited he thought, *Only someone with supernatural hearin' could have heard the thud* but he wasn't taking any chances. He waited a minute. Convinced no one heard the noise, he continued searching for a root or tree branch he could use to secure the stern line.

But supernatural hearing is exactly what the Hailer has. Viper just finished his second cup of coffee when he heard a sound over the system.

He sat up in his chair, held his breath, and commanded his heart to remain calm as he listened for the sound to repeat itself. He sat perfectly still in the chair, controlled his breathing and kept popping his ears to clear them. After a minute, he started to relax and allowed his breathing to return to normal. He reached for the night vision binoculars and quietly rose out of the chair. Staying low, he moved forward so he could look out the twelve-foot wide windshield that stretched across the front of the pilothouse.

Across the canal, Chino picked up his mask, snorkel and fins and slipped into the water. As he did, the water splashed against the Whaler and the Hailer picked up the sound and amplified it in the pilothouse.

Viper froze, certain someone was outside. Now he had to determine if the person was a threat.

Viper put the binoculars to his eyes and looked out the starboard side of the pilothouse windshield. He didn't see anything. He started scanning the harbour and the canal. He looked at the Channel Apartments and couldn't see anything unusual. He looked at the large grassy area in front of the apartments and the pool and patio area, to see if someone was taking an early morning swim.

He continued to scan until he reached the end of the Channel Apartments and then he saw it: A small black boat was resting against the seawall.

His heart began to race when he saw someone in the water next to the small boat.

The person was slipping the diver's mask on when Viper spotted him. Something was floating in front of the diver, but Viper couldn't figure out what it was because most of the object was under water. He looked closer and saw the object had a handle on the top.

Chino moved one of the gas cans so he could grip it with his left hand. Then, he grabbed the other with his right hand and used his fins to paddle across the canal toward *My Melody*. The yacht was docked with the bow facing out into the canal. Chino swam straight for it.

A second later, Viper realized what was in the swimmer's hand. *Shit. Those two objects look just like the plastic cans we use to store extra gasoline for our dingy.* Blood drained from his face, as he realized the swimmer planned to use the gasoline cans as bombs to set his yacht on fire.

The thing boaters fear the most is a fire. Boats are made of wood, fiberglass and numerous combustible materials. Plus, yachts like *My Melody* carry large amounts of diesel fuel, in her case, fourteen hundred gallons. Diesel fuel has a high kindling temperature of 195 degrees, but once a yacht catches on fire, it quickly turns into a roaring inferno, reaching temperatures of a thousand degrees or more, consuming everything in its path, including the diesel fuel.

Viper's reaction was instantaneous. He raced through the galley and down the stairs to the master stateroom where he kept his Mini-14 rifle. He didn't need the light to find the rifle. After cleaning it twelve days ago, he replaced it under the king-size mattress.

He removed the rifle and grabbed the cloth bag with the thirty round banana clip, and the spare, ten round clip. Melody stirred as Viper was preparing to go back up the stairs.

"Melody get up. There's someone in the water across the canal and he has two gasoline bombs."

Melody was awake instantly. Viper was in and out of their stateroom so fast it could only mean one thing. They must be in imminent danger, again.

She grabbed a robe and raced after him. When she reached the top of the stairs she saw Viper crouched down on the pilothouse deck. He held the rifle in his left hand and was slowly opening the port pilothouse door, trying not to make any noise. Melody's heart was pounding uncontrollably.

What should I do? she asked herself and for a second, her mind went blank. She couldn't go forward and talk to Viper for fear of making noise. Viper was trying not to make a sound, which meant the intruder was very close.

She couldn't get off the yacht through the stern doors—that would definitely make too much noise. She decided to raise the starboard window curtain a couple of inches and signal the police surveillance team in the condominium. *What can I use to signal them that wouldn't make any noise?*

They kept a small flashlight by the entertainment center to help look for CD and DVD's. She found the flashlight, crossed back to the starboard window and raised the curtain just enough to see the third floor condo. She held the flashlight in her left hand and placed her right hand over the front, covering the light bulb. With her left hand, she pushed the button forward and a small ray of light appeared between her fingers. She began moving her hand, to uncover and then cover the light. She sent out three short flashes, then three long flashes, followed by three short flashes, Morse code for S.O.S.

Detective Sergeant Rolle was sitting in a high back chair with soft, fluffy pillows in front of a large picture window overlooking the marina and the docks. He and his partner worked the midnight to eight shift. He thought, *This sure beats Bravo Team.* They were in the pool maintenance building, which had a pungent odor from the chlorine stored there.

Even though he was sitting in a comfortable chair, his body was numb. Surveillance was physically and mentally numbing work. Rolle turned his head to the left and then back to the right, as the vertebrae cracked in his neck.

His head snapped forward when he saw something flashing.

"What the hell is that?" he shouted. "Shit, It looks like someone is signaling us," he said. "Goddamn it!" he yelled, turning to his partner.

"Somebody on the yacht is signaling us. Call Bravo Team and alert them something's goin' down."

In a split second, Rolle went from lethargic to total adrenaline overload. While his partner called Bravo Team, Rolle called Inspector Jamison, who was in charge of the surveillance operation.

Jamison answered on the second ring and Rolle quickly told him about the signal.

"Are they still signaling?" Jamison asked.

"Yes," Rolle replied, "how do you want to proceed?"

Jamison was heading out his front door as he ordered Rolle to alert Bravo Team.

"Tell them do not, I repeat, do not leave their post," he said.

"We don't know how many bad guys are involved. Bravo Team needs to secure the rear perimeter of the marina while Alpha team secures the dock and *My Melody.*"

"I've already alerted Bravo," Rolle replied.

"Good work," Jamison responded. "Do you see anyone on the dock?"

"Negative," Rolle replied. "But I see a small boat in the canal directly across from *My Melody.*"

"Shit, how long has it been there?"

"I don't know, I mean it wasn't there a couple of minutes ago," Rolle replied.

"I want Alpha team to get to *My Melody*, and I mean now. Keep low and keep quiet. I want one man on each side of the yacht. See what's going on. I'm on my way and I'm calling for additional officers," Jamison ordered.

The two man Alpha Team raced down the stairwell at the rear of the building, hidden from the docks. Once they reached the ground floor, they moved as quickly and as quietly as possible, pistols drawn, a round in the chamber and the safety on.

Chino's plan was as simple as it was brilliant. He knew the yacht had three staterooms and all of them were on the lower level. He knew the engine room was on the lower level near the center of the yacht between the staterooms. He had seen the location of the staterooms and engine room the night they hijacked the yacht.

He planned to use duct tape to secure the five-gallon gasoline cans to the port and starboard sides of the yacht, next to the engine room. When he rode past the yacht on Saturday, he noticed in the midsection of the yacht, on the lower lever, there were three vents instead of portholes, marking the location of the engine room. He would tape the cans to the yacht and swim back to the Whaler.

Inside the gasoline cans were remote controlled ignition switches he bought at the hardware store. When he pressed the remote control button, the ignition switch would create a flash, and the gas fumes in the top of the cans would explode. One-tenth of a second later, the gasoline bombs would explode.

The force would be powerful enough to blow a hole in the hull and penetrate the diesel fuel tanks. Once the diesel tanks started to burn, the yacht would become engulfed in flames in a matter of seconds and Viper and his family would be unable to escape the blazing inferno. Chino imagined them dying a horrible, painful death, as they roasted in their yacht.

Viper had the port side door open far enough to crawl out onto the deck, which went forward to the bow. He had inserted the banana clip in the rifle, chambered a round, and put the safety on as he left the master stateroom. He was ready to shoot the swimmer with the gas cans as soon as he saw him.

Where the pilothouse door opened onto the deck, a solid fiberglass rail, one foot high, ran along the deck. Three feet above the fiberglass rail, a teak handrail extended forward and was joined at the bow.

Viper had a clear view over the side and into the water. He looked down but he couldn't see the swimmer. That could only mean one thing. *That son of a bitch is on the other side of the yacht.*

Viper wasn't going to let the swimmer get away. He wanted to capture him alive, if he could. This person could be the third kidnapper. If not, he would most likely know the identity of the third kidnapper. Either way, Viper didn't want to kill him unless he had to.

Chino decided to attach the first gas can to the starboard side of the yacht. There was a short concrete walkway that extended out from the main dock on that side of the yacht and the gangway was located there. If anyone tried to get on or off the yacht, he would hear or see them.

He swam under the concrete walkway and quickly located the vents amidship. The yacht had a rub rail running the length of the yacht, six inches above the waterline. He took one of the gas cans and pushed it under the rub rail.

Chino was about to tape the handle of the gas can to the rub rail when he heard a noise above him. He released the two gas cans and swam away from the yacht. There was just enough current from the incoming tide to keep both the cans pressed against the yacht's hull.

Chino saw Viper, but only for a split second. Chino quickly swam under the main dock. *How the hell did that bastard hear me? Maybe he's just lookin' around outside.* He thought, *As soon as Viper goes back inside I'll swim back to the Whaler and the ignition switches.*

Viper quickly walked to the gangway and stepped onto the dock. He kept the rifle pointed toward the water as he looked for the deadly intruder. He saw the current was coming in. He figured the swimmer would try to use it to his advantage to make the least amount of noise.

Viper walked down the main dock in the direction the current was flowing and then laid down on the dock. He looked under the dock, but it was dark and difficult to see anything. He thought he saw something move in the water, but he wasn't sure. He didn't want to fire the rifle randomly. Other people lived on neighboring yachts and random gunfire could easily wound or kill an innocent person.

The current was quietly carrying Chino away from the yacht. A moment ago, Viper looked right at him. *Thank God he didn't shoot me.* He only needed one or two minutes before he would be far enough away from Viper and he could swim back to his Whaler.

Just when he thought he would make it back to the Whaler unnoticed, he heard people running down the dock. He had no way of knowing if they were security guards or police. He thought, *How the hell did they get here so fast?*

Viper was laying face down on the dock, scanning the water behind *My Melody*. He watched the current as it moved from east to west. Then he got up, walked to the end of the dock and started searching the turning basin area. He heard footsteps behind him. Assuming it was the surveillance team, he decided he should identify himself before he got shot.

He turned around, just as Sergeant Rolle got to the yacht.

"Officer, it's me, Viper."

Rolle asked, "Are you OK?"

"Yes," Viper replied. "I've got my rifle and someone's in the water. I think he's somewhere under the main dock. He was trying to attach two gasoline cans to my yacht. He used a small boat to get here. It's tied up across the canal."

Rolle replied, "Yes, we saw it. Then we saw someone using a flashlight to signal us."

"That must have been my wife. I woke her when I went down below to get my rifle. I'll be right back."

In the adrenaline charged moments since he spotted the intruder, he'd forgotten his night vision binoculars. He ran onboard, grabbed the binoculars and ran back to where Rolle was standing.

Rolle asked, "What have you got?"

"My night vision binoculars."

Chino was close enough to hear Viper. *Shit, I have to do somethin' pretty motherfuckin' quick or the cops is gonna find me. I need to get back to the Whaler and ignite them gas cans. Then I'll race like hell up the canal and find a place to dump the boat. By the time the cops find the Whaler, it will have drifted far enough down the canal they won't have any idea where to look for me.*

There was nothing in the Whaler that would give away his identity. He bought all the clothing yesterday at a second hand store in Freeport. The gas cans and the ignition switches were from different stores and he paid for everything with cash. There was nothing to connect him to the crime scene, but he wasn't going to take any chances.

It was time to temporarily forget about Viper. He would go back to his apartment, pack some clothes and have Julio fly him to Nassau. He would stay with Eureka until Saturday. Once they were married and the deal with Blackbeard was done, he and Eureka would go someplace like St. Maarten's and get lost in the Windward or Leeward islands of the Caribbean. *I'll put Viper on the back burner for the moment. He's provin' to be a lot more difficult to kill than any of my other enemies.*

But first he needed to escape. All he had to do was swim one hundred feet back to the Whaler, grab the ignition switch and push the button. The cans would explode, and *My Melody* would go up in flames. That would create one hell of a diversion to help him escape.

V iper was disappointed with himself. He realized whoever was in the water probably heard him tell Rolle he had night vision binoculars. He walked back to the yacht and started looking for the gasoline cans. He spotted them pressed against the hull, and he realized his family and his yacht were still in grave danger.

Viper turned to his right and saw something moving across the canal. Chino was an excellent swimmer and he was able to swim across the canal under water. He got to the Whaler and lifted himself just far enough out of the water to reach his backpack. He was half in and half out of the water searching in his backpack for the ignition switch.

Viper raised his rifle just as Chino's hand found the ignition switch.

In a single movement, Chino let go of the boat and pushed himself away from the Whaler into the water.

Viper exhaled, aimed for the swimmer's arm that was holding something out of the water and fired one shot.

Chino felt something slap his right arm and then a searing pain shot down his arm and shoulder. He had shot enough people to know what had just happened. As his right arm was dropping, he grabbed the ignition switch with his left hand.

He looked across the canal and saw Viper standing on the dock, aiming his rifle at him.

A sick, crooked smile came across Chino's face, as he said, "Fuck you, Mr. Viper."

The instant Viper saw Chino, he knew he was the third kidnapper, he could feel it. *I know that's him.*

Chino never saw the bullet that ripped into the top of his head and exploded out his jaw. He didn't see any bright lights. There were no flashbacks. He was dead, instantly.

Viper was standing on the dock stunned. Just as he was about to pull the trigger and shoot the man in the other arm, his head exploded like a rotten watermelon.

Viper wasn't sure who killed him but one thing was for sure: The kidnapper, who had made his life a living hell for the past month, was dead.

Viper felt no remorse. He felt a profound sense of relief. This nightmare was finally over.

A police boat recovered Chino's body, but it would take a couple of days to identify the man because the front portion of his face and jaw were gone. Then, a police officer swam over to *My Melody* and removed the gasoline bombs from the side of the yacht.

Inspector Jamison questioned Viper and quickly learned he didn't fire the fatal shot. Next, he questioned all his people and none of them had fired a single shot.

Jamison was thoroughly confused. He couldn't determine who killed the man in the water. They waited until dawn and a search party scanned the vacant lot and area around the Channel Apartments. Divers found the trigger mechanism to the gasoline bombs half a mile down the canal, resting against a seawall.

By 9 a.m., Inspector Jamison and Sergeant Rolle had personally questioned everyone who lived in the Channel Apartments. No one had seen or heard anything.

Jamison was completely baffled. He had a dead criminal and no one knew the swimmer or who killed him.

By 11 a.m., the police were gone from Lucayan Marina and things were returning to normal.

Two miles away, David Thomas arrived at his office. After David fired the single shot that killed Chino, he drove his car from behind the Channel Apartments to the Casuarinas Bridge. He threw the Chinese made AK47 rifle, with the night scope and silencer Chino had given him two years ago, off the bridge into fifteen feet of muddy water.

Helpful Hints from The National Insurance Crime Bureau, a not-for-profit organization that receives support from approximately 1,000 property/casualty insurance companies. The NICB partners with insurers and law enforcement agencies to facilitate the identification, detection and prosecution of insurance criminals.

NICB estimates more than twelve thousand boats covered by U.S. insurance companies are stolen every year, including the three to four hundred stolen in The Bahamas. However, the NICB believes these numbers are significantly fewer than the actual number of thefts due to the lack of boat owners properly reporting a stolen boat.

Here are some tips from NICB on how to protect your boat.

Criminals typically avoid boats that take too much time to steal or create too much noise in the process. Make their job difficult. Be sure to:

- Dock your craft in well-lit areas.
- Secure your boat to the dock with a locked steel cable.
- Remove expensive equipment from your boat when not in use.

- Lock the boat's cabins, doors and windows when you leave.
- Chain and lock detachable motors to the boat.
- Remove registration or title papers in the craft.
- Disable the boat when not in use by shutting off fuel lines, removing the battery or distributor cap.
- Use a trailer hitch lock after parking a boat on its trailer.
- Install an alarm system and a kill switch in the ignition system.

Identification can help keep you afloat. Mark your boat and equipment with the vessel's Hull Identification Number (HIN). The HIN is a 12-character serial number that identifies your boat and can help law enforcement agencies more quickly recover your boat.

Engrave your driver's license number in a hidden location on the boat, as well as its engines, ship-to-shore radio, depth sounder, compass, stereo, trailer and other expensive components. Take photos or videotape of your boat, its HIN and equipment for documentation and identification.

The above information is from the National Insurance Crime Bureau's website *http://www.nicb.org* (or call 800.835.6422). If your boat is stolen, report it immediately to local authorities.

NAUTICAL TERMS

A-B-C

Abeam off the beam or on the side of the boat

Aft towards the stern of the boat; to move aft is to move back

Amidships In or toward the center of the boat

Anchor A heavy metal device, fastened to a chain or line, to hold a vessel in position

Astern in the direction of, or behind, the stern

Beam the width of the boat at its widest, usually the middle

Bearing direction according to compass

Berth sleeping bunk aboard the boat

Bow forward part of a boat

Bowsprit A spar extending from the bow

Bulkhead a partition below deck that separates one part of the vessel from another part

Buoy an anchored float marking a position on the water

Capsize to turn a boat over

Catamaran a twin-hulled boat

Cleat a two-horned fitting for securing a line

D-E-F

Dinghy a small open boat, usually 6' to 12' long, either towed or carried onboard, used to go ashore or short trips to explore areas

Ebb tide A receding tide

Fathom nautical measurement equivalent to a depth of six feet

Fender A cushion, placed between boats, or between a boat and a pier, to prevent damage

Flybridge An added set of controls above the level of the
   normal control station for better visibility. Usually open,
   but may have a collapsible top for shade

G-H-I-J

GPS global positioning system; uses satellites in fixed orbits

Galley The kitchen area of a boat

Hard over turning the wheel as far as possible

Head A marine toilet

Helm the wheel

Helm station one or more locations on a boat where a helm is
   located along with navigation equipment so the captain
   can operate the boat

Hull The main body of a vessel

Dingy (also called an Inflatable) small rubber boat used to
   transport crew and guest to shore. It may be powered by a
   small gasoline engine or by oars

K-L-M

Knot also see nautical mile (equivalent to 1.15 miles or 1.852
   kilometres)

Latitude an angular measurement or distance measured in
   degrees, north or south from the equator, which is 0

Lee the side sheltered from the wind

Leeward downwind

Longitude distance in degrees east or west of Greenwich,
   England meridian, which is 0

Main Salon the living room on a yacht

N-O-P

Nautical mile one minute of latitude; approximately 6,076
   feet, about ⅛ longer than the statute mile of 5,280 feet

Navigation The art and science of conducting a boat safely from one point to another

Pilothouse A separate enclosed area for steering and navigating the boat. The pilothouse is generally placed on the main deck, "flush" (on the same level) with the main salon

Port the left side of the boat when looking forward

Q-R-S

Rudder a fin under the stern of the vessel used in steering

Starboard the right side of the boat when looking forward

Stateroom bedroom that includes private or semi-private bathroom and shower

Stern the rear of the boat

T-U-V-W

Tender a boat, typically 18′ and 27′ long, transported with a larger boat or yacht and used to take crew and guests fishing, diving, or exploring islands and waterways

Trimaran a boat with three hulls

VHF Radio A very high frequency electronic communications system

Wake the swell caused by a boat passing through water

Winch mechanical device for hauling in a line

Windward toward the direction from which the wind is coming

X-Y-Z

Yaw, Yawing to turn from side to side in an uneven course

Bob Terwilliger is writing a series of mystery novels based on true-life adventures based in the Caribbean. Bob, his wife Melody, and their Havanese dog Viper spent two and a half years cruising the Caribbean on *My Melody,* their 68-foot motor yacht. When not cruising Bob and his family live aboard their yacht in Palm Beach, Florida, where Bob was born and raised.

Bob retired in 2001 from the computer industry after successfully starting five companies. A true entrepreneur, inventor, and successful businessman,

Bob uses his vivid imagination and first-hand experiences to take his readers to beautiful tropical islands with pristine beaches and crystal clear water. Join Bob as he takes you on the vacation of a lifetime.

Visit our websites:
Order *BETRAYED! Murder in the Bahamas* at:
www.springtidepublishing.com

Visit Bob and Melody Terwilliger's personal website:
www.MyMelodyYacht.com

Visit Bob's fishing gear and merchandise website:
www.ViperBob.com